She lay wit  *W9-CAI-227*
*wide across the pillow, her eyes half
closed in satisfaction.*

Her lips curved up as she felt his glance. They were swollen and chafed from his kisses. He would need to shave early in the morning if he intended another interlude—and he did.

Reaching out, he brought a curl to his lips. It smelled of musk and amber. Other women smelled of roses and lilies, but never Violet. He ran it against his cheek, enjoying the rasp of it against his beard.

Violet's hand reached over and caught his. She pulled it down and filled his palm with small kisses. If only he could close his hand and keep them safe for always.

"That was wonderful." Her voice was deep and ready for sleep. She moved over and curved her body against him, her curves melting into his own hard planes. She shifted and lay her head high on his shoulder, treating his neck to those same small kisses.

She was happy. He could always tell when he'd driven worry and thought from her busy mind. There was no greater pleasure in the world that knowing he'd brought her joy.

He brought his arms around her, treasuring her for the prize she was. "You never answered me," he whispered into her curls.

She stilled.

He pulled her tighter. "I know you haven't forgotten." He kissed the crown of her head. "Will you marry me?"

Romances by **Lavinia Kent**

A Talent for Sin

A
TALENT
FOR
SIN

LAVINIA
KENT

AVON

An Imprint of HarperCollinsPublishers

This is a work of fiction. Names, characters, places, and incidents are drawn from the author's imagination or are used fictitiously and are not to be construed as real. Any resemblance to actual events, locales, organizations, or persons, living or dead, is entirely coincidental.

AVON BOOKS
An Imprint of HarperCollins*Publishers*
10 East 53rd Street
New York, New York 10022-5299

Copyright © 2009 by Lavinia Klein
ISBN 978-0-06-173408-3
www.avonromance.com

First Avon Books paperback printing: June 2009

Avon Trademark Reg. U.S. Pat. Off. and in Other Countries, Marca Registrada, Hecho en U.S.A.
HarperCollins® is a registered trademark of HarperCollins Publishers.

Printed in the U.S.A.

10 9 8 7 6 5 4 3 2 1

For my husband, David,
who gave me the confidence to write
and who generously proofread my many drafts
until they were ready to be submitted.

A TALENT FOR SIN

Chapter 1

London, 1818

"**W**ill you do me the great honor of accepting my hand, becoming my bride, and living with me in endless delight?" Lord Winster proposed, settling to his knees before the beautiful and righteous Clarinda.

Oh, for God's sake, was that all anybody cared about? Marriage. Violet could not think of a more abysmal way to start a book. There was nowhere left to go. How was she supposed to care what happened to the heroine when it was finished on the first page? Even a proposal in the first chapter would certainly ruin a book. She slammed the novel shut, unconcerned about the noise. *The Duke's Darling*, indeed! She couldn't believe the Minerva Press had let her down so awfully, just when she needed them the most.

It was enough to make a woman cry, although of course Violet, Lady Carrington could count back the days and years, almost to the minute, to the last time she had cried. Tears were overrated. The only things they'd ever gotten her were a soggy handkerchief and a red nose.

She pushed herself up from the brocade chaise by the fire. Dark reigned outside her window except for the small glow of two gaslights far down the street.

Unsettled, she stared deep into the window. Her room reflected back at her in the black glass, elegant dark wood and plush velvet—a room designed to provide for every pleasure and comfort.

Violet gazed deeper. Her own image stared back at her—the russet curls without a single strand of gray to dull their fire; the round breasts that were only slightly lower than they had been in her girlhood; the waist, still slender; and the white skin, smooth. The reflection in the window glass was much kinder than her mirror. It didn't show the fine lines about her eyes and the skin that didn't pull as tight as it once had, that she knew the first light of morning would reveal. Thirty-one was not an easy year.

Oh, she didn't regret the years or the lines that marked them, but sometimes it was reassuring to see the softening the night window bestowed.

She looked further into the dark glass, not at her own reflection this time, but at the core of her problems, at the man splayed on the bed behind her. He needed no softening of his lines. He had none.

She turned to face him. Softening. It was a strange word to use in relation to Lord Peter St. Johns. There was nothing soft about him. He was all hard muscle and sinew. And youth and innocence.

She walked toward him. He sprawled diagonally across her entire bed in sleep, a sheet draping him modestly. Violet smiled at that. There was nothing modest about Peter. He could have walked naked through Piccadilly Circus without a blush. The bed linens must have somehow snuck up and crept about him. He jerked in his sleep, his massive frame unaccustomed to stillness.

She paused at the edge of the bed and ran a hand over him, a hairbreadth above his skin. Peace and splendor surrounded him. It would be a shame to wake him. Asleep he was everything she could ever want, and she could have kept him trapped in this moment forever.

Heat rose off his skin and caressed her hand. The smell of his herb soap tantalized her. She could see his chest fill and fall with each breath, and she had to resist the urge to lay her hand there to feel the steady beat of his heart.

He was so alive that even in slumber, motionless, his body exuded more vitality than she had ever known. Awake, he positively vibrated with it. He was impossible to keep still, an inquisitive puppy always after a new toy.

So young, so beautiful, so joyous. She started to turn away, disconcerted by her own thoughts, but iron fingers reached out and caught her.

"Don't you like what you see?" he asked, his voice coarse with sleep.

"You know I always like what I see when I look at you." Her own voice was husky—and not with sleep.

His fingers loosed and his thumb began to caress the tender spot at the base of her palm. Pleasure grew in the friction between their skin, and each stroke plucked at the firmness of her resolve. He tugged her toward the bed, eager as always.

"Again? I should think you would be tired after our earlier festivities." She resisted his urgings.

"Tired? I am more than refreshed after my nap. Would you like to examine for yourself?" He pulled her forward again, rotating his hips to loosen the covers.

She stood, withstanding his pull, and held the sheet steady against him. "Slower," she whispered as she bent her neck to rub her face in his black, wavy hair. The strands tickled her nose.

He tilted his head back until their lips met, rewarding her with the softest, sweetest of kisses—mouths closed, lips simply rubbing, pressing, feeling, endless—just the way she loved it; velvet softness. She parted her mouth in invitation, let his tongue glide along the crease, tasting her. The tip of her tongue slipped out to meet his, brandy and cinnamon, to begin their courtship dance. Brush. Taste. Retreat. Again.

They had kissed like this a thousand times, and still her belly quivered and her breasts grew tight with its perfection, with his perfection. She closed her eyes and sank into the moment. No past. No future. Nobody else had ever before kissed her like this, knowing every nuance of her desires. As if sensing the heat growing within her, Peter pulled back. She opened her eyes and found him staring up at her swollen lips and half-lowered lids. Watching carefully for her approval, he untied the belt of her wrap and let it ease across her skin. The rough weave of the nubby silk sent tiny sparks along her belly and arms.

When she was bare, he didn't stare at her breasts, although she could feel his suppressed desire, but instead pulled her toward him until his lips settled in the little hollow at the base of her throat. His tongue darted out and swirled in a delicious circle as his lips caressed. All the feelings in her entire body focused on that one spot.

His fingers swept her hair aside and began to knead the tight tendons of her neck until she relaxed into him, letting him pull her fully on the bed and spread her beneath him.

He paused for a moment, staring. His eyes swept over the swollen breasts, waiting for his touch, the gentle curves of her belly, quivering in readiness at his glance, and settled for a second on the fiery curls that hid how ready she was for him. She could feel the tension in his body, see how he held himself in check.

His gaze moved up and met hers. The desire she saw in his darkened eyes made all her earlier anxiety fade. In his eyes she was beautiful. There was no mistaking the adoration in his expression.

She arched her back, lifting her breasts toward him, needing him to ease the ache that grew within. He touched her reverently, the soft touch of the pads of his fingers sweeping in slow spirals from the base of her breasts upward. Her aching nipples were impatient for his touch, but still he teased her, drawing the flames of passion even higher.

She fought the urge to grab his hair and pull his head toward her, to bring his lips, his mouth to her. Instead, she tightened her fingers in the twisted linen, gripping so tightly she could almost feel the weave tear. She had taught him patience, now she must fight for her own.

Finally, his fingers reached the tight peaks and began to pinch, to pluck, each movement setting a quiver through her like the string of a violin. He was the maestro, and she his instrument.

She closed her eyes, waited. She knew what was coming, could sense almost to the instant when his mouth would descend, granting some release, while drawing the string still tighter. He sucked, he bit, he laved—the slight sting and then the soothing.

When she felt the coil drawing too tight, the end approaching, she pushed him back. He held himself above her, arms straight and solid around her. Their gazes met and held again, an unspoken contest of desire and withholding. He shifted, bringing his hips over her, pressing his arousal in the valley between her legs, but pushing no farther.

She knew he must feel her heat and moisture, but he gave no signal beyond a tightening of his fingers, a sharp intake of breath. He was panting with the stress, longing to move, but awaiting her cue. She lifted her hips, opening her legs more, granting him access, but still withholding her final permission.

The tip of his erection pushed against her still closed lower lips, and she moved, shifted until it ran against the bundle of nerves that were the center of her longing. She raised and lowered her hips, running herself against him, sending shivers of desire through both of them. She reveled in her moment of control. His jaw was clenched with the effort not to move, and the arms around her quivered with the strain.

He gasped when she tightened her legs about him, increasing the sensation. Her own heart was speeding and her body screamed for release. She tortured them both.

She pulled her head high, running her tongue up his neck, over the stubble of his beard, until she reached his chin. She nipped, a cat's love bite. He knew his cue.

He knelt, grabbed her ankles, and drew them up over his shoulders. Their eyes met, held, souls merged, as he sought her final permission.

In one long stroke he was in her, filling her, completing her. Her whole body shuddered as he rose up again and again, taking her with him to each higher cliff. Fast, slow, he knew her rhythms, her secret spots and deepest desires.

She closed her eyes and let herself slip into that place where only sensation mattered. She was lost upon the sea and he her only anchor.

When the waves finally crashed, reaching crescendo, she cried out loud and true. The world ended and was reborn in a single blinding instant.

Peter felt her climax around him, her every pulse surrounding him, blinding him, making it harder to maintain control. Sweat prickled on his brow, and he mentally counted backward, fighting for that last minute, last second, last moment.

He felt her convulse again, and let himself go. He knew he screamed, so intense was the pleasure, the release, but even as he circled back to earth, all he knew was her, the feel of her, the look of her, the deep feminine scent of her. Violet was his world.

He released her legs and collapsed upon her for a moment, enjoying her softness, then rolled aside, conscious of his great weight and her petite build. He knew she was not small for a woman, but always he was aware of how fragile she was next to his own heft. He turned on his side and stared down at her, this goddess who had opened new kingdoms to him.

She lay with her fiery hair spread wide across the pillow, her eyes half closed in satisfaction. Her lips curved up as she felt his glance. They were swollen and chafed from his kisses. He would need to shave early in the morning if he intended another interlude—and he did.

Reaching out, he brought a curl to his lips. It smelled of musk and amber. Other women smelled of roses and lilies, but never Violet. He ran it against his cheek, enjoying the rasp of it against his beard.

Violet's hand reached over and caught his. She pulled it down and filled his palm with small kisses. If only he could close his hand and keep them safe for always.

"That was wonderful." Her voice was deep and ready for sleep. She moved over and curved her body against him, her curves melting into his own hard planes. She shifted and laid her head high on his shoulder, treating his neck to those same small kisses.

She was happy. He could always tell when he'd driven worry and thought from her busy mind. There was no greater pleasure in the world than knowing he'd brought her joy.

He wrapped his arms around her, treasuring her for

the prize she was. "You never answered me," he whispered into her curls.

She stilled.

He pulled her tighter. "I know you haven't forgotten." He kissed the crown of her head. "Will you marry me?"

Chapter 2

Violet peered up at him through her burnished strands of hair. Her eyes opened wide at his question and then her lids slid down. She stared at the embellished edge of the sheet as if seeking her answer in its patterns.

"You are serious?" Her voice was low and careful, and an ache of disquiet took shape deep in his stomach.

"How could you think I was not? Marriage is serious. I would never tease you about such a thing." He must convince her. "I want you to be my wife."

"I am sorry." Her fingers traced an embroidered butterfly. He stared as her nail followed a line of thread.

"Why are you sorry?" he questioned. "I thought you would be pleased."

"I am sorry that I cannot give you the answer you want. I am not the wife for you." Violet kept her face angled down, refusing him a peek into her eyes.

"Why would you think that? You are exactly the

wife I want." Why was she responding like this? He worked so hard to please her in all ways, to anticipate her every need, desire. Why would she refuse him?

"But I am not the wife you need. Have you thought about this?" She removed herself from him, rising from the bed and wrapping the sheet tight about her body.

He still had not seen her face.

"Of course I have thought about it." Peter worked hard to keep the hurt from his voice. Too often she treated him as if he were a thoughtless child. He was not a child. "I would not have asked had I not considered the question with great care. I want to marry you."

"I am seven years older, have been married three times, am rumored to have taken many young lovers, and have little to recommend me except my fortune— of which you have no need. You cannot want to marry me." The rules of cricket would have been read with more tone and inflection than she used.

He followed her from the bed. He must see her face. She turned, finally. Her eyes swept his naked body and then rose to meet his gaze. They were flat and still, lacking the sense of play and adventure he so adored about her.

He stopped a handbreadth from her. "How do you know what I want?"

She moved forward and pressed her sheet-clad breasts and belly against him, rubbed her face along his chest. She arched her hips against him. Damnation, he felt himself stir again.

Her voice was husky. "It is quite clear what you want, but that is not reason for marriage. The passion between us is magnificent, but it is still mere sex. It blinds your common sense. You are young and guided by your loins." She placed a soft kiss against his throat. She had hidden her face from him again. All he could judge were her movements, and they spoke only of lust.

He could feel her desire rising in the heated breath against his neck. It would be so easy to give in, to pretend this had never happened, that he had never asked, never forced her to say these words. He only wanted to make her happy. He closed his eyes as the sheet slid down between them. Her perfect breasts begged for his caress. The full nipples pressed against his chest. He knew what she wanted, knew the response he should give, the gentle pluck, the sweet kiss, the sudden nip.

He had never refused her, not from the first time she had looked at him across his brother's crowded parlor and he had seen the invitation in her eyes. He had followed her from the room, from the house—a kitten chasing a string. And not once had he regretted it, until now.

He placed a hand upon each of her shoulders. God, why did her flesh feel like warm silk, the musk of her scent rising up to inflame him?

"No, we need to talk. Now. I need to know how you feel about me." He pushed her back.

If he imagined she would sulk, he was wrong. She pulled the sheet up again and knotted it at her breast. She turned and walked from him, her back straight—a magnificent queen.

She sat on the chaise, her legs curled beside her, but her spine still stiff. "How do I feel about you?" Again her voice was flat, and she looked anywhere but at him. "I do care about you Peter, perhaps I care too much, but surely you can see that does not matter. We are unsuited for matrimony. And truly I have no desire to enter the wedded state again. I value my freedom, as I am sure you value your own."

"Freedom is the ability to live the life you want, the life you need, and I wish to spend that life with you." He walked until he stood above her; he made no concession to his nakedness.

"I have not said that I will not spend my life with you."

"Then you will marry me?" he asked, hope sparking to fight the icicle forming in his chest.

She sighed. "No, I did not say that. Marrying me would ruin you. I will not do that to you—to either of us."

He wanted to be angry. She was so stubborn. But then that was part of the attraction. She was her own woman. He merely wanted her to be his as well. They would have such perfect lives if she would consent.

"Why would marriage ruin us? You are a lady, born and bred. We are well-suited."

She turned toward him then, and for the first he saw fire light her eyes.

"Well-suited." The word drawled from her lips. "At least you do not speak of love. You may be mistaken, but evidently you are not a fool."

She waited until his eyes settled on her and then stood, moving with slow deliberation that displayed each curve of her body. "We are well-suited—as lovers, perhaps even as friends or acquaintances. We are not that of which spouses are made. Let us leave things as they are and be content."

The sheet slithered over her hips as she walked, and he could feel the call of desire again. Despite the hardness of her words, her eyes had softened, and he could see care and concern in her voice.

"Peter, accept this for what it is—a young man's foolish moment. You will have forgotten it by morning, and if you have not, you will be glad that I have. What we have between us is a perfect moment—but it is a moment in a starry summer night. It is a dream from which we will both awaken and smile contentedly and then go on to meet the day. You cannot expect such dreams to last."

"Why?" It was such a simple question, but he felt his whole life caught up in it. "If what we have is perfect, what should ruin it?"

She turned from him, from his questions, and walked back to the window. She seemed caught by her own reflection. She reached up and traced a finger along her mirrored cheek. "Daylight. Daylight shows the flaws that night conceals."

Her eyes looked huge in the window. Their vibrant color did not show, but they filled her face, endless pools holding all the darkness of the night beyond.

He came up behind her and caught her in his embrace. He wrapped his arms tight about her, wishing he could hold her forever. His world was right when she was in his arms.

"I believe I understand your meaning, but sometimes daylight shows beauty in the details it reveals." He buried his face in her curls for a moment, then lifted one so the strand shone russet in the candlelight. "Right now this is a piece of beauty, a deep thread of hidden fire, but it takes the full light of the sun to become a thing of fantasy, true liquid flame and shining copper."

"For the moment, this magic moment, that may be true, but then the flame burns out and only ash is left."

They stared at each other in reflection. Peter wished with all his soul he could share with her all that he saw, all that he could imagine for them. Instead all he could do was feel the reflected stillness of her gaze. "I have never been a man for poetry and honeyed words. I grow lost in the illusion. It is a simple matter. Though you may call me a fool, Violet, I want to spend my life with you. With you, not some reflection. Why will you not have me?"

She closed her eyes and leaned back against him, her body limp and tired. Would she give in?

Then her eyes opened and he could see her strength. "I have told you why, Peter. It is not my fault if you do not choose to listen. I am half a dozen and more years older than you, and the experience between us is even greater than that. I know that we don't get everything we want in life, and you still believe in this fantasy that all is possible.

"I am free. I have a life, a good life. I have this home that I have designed, a place of warmth and succor. You are a wonderful part of it. You are, however, only a part. I have always belonged to some man—first my brother and then my husbands. Three marriages are more than enough. I do not want another. Why would I even think of it? Now, I am my own woman, and if I married again I would lose that and merely be some man's property."

"Not some man. Mine." Peter spoke firmly. He would not beg.

"I admit that you are better than most, but you are still a man. You do not even begin to understand why it is so important that I belong to myself."

"We can have settlements drawn up that would protect your interests. This can only be an excuse." He was beginning to feel anger. He had never expected such an argument. Did she not trust him? He would always put her first, do what made her happy. Didn't she understand he would do anything for her?

She pulled back from him, turned and walked to her dressing table. Lighting the lantern, she turned the flame high. She gathered her hair tight behind her head, coiling it into a knot.

She turned back to him. She let the sheet drop.

"Look at me, Peter," she began. "Look at me not with desire and the soft glow of candlelight, but really look at me. I am not a girl heady with dreams of love and marriage and babies." Her voice caught a little at the end, but she continued. "I am a woman, more than full-grown. When I dream, it is of properties I can acquire, of how my tenants are faring, of how long this peace with France will hold. These are the dreams and thoughts of a woman. Now, look at me and see me for what I am."

She raised her arms from her sides and held them out, daring him to examine her. He started at the bottom with her toes. They were pink and small. They could not be what kept her from him. Her legs were full and shapely—did she think he would prefer the slender sticks of a girl? Her hips were round and soft, the red glow of her curls hiding her secrets while allowing flirtatious glimpses. Her belly. He loved her belly. Its softness was his favorite pillow. Its velvet skin always ready to quiver at his touch. Even now he longed to blow a soft breath across her navel and watch her shiver in anticipation.

Her breasts.

He could not form a coherent thought about them. When his eyes traveled along their curves his mind simply stopped. Their red, pointed tips drew him, and even now his lips longed to taste them, to draw her nipples deep into his mouth, to suckle and lave until she began that soft moan deep in her throat that meant—

He moved his gaze up to her face. He knew desire was not the answer she sought. Her lips were full and beckoning, but the slight crease at the corner spoke of how strong and firm she could be.

Her nose was slightly uptilted, the most girlish thing about her. She tried to hide its sun-grown freckles with powder, but he knew each and every one.

He skipped over her eyes, afraid to meet them before he had finished his appraisal. Her brow furrowed at the top of her nose, and her forehead held the single whisper of a line that he longed to smooth away with deep caresses. He hated that he was the cause of her tension.

Even confined in its knot, her hair was the most beautiful he had ever seen. He doubted that it held the answer she felt that he was missing.

He moved back to her eyes. The crinkle of a thousand laughs edged them, and the thick black lashes that should have required kohl surrounded them. Violet. He had often wondered if she'd been named for her eyes. Eyes that should not exist, save in the tales of some long-dead goddess. Eyes of pansy purple and ocean blue, ever changing with her mood and purpose. Now, they shone at him clear and brave.

This was not easy for her. He could see the tension holding her shoulders tight and the breath drawing her belly in. Her eyes reflected that strain in the stillness of her pupils and forced wideness of their glare.

He knew she did not want him to see her difficulty, but he could read every clue to her distress. She was not as calm as she wished to be. He placed his hope on this. Why would she hide from him if it was as simple a picture as she painted?

Violet watched as his eyes edged over her body. She had thought this would be easy. She was not shy of her body. She wore the most revealing of gowns, the sheerest of chemises, and it had been years since she could remember the heat of a blush. Still, she fought the urge to squirm under his examination. She had not expected that he would be so thorough and—no, not cold, there was nothing cold in his look—but so detached.

She remembered how her first husband had examined her on their wedding night. She had stood before him, unhappy and unsure, but still strangely excited that she was finally going to know the secrets that were whispered of in corners. His watery eyes had trailed over her, taking in the voluminous white gown, proper for a virgin bride, and her wild mane of curls, unbraided for the first night since childhood. He grimaced. Pronounced, "You'll do. Good hips." Then he got into bed and settled back and looked over at her. "Come on then, girl. Get over here and pull that thing up. I don't have time for coyness."

She didn't even want to think of the remainder of the night.

This, however, was Peter, not Sir Dratton of Two Hills. He was not some old man who needed to hurry before his pride-and-joy shrank into his withered-and-unused.

She caught Peter's glance and held it. She was the one in control. She saw the anger in his eyes. He was not any happier at this than she. She drew in a deep breath, then relaxed and wished for strength. She let her shoulders bend forward, not the most flattering of postures for a woman. He would see what she wanted. See that she was not a young girl pining for matrimony.

And glad she was of it. Not for anything would she again stand before a man and seek his approval.

It was not approval she wanted now.

It was . . . acceptance. No, she did not need that either.

All she wanted was for him to see her as she was, not as some fantasy he had built up in his mind. She would let him have no illusions about what she was and who she was.

She truly was bare before him.

She let her stomach sag and her breasts fall forward. She dropped her chin, unmindful of the fullness beneath.

"You are so beautiful, so womanly."

"I am growing old, do you not see the lines? I am marked by the years of my experience."

"And . . . ?" He let word trail off.

"I could almost be your mother."

"Now that is an exaggeration."

She turned her face from him. "But only slight."

"If you gave birth when you were seven."

"You miss the point."

"No, I think you do. I know you are a woman. I know you have experience. I either do not care or love you the more for it. I do not want a young, marriage-minded chit. I want you. I want a family with you." He walked before her until there was a hand's space between them.

"And I want you, but I am not wifely or motherly material."

He placed a hand on each of her shoulders so that she was forced to look up at him. "I will need to change your mind."

Why could he not see that it was impossible? How

could he stand and stare at her faults and either not see them or pretend that they were attractions? And he did not even know the full truth, the truth that could not be seen. Perhaps she should tell him all. He spoke of starting a family with her, and that was impossible. He was too young to know his own mind. It would be her job to protect him from himself.

She turned and walked away, scooping up the sheet as she went. Her vulnerability had been for naught; like all men he saw only what he wanted.

Well, she'd had enough of it for one night. The discussion was too painful to continue. It was time to call him back to order. He would understand that some things were not up for discussion, and marriage topped the list.

She climbed up on the high bed and arranged the pillows behind her. This time she pulled her stomach tight and lifted her breasts to their most magnificent.

"Come back to bed. We can remove the flavor of this unpleasantness." She sprawled across the bed, letting the sheet fall to highlight her most favorable attributes, long, elegant calves and breasts lifted to almost obscene limits. She smiled her most alluring smile and beckoned for him to join her. She let the sheet slide another inch— even among familiar lovers a little reveal could heighten the mood. "Oh, don't be sullen, Peter. It will all be as it was before. Maybe we can sneak back into that perfect moment."

Peter stood. He let his eyes rove over her one more time. She watched the heat grow in them, the pupils grow large and deep. Tension built and spread. She let the sheet slip even lower. She was amazed that even after she'd stood naked before him moments before, cravings could grow from another bare inch of skin.

She resisted the urge to purr with pleasure. They would wrap this night in tissue and put it away, forever. She might sneak it out in the predawn hours when sleep eluded her, and relish that a sweet young man had once adored her beyond reason, but by morn it would be rewrapped and put away with the rest of her girlhood dreams.

"No." His single word drew her from her reverie.

She shook her head. "No?"

Peter padded toward her and with a grand gesture knelt before the bed. He reached up and took one of her hands between his much larger ones. "Violet, I ask you one last time this night. Will you marry me?"

She held in a sigh. "I thought we had been through this to its bitter end. No, I will not marry you, not now, not ever. Now, come back to bed—end this foolishness."

"No."

Peter stood, turned, and walked to his pile of clothing strewn over the bench of her vanity. He pulled on one leg of the trousers and then the other.

Violet sat up upon the bed. "What are you doing? I thought you were above pouting."

"I am not pouting. I am leaving. I wish you well."

"I do not understand. Do you want me to beg?" She slid onto her knees. "I can beg very prettily."

"You clearly do not understand. I am leaving you, Violet. An hour ago I thought there was nothing I wouldn't do for you. I always thought there was nothing you could ask that I would not do, but I was wrong. I cannot do this. I will not be your kept toy. If you cannot respect me enough to believe that I know my own mind and that I am no longer a feckless boy, then I cannot stay with you. You want an amusement, not a lover. That is not me. I will no longer play until you decide to be my wife." He pulled his shirt over his head, then grabbed his boots and jacket. "I wish you well, Violet. I hope you do find what you want."

He turned and walked through the door, closing it quietly behind him. The soft tread of his feet descending the stairs barely made a sound.

Chapter 3

"**I**f I ever let my husband within twenty feet of me again, please hit me with a vase." Marguerite levered herself out of a hardback chair and stood with a slight wobble. "Someone should have warned me it would be like this." She placed both hands on her distended stomach, pulling the delicate fabric of her summer dress tight.

Violet knew her gaze was glued to the firm protuberance of flesh. She normally avoided women in the later stage of pregnancy, but her need to know what had happened to Peter had driven her here, to his brother the marquess's home. If anybody could tell her about Peter it would be Marguerite, his sister-in-law.

By God, it moved. A distinct bump had appeared in the side of Marguerite's belly.

"Definitely a boxer." Marguerite pressed a hand against the bump, pushing back at it. "Tristan insists that he believes the baby will be a girl, but no girl could punch so hard."

If it moved again, Violet swore she would be leaving and would find out some other way why Peter had not visited her. She swallowed and kept her gaze fixed on Marguerite's belly, words forgotten.

"It is not going anywhere. I promised Tristan that I would not give birth while he was out of the house, so you are safe for now." Marguerite's words drew Violet's attention, and she forced her glance to meet Marguerite's.

"I used to be irritated that men would look at my bosom while speaking to me," Marguerite continued. "At least women used to look at my face. Now, everybody stares at my belly as if it were a bubble waiting to burst."

"I do apologize," Violet answered, resisting the urge to glance down again.

"Oh, I am teasing. You have not told me that I am glowing and have never looked better. And you are here. Everyone else seems to have fled Town for the summer. None of our dear friends remain. There seem to be a bounty of house parties and other frivolities at the end of the summer. Lady Westington was here for a while, but then her stepson asked her to return home to Aylsham. Clara never could refuse that boy. At least you remain and even visit. For that I will forgive you anything."

Violet turned and walked to the shelves. She stared at the titles without seeing. She did not wish to think of Marguerite and the small life within her. It was too painful. She tapped the spine of a book, it was blue, but her eyes would not focus on the words.

"So why did you come?" Marguerite never backed away from confrontation. "I daresay it was not to see me."

"Why would you say such a thing? Of course I wanted to see you, to talk with you."

"Then why haven't you visited these past months? You send the most delightful notes, but never a visit. I know when I am being avoided. And now, here you are with no explanation."

"Is it so strange that I would want to visit? And I haven't been avoiding you." Violet pulled the book from the shelf. *A History of Foliage in the Americas.* Why would anybody have such a book on his shelves? It fulfilled neither entertainment nor pretension. "I've been busy."

"That I would believe. But with whom?"

Violet slid the book back and tried to decide which smile to answer with. A knowing one always worked. "That doesn't matter now, does it? You know I am always discreet."

"So you are still involved with Peter."

"I certainly did not say that." Violet hoped she didn't sound shrill.

"It is all in what you didn't say." Marguerite shared her own smile, one of satisfaction. She sat back in the chair again, shifting from one hip to the other. "I don't understand why you keep it so secret. There is surely no shame in keeping company with the brother of a marquess. If Peter showed interest in me I'd parade him before all of society. He is quite adorable."

"Your husband might have something to say about that."

"It would be a little scandalous. I might enjoy that. I could use the excitement after being kept at home these last months. I do not understand why my condition should prevent me from venturing forth in society. Perhaps they are afraid there would be no more babies if women were allowed to see what this is like." Marguerite leaned back in her chair and lifted her feet from the floor, legs straight. She bent her head to the left. "I cannot see them, you know; my feet, that is. I cannot fit them in any of my old shoes and I cannot see them."

Violet wanted to close her eyes or to look away. She had expected that coming here, to Peter's family, might be difficult, but she had not considered this—that it might also be painful.

It was time to face this head-on.

"You know about Peter and me. I don't believe that anybody outside of my household staff realizes, except perhaps Peter's valet." She kept her feet firmly planted as she spoke. She refused to pace. "I would not normally come to you, but it appears I have no choice. I need information about Peter."

"Does this mean gossip and delicious tidbits?" Marguerite's cheeks flushed with satisfaction.

"I am not quite sure I would have phrased it that way. I merely wish to inquire as to his whereabouts. I have not seen him about Town these last days."

"I do not believe that is all you wish to know. If it were such a simple thing you would have sent a note of inquiry to his apartments. Have you quarreled? Why else would he not have informed you himself about his travels? He has taken Felicity to Brighton for a few weeks. His mother did not wish to travel alone." Marguerite straightened in her chair. "What did you fight about? Is there more you wish to know? I do love to play matchmaker."

Violet paused and considered. He had left Town without telling her. No doubt it was intended as some kind of punishment. "I have never known his mother to need a companion before. Felicity knows how to enjoy her own company. I've always admired that about her."

"So you want to know why he went and you avoid my questions about a quarrel." Marguerite was looking smug. "It was Felicity's suggestion, but I do believe he seemed rather relieved at the excuse to leave. He probably did not realize that Felicity was planning on visiting a friend and her four daughters. I do believe she means to find him a wife." Marguerite stared hard at her, and Violet could almost feel her searching for any response to that word—wife.

Wife. Peter with a wife. She had never considered it. "I would have thought Felicity would be content with her first grandchild on the way."

"On the contrary, it seems to have spurred her on. She sees how happy Tristan is and she wants the same for Peter."

"Happy, am I? And why would that be?" Wimberley strode into the room and walked straight to Marguerite. He bent and kissed her, much more fully than Violet would have expected from a couple married more than a year. It was still hard to believe the dashing marquess had become such a doting husband.

"I was telling Violet that I was never going to let you touch me again." Despite her words Marguerite nestled back against her husband.

"Now that would certainly not make me happy." Wimberley attempted a stern look, but the corner of his mouth twitched. "So, are you going to tell me what would make me happy?"

"Not you, Peter."

"Why are you worrying about my brother's happiness? I would have thought you had enough to fill your thoughts." Wimberley's hands slipped lower and rested on his wife's belly. He squeezed gently.

Violet had to look away. It was disconcerting watching the emotions playing between the besotted couple. She still had questions, but they would have to wait.

She shook her skirts and smiled at Marguerite. "I am afraid I must be going. I do promise to visit again."

Peter stared up at the roof of the carriage, his foot tapping against the edge of the bench opposite. Why had it never occurred to him that his mother had plans of her own?

The moment they had arrived at Brighton there had been a flurry of feminine activity, and then, before he could even descend from the carriage, a lineup of marriageable misses. One petite brunette, two almost identical blondes, and . . . He couldn't exactly remember the fourth, but there had been one.

He had not needed to see the slight smile pulling at the corner of Felicity's mouth to understand the situation. He was the boy in the sweet shop, but in this store it was the confections who grabbed and chose.

Before he knew it he'd had a blonde on each arm, another girl ahead, another behind, and two proud mamas sailing before. At least avoiding pointed comments and flirtatious looks had kept him from thinking of Violet.

Violet.

Damn.

He'd made it fifteen minutes this time without thinking of her and the real reason he was headed back to Town without spending more than a night in Brighton. He'd even left at first light to avoid his matrimonial-minded mother.

He'd love to tell Felicity that he also had a mind for marriage, but until Violet came around he would have to hold to his own counsel. And she would capitulate. Of that he was sure. She was being difficult, trying to make him want her more. Didn't she realize that would never happen? He was already hers in every possible way.

He leaned his head back against the well-padded squabs and closed his eyes. His fingers ran over the nap of the velvet seat—so very like Violet's skin. He could almost imagine it was she, lying beside him as the first morning sun began to peek over the trees in the park. He ran a finger down the indent of her spine, traced the dimpled swelling of her buttocks. It was not yet a touch of desire, still only one of exploration and morning greeting. He felt her stir beneath his touch. In a moment she would roll over and open those pansy eyes. Her gaze would still be heavy with sleep, but he'd see the fires beginning to burn in her darkened pupils. He ran his finger back along her velvet skin and . . .

The carriage shook and almost sent him flying to the floor.

He missed her.

It was easy to concentrate on the physical and pretend that was all he missed, but he knew the truth. The physical, the sex was easy. It was better with her than anyone, but if the state of his body was any indication, he could make do with a velvet pillow.

But his mind, his heart. They wanted so much more. They wanted her smile, her conversation, her quick wit and refusal to let him get away with anything. They wanted to trail her about the house picking up the scarves and gloves she left in her wake. They wanted to leave her gifts in surprising places, waiting for the smile that filled her face and wiped away every trace of sadness. The smile that was the same for a daisy plucked from his mother's garden as it was for the amethyst ear bobs that matched her eyes.

Why didn't she see that about him? Why did she try to act as if the sex was all he wanted? He couldn't deny that he did want it—what man wouldn't?

He was thinking in circles. He needed a plan, a way to make her see him and his desires in their entirety. He would show her he was a man, not a boy who cared only for one thing.

Violet slowed as she approached her home. There was a hired hack in front of her house. Who would come calling in a hack? Peter? Her heart gave one fast beat, before she pushed the thought away. He had both a curricle and a carriage. He would not arrive in a hack, and even if he did, she wouldn't be excited by his arrival. She would act as if nothing had happened.

She started walking toward the door, but more slowly. If it wasn't Peter, then who? A list of friends and acquaintances sped through her mind and were dismissed.

Well, there was one way to find out. She glanced at her dress, smoothed out a crease, adjusted the angle of her new feathered bonnet, placed a curl over her shoulder, tilted back her shoulders, pulled up the corners of her mouth into a society smile, and headed up the walk.

The door opened and a lady's half boot appeared, then the flounce of a sprigged day dress, a cinnamon curl, and then—Violet's smile loosed and then reformed. This time wider and more genuine.

"Isabella." She called her sister's name as she lifted the edge of her skirt and scurried forward. "What are you doing here? I thought that Masters had decided you were not to come to Town this year. I swear it took me a day to finish his letter describing all the estate's needs and how the heavy rains this spring had led to additional costs and that it would be impossible for you to come."

She stepped back and surveyed Isabella. "Your dress will simply not do, though. It screams country. I will take you to my modiste. I can't imagine that our dear brother will notice a dress or two. Do say you will let me? How long are you here for? It is late in the year for there to be much happening about Town, but I can always find a soiree or musicale. Have you had tea? I know it is still early, but . . ."

Violet sputtered to a stop as she watched Isabella toss her head back and release a bellow of a laugh. "I am rambling, aren't I? But I am so pleased to see you."

Isabella lowered her chin and stared straight at Violet. "And I too, sister. I hadn't been in Town an hour when I decided I must sneak out and see you. I cannot describe my disappointment when you were not at home. Masters would not be pleased if he knew I was seeing you alone. He is of the opinion that you have a scandalous reputation. Do you?"

"Is that glee I hear in your question? Do you want me to be scandalous?"

Isabella's nose wrinkled, and Violet knew she was trying to hold back a giggle. "I suppose I do. Life has been so boring in Derby and a bit of scandal sounds delightful. Still . . ." Isabella paused, more thoughtful. "I would hate to give our brother any further excuse to not let me visit."

"Perhaps you should have waited to ask him."

Isabella ducked her head, hiding the glint in her hazel eyes. "Yes, but you know it would have taken days for him to decide to call on you. From your surprise I don't believe he even bothered to let you know we were coming to Town."

"That's true—"

"Don't tell me to be patient." Now it was Isabella moving ahead and pulling Violet into the parlor.

"I wasn't going to. I was only going to say that sneaking out was not the best way to prove to Masters that you don't need to be watched."

"I know, but I couldn't resist. It's been over two years since you visited and you've given no indication that you've another trip to Derby planned." Isabella dropped into the seat that Violet waved to. "How long was I supposed to wait? You are the only sister I have—for all that you're old enough to be my mother."

The last words were said with mischief and a grin, but they still pricked at Violet's already tender skin. She'd thought she was tougher than this. Isabella and she had always joked at the dozen years between them, but now it was unpleasant reminder. Violet had said almost those exact words to Peter. In fact, Isabella was exactly the type of wife that Peter should be seeking— nineteen, sweet, and ready to believe in all that life promised.

"Oh, don't look so glum," Isabella said, evidently perceiving the shift in Violet's mood. "You're still well-preserved. I daresay you don't look a day over thirty."

Violet forced a smile and seated herself, gesturing for the footman who hovered at the door to send for tea. "No, I was thinking what a babe you still are, hardly out of short skirts. I am surprised it's not a nanny our brother has chasing after you."

"Don't even whisper that. He may get ideas."

"I imagine you're safe," Violet answered. "If Masters has finished with the services of a nanny, I can't imagine him loosing the funds to call her back. I imagine even your guardian maid and footmen have a host of other duties."

Isabella nodded at the truth of that statement. "I am happy to be here. I don't even want to think of him. I can't wait to explore. It is so seldom he brings me to London . . . even though it's time that I am out. Do you know I've never seen a menagerie or the Crown jewels? Would you take me to see the Elgin Marbles? Am I pretty enough to find a husband? It would be wonderful to move away from Derby. I could live in London, like you. I also want to go for ices. They sound so wonderful, and—"

"Slow down, little sister; only you would consider trying an ice and finding a husband in the same breath."

"I know, but I want to get it all said before I have to hurry home. I am still hoping that it will be assumed I am somewhere lost in the hustle of arrival. I don't believe it will occur to anyone that I have left."

Violet could not fault the logic; arriving in Town for a lengthy visit was always hectic. It was doubtful that anyone had bothered to keep track of Isabella. Still . . . "And what if Masters does realize you're gone?"

Isabella pursed her lips. "Then I will tell him the truth. He will not be pleased, but you are our sister. He cannot fault my eagerness to see you."

Violet stared across at her sister. The girl's cinnamon

curls were slipping loose from their knot. Her build was
far slimmer than Violet's had ever been, although the
curves were filling out. She sat still and quiet; not even
a toe tapped on the floor. Her eyes looked more brown
than gold or green in the light—large and placid. There
was very little, except years, to separate her from the
gentle sister Violet had always known and loved.

But there was something.

Something had changed.

She looked again, but could not say what was different. The sister she had known would never have dared
Masters's displeasure. Yes, something was different.

"You're staring at me. Have I grown two heads?"
Isabella raised a brow in question.

"No, you're still the same pretty girl as always."

Isabella nodded with the easy assurance of a girl
who had always been confident in her looks. That had
not changed.

"I am hoping my appearance will help bring me a
good husband." Isabella fluffed a loose curl. "I understand that is how it works."

"It is not quite as simple as that, but you are correct
that appearance counts."

"I am counting on you to help me with the rest. I am
sure you must have learned something with all your
scandals." Isabella grinned, and the calmness left her
face. "You managed to catch three husbands, so you
must have some clue how it's done. Although I am not

sure if you'll be able to chaperone me, we don't want to risk damage to my reputation should society wonder if you're lax."

Violet examined her sister again, and this time she saw it. There was a sense of self-importance and self-assurance that had never been there before. Neither was a bad thing in a woman, but they were mixed with a slight edge of calculation—there in the tightening of the lips, and a hard glow as she examined a crystal vase on Violet's table. None of that had been there two years before. Had Isabella been left too long under Masters's care?

Masters never missed the chance to better himself or his wallet, and for the first time Violet could see the same qualities in Isabella. They were perhaps not bad qualities to have, but they were not what she wished for her sister. Violet knew too well how much they could cost one.

She spun her feet to loosen her ankles and then placed them on the floor. "Isabella, dearest, surely it is too early for all this talk. Surely you can save your plans until later, when society picks up again?"

Isabella glanced down at her hands and then looked back at Violet. "No, I don't think I can. I am not sure that Masters will ever choose to come to Town at a better time. I must do what I can now. I want you to help me land a husband. I realize you're too old now to do so yourself, but I am sure you remember how."

Violet positively disliked her sister's mood. She'd felt nothing but warmth and gladness to see her, and now . . . She had to bite back the desire to inform Miss Isabella Masters that she had been proposed to only days before and by a most eligible, most handsome, most young man. She chomped down on her tongue to hold back the words.

"Oh Violet, I can see from your face that I have upset you. I did not mean that you are old, only old for marriage."

Violet had used that same argument with Peter, but it sounded very different coming from another.

Isabella lifted a hand and patted Violet's arm. "I am not saying this well. I know you have the life you want. The few times you visited you told me how wonderful everything in your life was. I could never understand how you loved those wrinkled hands, and drooping bellies, but you always assured me that you did. And now . . ." Isabella's gaze swept around the finely appointed chamber. "Now I can see how wonderful a life you have, the freedom you are allowed. It seems you have everything you ever told me you wanted. I imagine you even manage your own money. Do you wish me any less? I know my choices will be different, but I want what you have—plus maybe a babe or two."

That cut deep. A myriad of thoughts spun through Violet's mind. Had her sister really believed that she could have loved a gassy old windbag like Sir Dratton? Isabella had been only twelve the last time she had asked Violet about marriage. Carrington had been dead only a few scant years, and Violet had thought only of him when answering. What else was she supposed to have said when asked such questions by a mere child?

And, why did her "wonderful life" seem so empty when Isabella kept staring at gilt-edged frames and silk upholstery? Did her sister not understand all she had paid to secure what she had? And choices, there had been so few of them. How did you explain to a young girl who still had eyes full of innocence—and they were, no matter the touch of calculation—that life did not offer women many choices, and the ones they were offered must be seized?

"Isabella," she began, "I should have told you the truth about many things a while ago. I had not realized how quickly you would grow. I must explain—"

There was a rap on the door, and the tea she had longed for a moment ago arrived.

"Oh dear." Isabella sprang to her feet. "I had not re-alized how long I had been. I can't stay. I know I should have said something before, but you do understand I don't want to be missed. You'll have to tell me your secrets next time. Maybe we can start choosing my husband then too."

Without even a formal farewell, Isabella spun and dashed from the room. Violet sank into her chair and let the maid pour her tea. She cradled her head in her hands and rubbed at her temple. She refused to have a headache.

She still hadn't decided how to deal with Peter, and now this. There must be a way to resolve both dilemmas—to get Peter back in her bed and to stop her sister from precipitously trying to trap a husband.

She took the cup the maid offered and sipped. If only she could turn back time a week or two.

Or a week ahead—she had forgotten Lady Smythe-Burke's famous midsummer party by the river.

It might present the solution to both her dilemmas.

Chapter 4

"**T**his is marvelous. Thank you so much for bringing me. I don't know how you persuaded Masters to let me come, but I am so grateful." Isabella alighted next to her sister, spreading her skirts across the blanket. A deep bonnet shadowed her face, but glee played across her features as her eyes darted around her.

"It's not hard to persuade Masters if you do it before he's made up his mind." Once he'd made a decision it was a far different story, but Violet didn't want to dwell on that or on the complexity that made up her brother. "Besides he could hardly object to your attending any function held by Lady Smythe-Burke."

Lady Smythe-Burke had thrown summer soirees at her late husband's home in Richmond, only a short ride from Town, for longer than Violet could remember. The lady claimed that if she was in Town during August, she didn't understand why anyone else wouldn't be.

"It is rather a wonderful afternoon. I am surprised at how many gentlemen have shown up," Violet said, keeping her tone gay. She had chosen this venue to assure her plans unfolded in respectable society, hoping such a venue would not appeal to the younger, more thrill-seeking crowd. She'd been right on the first account, but wrong on the second.

She peered around the edge of her bonnet at her sister. Isabella was avidly looking about, her gaze full of exhilaration—and an unmistakable desire for adventure. Maybe Violet had been overeager to see how shallow and foolish her sister's plans were and had not considered that they might make sense.

Why shouldn't a sweet, young girl dream of a handsome husband? The fact that her own youthful dreams had not come to fruition was no reason to punish her sister.

She looked around the garden with new eyes. There were several young men present who, from what she knew, would not make bad husbands. They might not be as dashing and gallant as the man in her sister's dreams, but they were of good countenance and solid means.

She leaned over and took Isabella's hand. "I am glad you are here, dearest. You are right. It is time to find a husband for you." She patted the slender fingers resting between her own. She'd never considered herself a matchmaker, but she suddenly felt a sense of purpose. "You must tell me whom you find appealing. I am sure there must be someone here who meets your fancy."

Isabella pushed back the brim of her bonnet so that her features could be seen; her deep gold curls burned red in the fading sunlight. "Who is that over by river's edge? He is standing next to the table with the sandwiches."

Violet loosened the ties of her own hat and let it fall back. As the daylight faded many of the ladies present had already lost their headgear. Free of the encumbrance, she looked over her shoulder in the direction that Isabella pointed.

Langdon.

He had been involved in some unfavorable events the year before, and what little she did know did not make him husband material. Even as she watched, he grabbed four glasses of champagne and downed them two at time, not minding the amount he spilled across the hemlines of those nearest him. When one of his neighbors spoke in protest, he only laughed and called the waiter back.

"He looks like such fun," Isabella chimed in as she waited for Violet's answer.

"That is Langdon. He is the oldest son of the Earl of Linster. I don't believe he's entered the marriage market. He still enjoys other pursuits." Violet had a sudden distinct remembrance of Langdon staring down the front of her dress and trying to pull her closer for a better look.

"Well, then, we'll have to change his mind. Is his father rich?" Isabella's voice took on that strange quality. Once again, Violet was afraid it was calculation she saw shining deep in her sister's gaze—but perhaps it was only the bright glow of the sinking sun.

"I just don't think he's the right man for you. You don't want a husband you are always wondering about."

"Wondering what about?" Isabella sounded genuinely confused.

Her sister was still a little innocent, a fact easy to forget when Isabella's voice rang with that manipulative tone.

"Don't you worry about that. Trust me. He's not a good choice for a husband. How about the one standing before the willow in the deep blue superfine? He's Lord Tom Wesley. I've heard he has wonderful manners and is always polite to his mother."

"Polite to his mother." Isabella's tone made it clear that this was not a recommendation. "He appears a little short and I've never been partial to blonds." Her gaze turned back to Langdon.

"Don't be too hasty to judge." Violet tried again. "He may be a third son, but his aunt has settled a fine estate upon him. I am surprised he's not there now. I know he takes a hand at running it."

"I daresay that would mean spending too much time in the country. I don't think I'd mind a house party or two, and the countryside is lovely at Christmas, but once I am away from Masters I don't ever want to spend more than a week at a time away from the joys of Town. And I don't like travel so it would be silly to spend more time at it than necessary."

Violet could not remember being young enough to care about the length of a carriage ride.

"Oh, who's that? Over there talking to Lady Smythe-Burke." Isabella caught at Violet's sleeve and gestured. "He's a bit large, but his coat is wonderfully cut."

Violet turned and, following her sister's gesture, looked back over her shoulder. Her stomach dropped as if she'd consumed Christmas dinner thrice over.

Peter was here.

She expected he would be, even looked forward to the chance to lure him back, but still her heart sped with surprise.

She had not seen him since he'd stormed out of her chamber. She allowed herself to soak in the sight of him as he stood there, strong and vital, his dark hair waving in the soft breeze. He bent forward to catch something that Lady Smythe-Burke said, and Violet found her gaze drawn to the tight twill of his breeches as they pulled across his muscled thigh. She could see the delineation of each muscle through the fabric, almost imagine the spread of dark hairs growing thicker as she ran her hands upward. Her fingers twitched and she caught her breath deepening. It really was time—

"So who is he? You're staring right at him." Isabella's voice penetrated Violet's thoughts. "He must be acceptable if Lady Smythe-Burke is spending so much time talking with him, although how anybody would wish to talk with her for so long I don't know. Do you know what she said about my reticule? She described it as—"

"He is Lord Peter St. Johns. His older brother is the Marquess of Wimberley. Surely I have mentioned him."

"No, I don't believe you have, but then we haven't had much time for talk. Even at the mantua maker's we talked only of clothes. You haven't told me anything of your acquaintances. You must tell me more if I am to decide whom to wed. I do want to make the right decision."

"I wish that too," Violet said

"Well then, tell me all about Lord Peter."

She was here.

He hadn't seen her yet, but he knew. Peter tried to keep his attention on Lady Smythe-Burke as she chattered on. His foot tapped restlessly. So far she had proclaimed why the season should be held in the summer, why all girls should attend school—boys apparently should be tossed out of doors until they reached their majority—why eating French style was unhealthy, and, oh yes, why the new lighter corsets that were in fashion would lead to bad posture and sagging. Lady Smythe-Burke had shared far more details on this last than Peter cared for.

Where was she?

He looked over his hostess's shoulder at the slew of bonnets covering her lawn. He spotted Violet even before she loosed the strings and let her headgear fall back. He knew those creamy shoulders anywhere. He would have noticed her sooner except that he hadn't recognized her companion. The girl was gesturing animatedly. As he watched, the chit turned and pointed at him, or perhaps at Lady Smythe-Burke. He had only a moment to fasten his gaze back on Lady Smythe-Burke before he felt Violet's glance lift toward him.

Even without looking back at her he felt her eyes travel over him. He shifted as his body answered their call.

It had always been like this. She had only to look at him and he responded. He closed his own eyes and concentrated on not embarrassing himself in public.

How did she do this to him when he still felt the pain of her rejection?

"Do you have a headache?" Lady Smythe-Burke asked. She must have caught his grimace. "Does the light pain you? I've always enjoyed a good sunset. It isn't quite upon us yet, but there's nothing like a good rosy glow to make the world attractive. Even an ugly girl looks good when the sky turns red . . ." Lady Smythe-Burke continued on, but Peter's full attention was required to ignore Violet.

"Large grayish spots." Lady Smythe-Burke spoke the phrase with vehemence and then repeated it. She paused then as if waiting for a response.

Peter didn't have one. How did one respond to spots? And how had she gotten from sunsets to spots? Listening was clearly not his forte. He could still feel Violet's gaze upon him. What would she do if he turned and met it head-on?

"You're not answering." Lady Smythe-Burke persisted. "Either you truly do have a headache, you're foxed, or it's a woman. I am guessing a woman. It's always either whiskey or women with men your age, and I've never known you to indulge this early in the evening. It does take whiskey with a man your size.

"You're still not answering. So, it is a woman. Now, which one? My eyesight is not what it was, but I'd have to be blind to miss the glow of that carrot hair."

"It's not carrot," Peter answered. "It's sunrise and sunset and every moment of glory in between."

"Gads, it really is a woman. Nothing else could be responsible for such syrup. Now, which one is it?"

Peter swallowed and turned to stare at Violet. "I thought we'd just decided that."

"Nonsense. There are still two of them. Is it Lady Carrington or her sister, the Masters girl? They both have red hair and your . . . whimsical . . . description does nothing to differentiate between Violet's deep red and her sister's more strawberry color. Hmmm."

Peter studied the girl who sat beside Violet. Her sister? He hadn't been aware she had one. He'd known there was a brother, of course. He'd heard enough of the story of her first marriage to know about the brother. But a sister?

He examined the girl with care. Lady Smythe-Burke was correct about the color of the hair, if not the shade. He would have called it ginger. That was the only resemblance he could see between the women, however.

Where Violet was full, lush, this girl was—well, he wouldn't say scrawny, but she lacked the padding a fellow liked. And her mouth looked pinched, not relaxed and succulent like his Violet's.

He couldn't imagine the girl ever opening those lips to trail soft kisses down his belly, pausing, licking, laving, her tongue trailing back and forth in ever slower patterns, the teeth stopping to nip at his short hairs. And that final smile. She always looked up at him in mirth and power before that final lick and kiss that started it all . . .

"Lord Peter, I do not know what you are thinking," Lady Smythe-Burke interrupted, "but I can tell it is not appropriate for one of my evening entertainments.

Turn away from her at once, and pull your coat forward. Disgraceful. I will have to talk to Wimberley about this."

Peter had a sudden vision of his brother's face on being presented with such information by Lady Smythe-Burke. It was not pleasant. "Surely there is no need to bother—"

"Every need, I should say. But perhaps there is another way. I will talk to the girl, give her some hint of your admiration, while being sure to warn her of your methods, inclinations, tactics—talking to the young is so difficult. But I will manage. I'll talk to the girl, try to be gentle as I warn her of the dangers of men—and you, my lord, will take the older sister aside and tell her of your feelings. I am sure once you explain your interests to Violet she will know to keep a sufficient eye on her sister. The dear girl, Lady Carrington, that is, always did have a grasp on how to treat your sex. Now, if only it had been her you were staring at. I always did fancy finding her a good match. I might even have decided to help if it had been her you were after."

"But it was, it is. My affections are held by Violet," he blurted out. God, it felt good to say the words. "I don't even know her sister's name."

"Isabella, but don't think I don't see through you. Come now."

Peter could only follow. At least she was leading him over to Violet.

*   *   *

How had this happened? Violet looked at the dark shrubbery surrounding them as she followed Peter along the little-used path. It should have been stretching the bounds of all propriety for them to be walking alone here, but Lady Smythe-Burke had verbally shoved them off together and left little choice of destination. What had the lady been thinking?

"I am supposed to reveal my lusts for your sister and promise to behave in the most honorable fashion," Peter explained.

As if that was an explanation.

"Isabella? You don't even know her." Violet hoped her irritation didn't show as she stepped down hard upon a sharp pebble. Her light slippers, while fine upon the lawns, were no match for roughness of the path, and Peter's pace had left little room for care.

"I tried to explain that to Lady Smythe-Burke, but she remained unconvinced." Peter stopped and looked around. "Where has she sent us off to? This looks more a woodland hike than a garden stroll."

Violet was inclined to agree. The foliage had grown increasingly dense, and she could hardly hear the chatter of the party. "Perhaps we took a wrong turn."

Peter didn't answer, but turned to continue down the path. He paused occasionally to hold back a branch for her or to kick a rock out of the path.

This was not the meeting she had imagined. Even

with her experience it was hard to be seductive when trudging over tree roots.

"Oh, do slow, Peter. You can't still be angry with me. It's been over a week, almost two. I am sorry that my answer was not what you wanted. But you must have realized by now that I was right."

Peter remained silent, but he did slow. Perhaps he could be brought to listen to reason. She had always admired his intellect.

Damn. It was getting dark. When her knee hit against a broken branch Peter had missed, she stopped.

The sun was setting, the bugs were coming out, and she'd had enough of this. Marching off into the woods was not going to solve anything.

Peter must have been listening to the rustle of her walk, because he turned and walked back to her.

He turned toward the sun still shining low through the trees so she could read his face. There were so many emotions warring over his countenance that she hardly knew what to think. There was anger in the pursing of his lips, and the tight furrow of his brow, yet a hint of humor hid at the corner of his eye and lust, yes lust, burned there too. She could see it as he let his glance trail down her body, pausing in all his favorite places.

It grew and spread, his lips softened, and she could feel the heat of his breath as he leaned closer. He pupils grew large and dark as he stared. His mouth parted further, and she could see the tip of his tongue as it darted out to moisten dry lips.

She drew closer in response, a moth to the flame. His gaze was focused on her own lips now. She let them part, drew a deep breath in and released it, watching it ruffle the folds of his neckwear. She pressed even farther forward, fitting under the strength of his chin, her face almost brushing his shirt.

Almost. It was almost. They did not touch. They did not speak. She had never been so aware of another human being, of another body. She closed her eyes, inhaling his scent, leather, sandalwood, the crispness of a lemon. Why did he always smell like home, like safety? She cast the thought aside. It did not belong in this moment.

She could feel his heart beat. Even without touching she could feel the air move with each beat, each pulse. She longed to press her lips to that spot, to lick at the linen of his shirt until it dampened and she could taste his skin though it. She longed to curl her fingers into the fabric and rub it across his finely-haired chest, feel the flickers of emotion run through him as the fabric delicately chafed.

But she did not. She stood and breathed and waited.

She did not know how long they stood—not touching. It could have been a moment or a month. Her hands had curled to claws at her sides with the effort not to move, and her legs were pressed so tight it was a wonder they had not fused. She was a statue—did stone so long to move, to feel?

There, she felt it. First a twitch and then a shift. He hauled her forward, strong hands grasping her waist and lifting her to him. His mouth pressed down upon hers, forcing it open. He was all heat, passion, and speed. Her back was flattened against the tree as he took possession.

But it was not all his possession. From the moment she'd felt him move her own desires had run free. Her hands cupped his face, holding him tight. She opened her mouth wide beneath his, welcoming him in, before her own tongue darted out on its own forays.

She tasted, nibbled, devoured. It had been too long. It felt so good to feel him against her. She pushed forward against him, rubbing her breasts back and forth against the linen of his shirt. Her fingers ran through his hair, tangling in the strands at his neck before sliding to find the bare skin beneath his cravat. She ran a finger around, enjoying every tiny shudder coursing through his body. She pulled back a moment to stare into his eyes, they were so deep and brown she felt she could drown in them and never return.

It was a moment of stillness in the midst of a storm, a moment of peace as their eyes met and took measure—well, except for her fingers, which were all the while working skillfully to bare his neck before her.

Still keeping her gaze locked with his, Violet leaned

forward and nipped at his chin, her teeth grating on the stubble he could never shave completely away. His body jerked and trembled, his fingers grasping more tightly into her waist.

She kissed the nip away, and then, finally releasing his look, she kissed and licked and laved her way down his throat, she could feel the rush of his pulse beneath her lips, the tension that shook him with each swallow. She lingered slowly, endlessly.

She could feel her power over him, relished it. His fingers tightened again, beginning to gather her skirts, but with the slightest swish of her hips she discouraged him. Slow. Easy. Gentle. That was what she liked and as always he seemed to know her every wish before she formed it.

His hands released, and then began to form slow, easy patterns up and down her back as he buried his lips in her hair, breathing in her essence.

She unfastened his shirt, her mouth continuing its dance down his chest. She caught the short hairs between her teeth and tugged. She tasted the salt, the sweat, the flavor that was all him. She reached his left nipple, and ran her closed lips around it before letting her tongue dash out to play. She could feel his heart beating beneath her mouth, feel its strength, his strength in each pulse.

She pressed her cheek against him there, loving that sign of the life that filled him, wishing she could stay like this forever—but still her hands moved on, dipping beneath the waistband of his trousers, before seeking the fastening.

One of his hands came forward then and caught hers, stilling them, while the other caught her face and tilted it up to meet his gaze.

"You do know what this means. Remember what I said the last time?" His voice was husky with passion, with desire, but his eyes stared into hers, seeking.

God, what did he want? Violet tried to gather her scattered thoughts, while her body cried for more. She knew whatever he was asking was important to him, could see that in the stillness of his face, but all she could think was, *Don't stop now.*

She nodded in agreement as her hands fought their way free from his and released the flap of his trousers, her hips pressed forward against his heavy arousal. His eyes flared, and his body jerked, but even as she rubbed against him, her body wanting him, wanting to forget everything but him, he held her gaze and refused to continue.

"Do you remember? I need to hear the words." His voice strained with effort. She pressed tighter, testing, wanting. Everything was so perfect when she was with him—why did he force this pause in the midst of the magic?

"Yes. Yes," she whispered as her forward hands crept around him. She didn't know what she affirmed, but she knew this was not the moment for talk. She would have said anything to feel his arms about her again.

Peter watched Violet's eyes glaze over as she moved her hips against him. She was so beautiful in her passion, her lips parted and swollen and pink, her face flushed and rosy.

When her fingers wrapped around his erection, it took every ounce of his being not to give in to her, not to get swept away. She was all he wanted, all he needed, and it went against everything that he was not to answer her.

But he needed her answer.

"Yes." Her voice murmured around him, surrounding him, lighting each particle of his being as if with static shot. His eyes closed with the sheer pleasure of it. Even the soft movements of her hands brought not the pleasure of that single word.

She was his.

She had finally agreed.

He would have crushed her to him then, but he knew what she liked. He forced his hands to relax, pulled her to him gently, as he tilted her face up for one more infinite kiss. Sweet, caressing—perfect.

He allowed his hands to run down her back, to cup her buttocks to him, to gather the fabric of her skirts. The rough bark of the tree behind her rasped his knuckles with each gather.

Finally he slid his fingers beneath her skirts to find—
"What's this?"

"What?" Her voice was blurred with passion, her
eyes unfocused. She shook her head as if to clear it.

"You're wearing pants." Where was the velvet skin
his fingers longed for? What was this cloth blocking
his desires?

She laughed then, soft, husky, and all Violet. "They're
my drawers. Have you never seen them before? The
very latest fashion, but also a bit of warmth should the
evening cool. But never mind them." Her hips pressed
forward and rubbed hard against him, showing him
how unimportant they were.

His gaze moved down, capturing the measure of her
long legs in the fine linen. The drawers did not block
his view, merely shadow it. He could still see the curling red that marked her sex at the apex of her thighs.
And as she moved, the hint of that true flame peeking
out.

He pushed her back against the tree, sinking to his
knees to get a better view. "What if I want to mind
them?"

He ran his hands up and down her legs, enjoying the
rub of the fabric against them, imagining how it must
feel on the even more sensitive skin at the top of her
legs.

There. He was right. The whole center seam of the
thing was open, inviting. He'd always loved her long,

naked legs surrounding him, but this—the chaste linen with her curls shining through—

He ran his hands outward, toward her hips, causing the fabric to pull tight, and separate. Then he blew. The barest puff, it would not have disturbed a lit candle, but she shuddered and cried.

He blew again. Her hands found his hair, tangled, pulled.

He leaned forward and kissed her, not pressing or demanding, but barely denting the surface of her curls.

He didn't know how he held back when his own body screamed for completion. He was one endless sensation, centered in the hard arousal that longed to be buried deep within her.

But this was about her. He gripped his own thigh with one hand, the nails biting deep as he fought for calm, while with the other he held the seam of her drawers open. He moved carefully, precisely, opening his mouth on the second kiss, letting his tongue move out to taste, to savor.

"Oh, Peter. Yes." Her voice moved about him as she raised up on her legs, spreading herself further. "I am so glad you've forgotten that foolishness and come back to me. I was insane without you."

"What foolishness?" He spoke against her, feeling her response to each breath of his voice.

"Ah, that marriage nonsense," she rasped. "We are so perfect like this. Why should we need more?"

Peter felt all the air leave him. Nonsense. He was a fool. She had spoken the truth. He had been so eager to believe she remembered his words that he would not do this again until she agreed to be his wife, so eager to believe that she took him seriously, so eager to believe—in her.

Anger ground though him—not at her, at himself. He had been betrayed by his own eagerness. It still betrayed him.

He should stand and walk away.

But he could not.

In one move he rose and, lifting her around him, dove in, impaling her to the core. "Then let's give the lady what she wants."

He pushed forward, pulled back, thrust again. Hard. Fast. Unmindful of the care and gentleness of a moment before. Who cared what she wanted. This was for him.

But even as he thrust again, felt the climax coming, saw the flashes of light against the closed dark of his lids, he felt her quiver around him, heard her cry, that sound he knew so well.

Then it was upon him and he could think no more.

The world came back slowly, and then in a rush.

He'd played this scene before. Peter unwrapped his cravat from the branch it had tangled about and pulled back.

Violet leaned against the tree. Her skirts had fallen with his departure, and, aside from the flush on her cheeks and a single leaf in her hair, she looked unchanged—if very contented.

He stepped away.

Then walked away into the dusk.

"Peter?"

He did not answer.

He did not have the words to explain the turmoil within.

Chapter 5

How could he have done that to her?

Violet picked up a jeweled hairpin from the tray before her. Tonight would be her first night out since the episode in the woods two weeks ago, and still the incident preoccupied her. She smoothed her hair back and threaded the pin through it. She would have jammed it into the side of her head if she hadn't already made that mistake with the first pin. She would have cursed, but she'd run out of curses.

How had this happened to her? She was the one in control. He was the boy. If anyone was going to walk away it would be she.

Only he'd done it to her. Twice.

She pushed away from her dressing table and stood. Her light skirts flirted around her ankles, moving of their own accord. It should have pleased her. The dress was spectacular. It cut across her shoulders, revealing the full curves of her breasts while still shielding her upper arms, and its silk-gauze overlay smoothed any imperfections in her figure. The gold iridescent fabric reflected light up toward her face, giving her a radiant glow.

It was perfection.

She looked almost girlish.

She had chosen it with Peter in mind.

Damnation.

Not only did the boy walk out on her, she couldn't stop thinking of him. She refused to think of him.

There were numerous young men who would be all too happy to take his place. She did not need him. She wished the thought did not sound so childish. She was determined to be mature about the situation.

If she sought the company of other men it was because the time had come. If Peter didn't want her she would not waste any more time waiting for him, wishing for him.

A woman did not always get what she wanted.

She had wanted Peter, but she could not have him.

Therefore, it was time to take what she could have.

She selected a necklace heavy with sapphires. It was a bolder piece than she would normally have selected, but tonight was a night for boldness.

It took a woman of a certain ilk to intrude upon the men in their gambling hells, one who could hold her head high and stare down anyone who would question her right to be there.

Even at her wildest moments she had never felt the

need to be such a woman, to attend such gatherings, but now . . .

Now, the time had come. Whispers had surrounded her for years—she killed three husbands, had hundreds of young lovers, spends a fortune without a thought, never gives a damn what anyone thinks. There was a pinch of truth in all of them—there usually was—but now she was ready to make them all true. Well, she hadn't killed any of her husbands and it did seem a little late to start now, but otherwise taking another young lover and recklessly spending some of her well-cared-for funds didn't sound like bad ideas at all.

She took one last glance in the mirror. She glittered and glowed. One deep breath. One glass of sherry. She shook an invisible wrinkle out of her skirt and left.

How had he gotten roped into this?

Peter looked around the room and resisted the urge to hide. He hated this kind of house party, always had. The only good social gatherings involved horses, hounds, and very fine French brandy—with nary a lady in sight. Here, there seemed to be nothing but women, and young giggling ones at that.

The only thing worse than staying at home thinking about Violet was being abroad—thinking about Violet.

A group of tittering chits stood before him. One of them had her eyes glued right to his—gads—he glanced down, everything was fastened and there were no embarrassing crumbs of food or spills of drink. What was she staring at? Everything he knew of young women—which was not much—indicated that they avoided the very mention of body parts. But there was no doubt where her eyes were fastened.

He did the only thing a man could do—he turned his back and pretended that the portraits of Summerton's ancestors were of unsurpassing interest. Unfortunately, the titters increased. Hopefully, they'd grow bored, and in a moment he could slip away.

"Have you found her yet?"

Peter turned to see Henry Edwards, a friend from Cambridge, peering up at him. The crowd of giggles seemed to have moved on. Henry's pronouncedly larger backside was not the attention grabber that his own had been.

"Well, have you?" Henry asked again.

"I don't know what you're talking about, I am afraid." Peter relaxed, leaning back against the wall, careful to avoid whichever Summerton grandmother hung on the wall to his side.

"My mother said you were here looking for a wife. Why else would anyone come? Lady Summerton isn't even pouring brandy since she feels that it will only muddle the situation—and she didn't even explain what the situation is. I am afraid that we are going to have to force Summerton to take a wife so that his mother becomes the Dowager Lady Summerton and can be shipped off to a cottage. It is cruel of him to allow her to hostess his parties, and therefore it is only fair we help him find his own leg-shackle."

Henry smiled up with round-faced good humor, looking as harmless as a man could. Peter, however, had known him for too many years to be taken in.

"You've thought this all out, haven't you? You truly do mean to find the poor man a wife?"

Henry continued to grin, his cheeks stretched and glowing. "Of course I do. The man has reached his middle thirties and is allowing his mother not to serve brandy. If he is not careful the port will go too. It will have to be the right type, of course; men with controlling mothers often end up with controlling brides—and that would defeat the whole purpose."

"I'm going to feel sorry for Summerton if you keep this up, and I don't believe he'd take kindly to the sentiment," Peter said.

"We must deal with you first, of course," Henry answered.

Was it possible for the man to keep smiling for much longer? "Again, I am not sure what you mean."

"Oh, no need to be bashful. Your mother told my mother that you had decided it was time to enjoy matrimony. So, who is she? Even when you were a boy you always knew what you wanted. So, which one? We'll mount a campaign."

Peter was about to exclaim with great vehemence that he certainly had no interest in marriage, when he caught himself—he *was* interested in marriage.

"My first thought was that you'd like one of the Breyers girls—very sweet and pretty, with good portions," Henry continued. "I'd probably pursue one of them myself—if I were of a matrimonial mind. The only problem is that they are too sweet. I am of good acquaintance with your mother and she is definitely not sweet, so you will not want a sweet wife."

Peter happened to think Violet was quite sweet, although perhaps not in the way that Henry meant. He doubted Henry expected him to walk through the room licking all the young women. "I am not looking for a wife who resembles my mother."

"You are seeking a bride, though."

Peter considered. Even here, a day's ride from London, surrounded by—he took the time to look around the room at the beautiful girls spinning and dancing and laughing—the choicest damsels of the year, all he could think of was Violet and how she tasted of honey.

If he couldn't have Violet, why not choose another?

"You know what, Henry, I think I am. A sweet fiancée may be what I need."

This was supposed to be exciting and risqué? Violet peered around the room—it was too smoky to do anything but peer. Small groupings of men sat around tables pouring large quantities of brandy and whiskey down their throats, something most of them should have stopped doing hours ago.

There was some thrill in watching fate turn on the flip of a card, but it had taken only one look at a loser's face for Violet to decide that stupidity beat out adventure.

Maybe the excitement was in the personal risk. Did she need to substantially risk her own funds to find the attraction? She swigged her brandy, letting the burn fill her mouth and throat. The sweet aftertaste soothed her.

She shook her head at the dealer, gifted each gentleman at the table with a smile, and stood. She needed to find a different table if she wanted higher stakes, since it had become clear that the two older men at the table were there merely to pass the time and that the younger ones didn't have the funds to play deeper.

And she wanted deeper. It might be stupid. It might be a step on the road to true ruin, but she needed to feel something.

She must stop looking about the room and imagining Peter there. She must stop seeing him grinning up at her as he turned his cards—sharing the secret that he knew he was going to win and didn't care.

She closed her eyes to collect herself—then opened

them to find her spot. She wanted high stakes, but not desperation.

There under the window—Struthers, Lord Burham, and Jackson, all men of sizable means and discretion. It took only a moment to determine they were driven by competition, not a need for funds. Male competition, that was something Violet knew how to work with.

She watched them for a moment, picking up the game and the pace of their play. Then she sidled over to the table. "Do you mind if I join you, gentlemen?"

Jackson looked up first. She'd flirted with him after the death of her first husband. His eyes gleamed as they traced the lines of her figure, settling on the deep cleft between her breasts. "Why, Lady Carrington, I can't recall ever seeing you here before. I thought you only indulged in cards after dinner in much more respectable locations."

"When have I ever been held by respectability? Although you are right, this is my first time." Violet purred the words. She might only have played cards among friends, but she knew well that distraction was always key.

"I doubt that. I've heard you know how to play very well," Lord Burham spoke up. "Your friend Lady Westington has joined us on occasion, and she speaks most highly of your play. Do you play the way she does?"

Struthers leaned back in his chair and watched.

"Yes, my dear Violet, what brings you into our company? And do you enjoy the same games as Clara Westington?" Jackson asked. "I'd heard you were more exclusive in your tastes."

Violet did not miss how quickly she had moved from being Lady Carrington. She leaned forward over the table, granting the men a better view. "I don't know about Clara and her games, but perhaps I've tired of being exclusive. Would you like to show me what I've been missing?"

Burham choked on the whiskey he'd been swallowing.

"Take a seat," Struthers finally spoke. He picked up the deck and shuffled the cards between long, elegant fingers. "I've heard much about you, my lady. I'll enjoy learning what's true."

Violet could not keep her eyes off how those fingers manipulated the cards—easily, deftly. She tried to recall what she knew about Struthers. Not much. He'd inherited a fortune from an uncle who'd gone off to India. He never attempted to pretend to be more than what he was, the younger son of a younger son. But still he held respect and position.

He watched her with half-closed blue eyes as she edged around the table to the one empty seat. When she was settled his lips curved up—a cat granted a dish of cream.

He was the man to watch.

"You do remember how to play, don't you? Or do you need lessons? I am always happy to help," Jackson said as he leaned far too close. Their thighs were almost brushing.

Violet slid the other way on her chair, only to brush against Burham, who clearly thought this was a signal.

"Gentlemen," Violet began, "the cards haven't been dealt and already you're trying to sneak a look. A lady needs some space and privacy to plan her bets. Please grant me some room—unless you're already planning to cheat. I should warn you I only deal with those who play fair."

"A wise strategy. But how do you enforce it?" Struthers asked, as his speedy fingers tossed the cards around the table.

Violet sat up straight. "A woman quickly learns how to remove herself from trouble or she doesn't manage to play for long. Would you like me to demonstrate?" It took only the slightest indication that she would rise for all three gentlemen to assure her they would never dream of cheating. A further glance at Burham and Jackson had them moving a proper distance.

She picked up her cards and considered.

"What do you wager . . . Lady Carrington?" Struthers hesitated before addressing her. His eyes lingered as he let her name glide between his lips. It might have been seductive if it wasn't so practiced.

"What are the stakes?" She was not fool enough to venture in first.

"On the last hand, Jackson here relieved Burham of a rather spectacular matched pair. I myself am out a rather hefty amount of coin," Struthers answered.

"Oh dear," Violet cooed—God, she'd always hated women who cooed—"I am not sure I am ready to match that. Do you think we could start out slowly and then bring me up to speed? Fifty guineas, perhaps?"

That met with quick agreement and they were off. The men played at blistering speed, and Violet was amused to see they cared as much about scoring off each other as trying to impress her. She did have to push Burham away a further time or two, but Jackson became so involved in the cards that she wasn't sure he remembered her.

Struthers played a quiet, but deadly game, and it took all of Violet's wits to keep her losses to a minimum.

It should have been fun. Gambling was fun. She'd always enjoyed it. And male attention. Who could complain about being at the center of three attractive males? And they were attractive; even Burham's undistinguished chin did not detract from his height and strength. Jackson glowed with the easy charm he always had, and Struthers—Struthers shone with masculine allure and danger. Each time the stakes rose, so did the edge of his attraction.

Flirting and double entendre were her specialties.

She leaned forward in her chair again and let the barest hint of a smile cross her lips as she stared across the table at Struthers. She looked at her cards, glanced at him, touched the tip of her tongue to her lower lip. He swallowed hard before concentrating on his own cards.

Beside her, Burham actually dropped his cards and had to move quickly to gather them up.

Yes, it should have been a prime moment of her life.

But it wasn't.

She didn't know why, but the whole evening felt flat and tarnished. One more hand and then she'd go.

She'd look for a new . . . friend another night. Any of the men at the table would be a likely prospect, and yet none appealed. It would be a waste of her time and theirs to continue.

"You're out of coin, my dearest Violet? Do you have more?" Struthers leaned forward as he asked the question. "Or perhaps you'd like to wager something else?"

"I didn't bring anything else. I do want to play one more hand. Perhaps I could give you a vowel?" Violet answered.

"Unfortunately, we only play for what we can see." Struthers leaned across the table and let his hand brush over the top of hers. His meaning was unmistakable.

Jackson looked up from his cards, his interest caught. "I'll put it all in for an offer like that."

"I am in too," Burham added.

"Well." Struthers pushed forward his full pile of winnings. "Are you with us?"

Violet lifted her hand and brought it to her lips. Struthers's touch lingered, and not in a particularly pleasant way. She watched as all three gentlemen focused on her hand. She blew on it gently, then trailed it down her chin, her neck, and paused at the lace-edged top to her dress. She fluttered her fingers and almost laughed at the fixed quality of the three male gazes.

"You like what you see?" She lowered her voice and added a rasp. "This is what you want in return for all of that?" She waved her hand over the pile of notes and coin that spread across the table. Their eyes followed her gesture. "Are you sure, Burham? That matched pair you've tossed in are worth a pretty penny."

Three heads nodded in agreement.

"Well, if you're sure. I wouldn't want to disappoint three such fine gentlemen." She pulled the large sapphire ring off her finger and dropped it on top of the pile. It landed with a clink.

He had danced with five marriageable children and brought lemonade to three more. The more he tried to speak with them, the more he felt he had nothing to say.

"How did you enjoy last season?" he would begin.

"Can you believe that hemlines are coming down again?" was the reply.

"The weather has been very favorable this season," he tried again.

"Oh, I think not. I've got three freckles on my nose. Oh dear, I am not supposed to speak of appearances. You'll think me awfully fresh." And then the titter. There was always a titter.

This finding-a-wife thing was not as easy as he had imagined. He'd thought he'd show up at the proper engagements. The mamas would send their daughters to parade before him. He'd choose one and call on her family. An announcement in the papers. A ceremony at St. George's, and within the year there would be an addition to the family Bible.

That was how it was supposed to work.

He'd never considered that he'd actually have to talk to the girl. He'd imagined the bedding part a thousand times before Violet, but never this blasted need for conversation.

"Well, my dear chap, you seem to have found the cream of the crop, every one sweet and beautiful." Henry had found him again. "Summerton does throw a good bash—even without the brandy. I keep hearing rumors there will be champagne soon to cool us down."

Peter had a sudden overwhelming urge for a very large whiskey. "That sounds lovely."

"You must have been talking to Foxworthy. He keeps staring at young bosoms and saying, 'Lovely, lovely.'"

"I've actually managed to avoid the old coot, but he may have a point. This whole evening is just lovely."

"If a fellow didn't know better he'd think you were being sarcastic—maybe even being a bit of an ass." Henry was smiling again, but his gaze was sharp as it swept the room.

"Why ever would one think that? Don't I look like I am having a wonderful time?" Peter answered.

"You keep choosing the sweet ones. I tried to warn you, you need a bit of a bite." Henry's glance settled across the room. "There, that's the one for you. Miss Isabella Masters. She doesn't have much of a portion, but you don't need one. She's clever and pretty and only a little bit sweet once you get to know her—don't be put off in the first five minutes. They all think they have to drip with honey to catch us, but they can only keep it up for so long."

Honey. Violet's skin. Keep it up for so long. Oh, he'd keep it up all right. Peter's mind wandered along familiar paths.

"I say. You don't seem to be listening. Isabella Masters is the perfect one for you, although from what I hear Langdon is playing the bee to her flower, so you may have some competition. And I shouldn't forget Foxworthy. He looks at her with ownership glinting in his glance." Henry sounded most insistent.

Peter glanced around. Miss Isabella Masters—it sank into his soul. Violet's sister. He could only stare.

What on earth was the chit doing here? Shouldn't she be safe in London?

Almost as if reading his mind, Henry answered. "Her brother decided to put her on the market more obviously. I am not sure if he's going for the highest price or has something more particular in mind. It was strange of him to wait until August to bring her to Town, but maybe he wanted to get her some dresses before bringing her here. That's a very fine one she's wearing. It certainly shows off her . . . complexion."

"I am sure that's what you were about to say, Mr. Edwards." Lady Summerton joined them. "I do hope you're not foxed. I can't abide a drunken gentleman. I had considered having the champagne brought in, but now I must reconsider. It's clear you gentlemen have been tippling on your own."

Lady Summerton sailed off again, having said her piece.

"No champagne. I may have to develop stomach troubles that demand an immediate return to Town. I am not sure I could handle this without some recourse." Henry had lost his smile.

Peter was only half focused on him anyway. He continued to stare at Violet's sister, trying to see the similarities between them, trying to decide if her presence there was a curse or if he could turn it to his own advantage.

Maybe if he did pay court to her it would bring Violet

around. She certainly wouldn't want him to marry her sister. She might say that he should marry somebody fresh and young, but how would she react if confronted with the reality?

It might be worth a try.

Besides, Violet's sister couldn't possibly be as full of titter as his previous companions had been.

He turned back to Henry. "I'd appreciate it if you'd introduce me to Miss Masters. I've decided to take your advice."

She'd almost lost her ring. Violet stood in the doorway waiting for her carriage to be brought round. Peter had given her that ring. It was the only gift of any value she'd ever allowed him to give her, and she'd tossed it in a pile of coins without a thought. She'd even felt a moment of victory as the men had looked up at her in confusion and then understanding. She'd played them well.

Only she'd almost lost her ring. She understood for the first time how insidious gambling could be. She'd been so busy looking at the prize, she hadn't even noticed the risk.

Damn. She shouldn't care anyway. She had much nicer rings. Her third husband, Carrington, had loved giving her pretty things. Why should it frighten her so that she'd almost lost it?

And it was *almost*. She had come out the winner.

She shook her heavy reticule, hoping the seams would hold. She could probably bring down an elephant—should she ever happen to meet one—with it.

"Can I help you with that? It looks like you may end up with one arm longer than the other if you're not careful," a hesitant voice spoke up.

Violet turned and beheld a most beautiful young boy. He had the haunted perfection of a Renaissance saint combined with the barest hint of mischief. He looked barely old enough to shave, much less frequent a place like this.

"Forgive me. Do I know you?" Violet answered.

"Oh, do pardon me. Yes, I met you at one of my brother, Lord Chandler's, soirees. I am Ian Winchester. My brother is a close acquaintance of Lord Peter St. Johns. I had the pleasure of a country dance."

"You are quite correct, sir. Please, do forgive my forgetfulness. I've had a long evening."

"Would you be interested in making it a longer one? My brother mentioned that you and Lord Peter were no longer—"

"And what on earth makes you think that Lord Peter and I were ever—" Violet was almost speechless; not only was it clear that her relationship with Peter was much less secret than she had imagined, now she was being propositioned by schoolboys.

"This is about to become a conversation full of apologies." Ian—it was impossible to think of the boy as Mr. Winchester—blushed furiously. "I was going to say that my brother mentioned you were without an escort with Lord Peter out of Town. I only sought to offer my services."

Violet was not convinced of the innocence of the remark. "And the later night?"

"It is merely that it is such a warm and beautiful evening that I thought to invite you for a late ride." Ian gestured out the open door. "My barouche is open so there would be no impropriety. The moon is full, the air is warm, and the city is empty. After a night in such a smoke-filled—I believe the word is hell—I thought you might enjoy a bit of fresh air. I know it's not conventional, but I am afraid I am not a conventional type of fellow."

She should say no. Any woman with a whit of common sense would say no. Still, he was harmless and she had always been partial to young, malleable men.

She lowered her chin and met his eyes for a second. His gaze did not even dart to her breasts. She handed him the heavy bag. "It sounds lovely."

Chapter 6

It was the dream of every girl during her first season—flowers from each man she'd met the night before. Violet glanced at the four perfect bouquets of fresh spring violets that lay on the tea table—expensive in late summer, if not original.

Ian's were white with purple edges.

Struthers's contribution was the grandest. The florist must have emptied a hothouse.

Jackson and Burham had both sent small dainty offerings—it would have been hard to distinguish between them.

There was only one problem. She detested violets. She loved roses, lilies, even lavender. She wanted vibrancy and color, lush scent and sensuality. Violets offered none of that. They were demure and sweet.

She was not sweet and never had been.

Even at seventeen, before she started on the road that had led to her present position, she had not been sweet.

So why did men always send violets?

Oh, she knew why—but still she wished for some true thought and deliberation.

Peter had never sent her violets.

He'd favored peonies—huge, rich peonies of a pink so deep it put a baby's lips to shame.

She could close her eyes and smell them now.

But of course she wouldn't.

That was the past. This was now.

She picked up Ian's flowers. White was different. She didn't remember ever being sent white blossoms before.

She placed them back on the table.

Struthers's arrangement was too large to lift. It was not dainty and demure.

She tapped a finger on the table between the two.

Struthers wanted to ride in the park.

Ian wished her company on a walk.

She tapped again.

If she couldn't decide, why should she? Let them compete.

She wasn't in the mood for either a walk or a ride. Perhaps a little culture. It had been some time since she'd visited the British Museum. Isabella had wanted to go, but Isabella was out of Town.

She wondered whether either of the men would even pretend an interest in art or history.

With a smile she moved to her desk and picked up

a quill. Should she acknowledge it would be a group endeavor? No, it would be more telling to take them by surprise.

Isabella Masters was an entertaining girl. From the first time Peter had drawn her into a dance she never failed to entertain, and she never, not even once, simpered.

If it hadn't been for Violet, Peter might have sustained an interest.

But no matter how desperately he tried to pretend there was no Violet, she never left his thoughts for long.

"I've heard that Summerton has a Rembrandt," Isabella cooed as she led him down a candlelit corridor. "I do so adore art. Don't you? It makes us see so much more than ourselves."

"I've never thought about it." Violet had tried to interest him in art and music, but he'd never taken much notice. He liked his entertainments to be more vigorous—horses, boxing; he didn't even dislike fishing, but looking at pictures . . . not the entertainment for a man in the prime of his life. No, there were much better entertainments. He'd had such fun showing Violet how a man liked to be entertained. He could see her, leaning over him, her face flushed, her lips damp and swollen as she leaned forward—

"All you need to do is look at the faces in a painting," Isabella continued. "They speak without words. When I look at a canvas I can see what they're thinking, even begin to imagine what their lives were like. Sometimes I can even feel that way about a landscape. I look at it and imagine that I am there—that I can feel the breeze, smell the scents. It reminds me that the world takes place in viewpoints other than my own. Do you see what I mean?"

He didn't really, but it would be ungracious to say so. He nodded and shifted his hips to the side, nearer the wall, so that he would not shock her with the effects his thoughts of Violet had on his body.

"Come look at this one," Isabella said, walking ahead. They entered a long gallery, and she stopped in front of a large canvas.

Peter drew closer. It was a picture of one of Summerton's ancestors and his family. The past earl stood proudly at the center of the canvas, his family arranged around him in adoration. Even the dog in the lower corner seemed to be looking up with worship in its gaze.

Isabella was not to be daunted. "Look at the girl, the oldest daughter, there. Do you see how she looks at her father, but leans the other way? I think she's eager to be gone. Her eyes are on her father, but I doubt she thinks of him. Do you see the glint there, and the hint of a smile at the corner of her mouth? She's thinking of a lover. What do you think?"

As she spoke, Isabella moved closer to him, and Peter could smell lemons. She must have used them to wash her hair. Violet never smelled of lemons, her scent was more primal. Isabella edged even closer, and he felt the heat of her body. He would have stepped away, but somehow he was sandwiched between her and the wall.

He tried to step to the side, but she moved, blocking him. She was so close the air vibrated with each breath she took.

She rested her cheek against his coat. "I know how the girl must feel, trapped in one place while thinking about another."

Her hand was planted on his chest, her fingers tangled in the soft folds of his cravat.

His first impulse was to push her away, but she was just a child and he had invited this situation. He was so busy thinking about how to even the score with Violet that he had never even considered the possibility that he might be engaging Isabella's emotions. He would have to tread carefully.

He took her hand between his own, bent his head, and kissed her fingertips. "I think we had best be getting back. We wouldn't want to do anything to damage your reputation."

She gripped his neckwear tightly. "I am sure a moment or two won't matter. I feel so safe when I am near you."

"Yes, but—" His further words were cut off as she yanked his cravat, pulling his head down toward hers. He saw the intent in her eyes as they focused on his lips.

He tried to pull back but the damn wall was behind him. She pulled harder. It was either return to the ball with ripped threads of linen wrapped in shreds about his battered neck or give in.

He gave in.

The kiss was not bad. It was soft, sweet, and all woman.

It was one of the worst experiences of his life.

He felt as if Violet stood behind them watching.

The moment Isabella's hands moved from his cravat to his shoulders he thrust her away. She stood before him, bosom heaving above lowered bodice, one of her breasts staring at him, its rosy tip taunting.

Gads, he had not done that, had he? The lace edging of her dress must have caught on his buttons.

He reached over to pull up her gown and restore them both to dignity. She caught his hand and held it there, her eyes shining.

"Oh, Peter. I am so glad that—"

A cacophony of voices echoed down the hall. He grabbed Isabella and yanked her behind the heavy drapes of the nearest window. The poor dear was so confused she was pushing her dress back down. She started to speak again and he was forced to cover her mouth with his hand. She squirmed hard against him, and it took all his strength and agility to keep her from pushing out against the curtains. She really did not understand the possible repercussions of the situation. Or perhaps she was frightened by his strength. He almost released her in the fear that she felt attacked.

Only the shrill sound of Lady Summerton restrained him.

"Now do let me show you the Rembrandt. I know somebody was asking about it and I did promise a tour after the first waltz. I wish I could remember who it was. Tell me, Langdon, what was the name of that blonde you were speaking with earlier? It might have been her."

Isabella bit down on his hand, and Peter subdued his curse as comprehension filled him.

Violet leaned back on the settee and admired her suitors. They were magnificent men. Over the past few days as she'd gotten to know them she'd become increasingly impressed.

Struthers had not only inherited money from his uncle, he'd spent years traveling through India helping his uncle increase profits. He'd developed a tolerant view of the world during his travels, not at all the biased outlook she'd found so common in others returning from the East. She found delight in sitting with him in the evening, sipping port and discussing world politics.

He'd also hinted on more than one occasion that the vast knowledge he'd developed in the East fell into more intimate categories. Violet worked to contain a blush as she remembered a book of erotic drawings her last husband had imported from India. They were gorgeous and lush. She wondered if some of the positions drawn were possible.

She could almost feel Peter behind her, lifting her, seating her on his lap, drawing her legs backward around him, her ankles locked—he'd stand then, moving her, rubbing her—

Damn. She shook her head hard and then had to fake a cough as Struthers and Ian turned to stare at her.

Ian was even more beautiful than Peter. She could stare at his long, refined features for hours. His eyes alone were enough to fill her fantasies, so dark a blue as to be black and lashes longer than her own, even when she darkened them. And if eyes were the windows to the soul, then his soul was deep and dazzling.

How different from Peter's solid brown eyes. Eyes that were not all that extraordinary, in fact they were a rather ordinary brown. Oh, it was a deep, warm brown, and when he stared down at her his glance made her toes curl. That look was all for her. When he stared at her it made her feel the center of the world, that there was nothing else he would rather look at. In his eyes she was more beautiful than a perfect sunset or a radiant gemstone. And she'd felt such power, she'd only to lower her lids and smile for his breath to speed and his eyes to darken in desire.

Blast. She was doing it again.

She was sitting in her own parlor with two interesting and eligible suitors, and all she could think of was Peter. It was definitely time to take another lover.

It might even be more fun with somebody new, somebody who didn't already know every nook of her body, who didn't know how to run a single finger up the back of her leg, slowing to draw intricate designs on her ankle, moving again to the back of her knee—

Double blast. If she didn't stop this then—

"You seem rather distracted, my dear Violet. Are we not entertaining enough for you this evening? Is it time for me to seek my pleasures elsewhere?" Struthers leaned forward in his chair and placed his glass on the table with a decided clink.

Ian reclined further and let his eyes roam over her. "If my good friend Struthers is ready to look elsewhere, then perhaps it is time for us to become better acquainted? I can assure you that when we are alone you would not be bored in my presence."

Struthers picked up his glass and took another swallow. He glared at Ian. "Are you going to offer to read to her from your schoolbooks? Or perhaps you have some new toys you'd like to show her? I am not sure that's the type of entertainment this lady needs."

"If, and I say *if*, I had new toys that I wished to share

with Violet, I can assure you she would enjoy them."
Ian leaned forward in his chair and brought himself
eye-to-eye with Struthers. "Tell me, Struthers, do you
never play with toys? If so, I can understand why you
worry that you bore women."

Struthers leaned away from Ian, bringing himself
closer to Violet. He reached over and took her hand
and brought it to his lips. He laid soft kisses across the
back of her hand and then turned it, opening her palm
and laying firmer kisses there.

Violet gasped as his tongue darted out and worked
its way between her fingers. She tried to pull her hand
back, but Struthers held it firm and, with a smile at Ian,
drew her index finger into his mouth.

She turned toward him in protest. "Really, that is
not—" Her words were cut off when Ian slipped onto
the settee beside her and took the opportunity of her
turned head to begin tracing faint designs on the side
of her neck. He drew a single finger across her collar-
bones. She shivered with the intimacy of the gesture.

Then, in one sudden movement, she pushed herself
to her feet, pulling away from both gentlemen. She
turned to face them.

"Really, boys, I have never in my life seen men behave
in such a childish manner, not even when I myself was
in the nursery. If you cannot comport yourselves in a
more seemly fashion, then I suggest you depart and I
will find myself more polite entertainment."

Struthers leaned toward her, letting his eyes maintain their connection although she had broken the physical one. "Perhaps we act like children because you treat us like children. Why else all the games?"

"Games?" Violet was thrown by his comeback and needed a moment to regroup. How had she lost control of the situation?

"I must confess that while my friend Struthers and I may disagree on many issues, I do take his point on this." Ian stood and moved between her and Struthers. "You have led us both a merry chase these last days. I can assure that I have rarely left my bed before noon in the past years, but at your request I did—only to find I had unexpected company. When a lady requests the pleasure of my company for a stroll through the parks, I expect it to be a chance to get to know her, not to discuss the merits of the foliage."

"Yes," Struthers took up the conversation. "And when I am invited to examine art and discuss the newest sculpture the museum is exhibiting, I do not plan on spending the afternoon trying to decide whether marble or granite makes a better medium. My discussion tends to include more . . . provocative . . . elements of the works. And"—he glared at Ian—"I don't need a chaperone for the outing."

The two men strained with tension, and Violet was not sure whether it was aimed at her or at each other. The air felt heavy with their scent and the raw masculinity their posturing presented. They were two dogs with a bone, unsure whether to fight or to try to steal the bone and run.

"Gentlemen." She softened her voice and moved away from them to sit on the bench of the pianoforte, spreading her skirts so there was no available space. "I am sorry if you feel I am being less than honest with you. The truth is that I find pleasure in the company of both of you. I meant no disrespect. Forgive me if I thought only of my own pleasure."

"Pleasure." Struthers let the word hang in the air, but did not seek to move closer to her. "Pleasure. If I was assured there was to be pleasure involved, I would not have any complaints."

"And is the lady's pleasure not enough for you? Do you not find the enjoyment of your partner rewarding?" Ian took a step closer to Struthers, and again Violet could not mistake the smell of power and competition that flew between them.

She wished Peter were there. He would have disarmed the conflict with a smile and a clever word. And if he hadn't . . . The thought of his standing here, ready to fight for her . . . She closed her eyes and she could almost feel him here . . . Never before had she realized that masculinity had a scent, musky, smoky, and overpowering, but not without its own allure.

Struthers pushed to his feet, bringing her attention back to the present. He stood facing Ian, his hands curling into fists. "Do you want to say that again?"

"Ian. Struthers. I can assure you this brings me no pleasure, entertainment, or enjoyment." Violet hoped the quiver in her voice didn't betray that her words were not fully true. There was something quite exciting at having men almost fight over her, and her thoughts of Peter had only added to her body's tension. She just wasn't sure it would be alluring to have them actually exchange blows. She'd never been partial to blood sports.

"Please be seated," she continued, "and you may each have a turn to tell me what it is you want, to express your desires."

Something flared in Ian's eyes, and Violet realized sex might not be the best way to control men who were already straining to break free from civility.

"Sit." This time it was command and not sensuality that filled her voice.

The men did not move.

"Sit or leave. There is no other option."

For a second she was afraid that they would not move, but then inch by inch, measuring each other's movements, they both sat, their glances locked together.

The tension in the room was palpable, and Violet wished she could close her eyes and have them gone. This was supposed to be fun—fun and easy. If she'd wanted difficulty and argument she would have stayed with Peter.

Peter.

She was never scared her carpets would be bloodied when Peter was around. No, if her carpets were stained after one of his visits it would be because—

Damn it. She was here in a room with two bristling hounds and she had to stay focused. "So, gentlemen, what is it that you find unsatisfactory about this situation, and how can we resolve it?"

"Don't sound a fool." Struthers was the first to speak. "You know what the problem is."

"Do you think calling me a fool is going to further you in my affections?" Violet kept her voice cool.

"Struthers is right, if not diplomatic." Ian leaned toward her, as if realizing for the first time that the object was not to beat Struthers but to win her. His glance moved over her, pausing at all the crucial spots. Without a single word he told her just how desirable he found her and just how ready he was to adore her.

Violet drew in a deep breath. "Then forgive my foolishness, but what is it you want?"

Struthers stood again and walked toward her. He stopped at the moment before his knees brushed her skirts. He leaned forward until she could feel his brandy-scented breath on her cheek. "I want you." He held his face inches from hers. His glance dropped to her mouth and to her eyes and then back.

She felt the force between them with each sweet breath. "I want you to myself—no little boys as competition. Send him away and let me show you what a man is like."

"A man is not measured by years, but by action and maturity." Ian still reclined in his chair across the room, but his gaze had never left her. "I can assure you, my lady, that I am no boy, but with youth comes a certain vigor. Send Struthers away and I will demonstrate why a young lover is preferable."

"Choose," they spoke in unison.

He was going home. Peter smiled as his valet signaled that the last bag was packed and that the coach was ready to depart. He walked down the stairs and took his horse's reins.

He was free. He looked back at the grand house as he swung into the saddle. He'd spent the last two days avoiding Isabella, and with each passing hour he had become more convinced of her manipulations. Every time he looked at her it seemed some dowager matron was there to witness the act. The single time he gave in to her pressures to walk in the garden, she tripped into a rosebush. Her brother appeared a minute after Peter set her back on her feet. If Masters had arrived seconds earlier, he might have caught Peter with his arms full of wiggling virgin.

There was only was possible conclusion—Isabella

Masters was husband hunting and he was the target, or at least one of them. Peter had been staying out of sight in the garden and saw Isabella pull the same trick with Langdon. Either the girl was beyond clumsy or she was indiscriminate in her goal.

He chose the latter.

Isabella wanted a husband and didn't care who. He wasn't even sure that she liked either of them. She had the right reply in conversation, but he no longer felt genuine interest. Could there be a fate worse than a bride who didn't like him?

A week ago he would have said yes, he could think of plenty of worse fates. Now he wasn't so sure.

So he was going home—not to London, but to Glynewolde, the country home of his childhood. It might belong to his brother now, but Wimberley would not mind, and it was far better than London, where he might run into Violet.

He would have weeks of quiet and peace before he had to face society again—weeks to recover his sense of equilibrium and to decide what to do about a certain redhead he couldn't keep out of his thoughts.

The carriage rattled into motion, and he eased the horse into a trot. He spared one last look at the house. He wondered how Isabella would react when she realized he'd left before the masquerade that evening.

Poor Langdon.

* * *

Violet sat and stared at the two men, frozen. How was she supposed to choose? She didn't want to choose. Violet swallowed as a deep certainty settled in her belly. She loved the attention. She loved the flirting. But the thought of either of these men in her bed brought only a sense of discomfort.

This was not right.

Her eyes darted from one to the other. Seconds passed as she waited for the words to come to her, the words that would somehow make everything right again.

Only with each second that passed she could feel the tension rise and grow. The men were looking at each other again and violence was in the air.

She had to think of something.

Even if she did chose one she wasn't sure the other would leave peaceably.

She had to find a way to play for time. If she could delay things long enough, surely boredom would set in—no, that was foolish. She'd played enough games of cat and mouse with men to know that they only grew more eager the longer the hunt.

Maybe if she chose one quickly.

Ian was younger—more trainable—but more unpredictable.

Struthers she understood—but she could feel the danger in him.

She didn't want to choose. She didn't want either of them.

There must be a way to delay without leading them to believe it was part of the game.

As if sent by the angels, there was a light tap at the door and her porter entered. "Forgive me, my lady, I know you wished to be left undisturbed, but an urgent note has come from the Marquess of Wimberley. The messenger is awaiting your reply."

She was handed a heavy piece of folded parchment. Rising from her chair, she moved to the window, away from Struthers and Ian, before breaking the wax.

Marguerite was poorly.

The doctors were insisting she move to the country for the remainder of her confinement. She could not delay or she would not be able to travel.

She wished Violet's company—could not bear to be without a female friend in this hour of need.

Wimberley's mother was still in Brighton.

Each thought moved through her mind individually. Confinement. There was no place she had less desire to be. Marguerite was a friend, but Violet wanted nothing to do with birth and babies.

She would send a refusal. Marguerite would have to understand.

Then Violet looked up. "I am sorry, gentlemen,

but I must depart as soon as possible. A dear friend needs me."

"I can guess what kind of need." Struthers stepped toward her.

"Actually, I am attending a confinement. Would you like to come?"

Chapter 7

Rain.
    Rain.
  Rain.

Violet pulled back the heavy curtain of the carriage and peered out.

Rain.

She'd known it was raining from the steady pound on the roof, but she was beside herself with boredom, and even the brief moment of adjusting the curtain was something to do.

Marguerite slumbered on in the corner of the opposite bench, well packed in with a multitude of pillows that cushioned and cocooned her body. Violet was glad her friend had found escape in sleep. The trip had been miserable for Marguerite. She'd been queasy from the start, and an extra day of slogging through the mud was certainly not helping the situation.

Violet pounded her hand into the plump cushions. She'd been insane to come. She disliked the country.

She hated long carriage rides, even when they weren't delayed by rain. And she really was not comfortable around Marguerite.

She knew that was really the problem. She was distressed by the whole idea of delivering a baby. She pressed one hand tight into her own belly and with the other pulled back the curtain again. She pressed her face against the cold, foggy glass.

She hadn't always felt like this.

She pressed her face harder, wishing the cold would seep into her brain. Her cheeks were damp, and she told herself that it was the condensation on the glass.

She'd married for the first time expecting babies of her own, just like any young bride. It wasn't Marguerite's fault that such thoughts now turned to blood and loss. And pain.

Her whole life could have been so different, if only—

No, she was not going to dwell on that now. It was depressing enough sitting in a swaying carriage on such a dark, dull day. There wasn't even enough light to read. She'd packed *The Duke's Darling* in her bag in the hope it could redeem itself, but so far the strain of reading in the dim light had proved too much.

Violet wiped her cheeks on her sleeve and turned back to look at Marguerite. She looked so beautiful and contented despite the slight gray tinge her skin had taken on over the past week.

Violet hoped that the country air would prove as beneficial as the physician had suggested. Marguerite deserved happiness. As if she'd picked up on Violet's thoughts, Marguerite shifted and finally opened her eyes. She smiled as she caught sight of Violet and then grimaced as she pushed her body upright. She rubbed her eyes and then pushed back the curtain to stare out her own window.

"We are almost there," she murmured, her voice still husky from sleep. "We're coming upon the village now and then it's only a few more miles."

"It can't be soon enough." Violet kept her voice light. "You are such a dear friend coming with me. I know you would probably have been happier staying in Town and this journey has been miserable, but I am still so glad you came."

Violet reached over and patted Marguerite's hand. "Of course. I would never have dreamed of refusing." That was not strictly speaking true—or, well, maybe it was. She would just never explain to Marguerite exactly why she hadn't considered refusing for more than a moment.

"As I said, you are a dear friend," Marguerite replied. "You did not even complain once about the inn last night, mutton that couldn't be cut with sharpest knife, and damp beds that must have been stuffed with rocks."

"It really wasn't that bad. It was only your condition that made it seem so dreary. I was quite comfortable."

"You are lying, but I will not hold it against you. Besides, we are almost there. Do you hear the pounding of hooves? Tristan must be racing ahead to the house to be sure all is prepared. He is such a wonderful husband, riding all day in the rain just to be sure I have enough room in the carriage."

With any other man Violet would have taken a much more cynical view of why he would choose to ride in the fresh air instead of closed in a carriage, but she'd watched the way Wimberley looked at his young wife and had to admit Marguerite was probably right in her reasoning.

Peter looked at her that same way before he brought her chocolate to the bed or rubbed the aches out of her feet.

The carriage slowed to a halt, and Violet was glad of the interruption of her thoughts. She was not going to think of Peter any more today. Maybe sometime during her stay she'd sit down and figure out what to do, but not now.

Now she would be glad that the trip was over and that things could only improve. She felt a distinct lightening of spirits as the door opened and she took Wimberley's hand to step out.

It was time for things to get better.

Peter slammed a billiard ball into the corner pocket, almost scoring the felt. Why had he decided to come to

Glynewolde and not return to London? If he'd had any idea that it was going to rain for days without ceasing, he certainly would have headed for Town.

If he'd gone home to London he might be ensconced at his club right now, enjoying a large brandy and a warm fire.

It was true that he could find both brandy and a lit hearth here, but it just wasn't the same when he was alone in the house with only the sound of the rain for company.

Even the house party would have been preferable to this. He could have survived a few more days being chased by Isabella. It wasn't as though he was unpracticed in avoiding marriage-minded young misses. If only Isabella had been more like her sister.

He chose another ball to target and, with the click of the stick, sent it careening across the table. He wasn't even playing well. He should have had at least a couple of drinks before his play hit this level, but he'd had no desire for solitary whiskey.

He took a deep breath and spent more care choosing just the right angle of attack. The cue bounced at the opposite corner of the table before rolling straight into the pocket.

Violet would have laughed, that deep, husky laugh that filled the room and echoed in the hall. That deep, husky laugh that lit fires within and made him feel that all was right in the world.

She'd lean over the table, fully aware of the display she was making, and ask if he needed help with his stick work. She'd lick her lips and smile that full smile that made him think how much he'd enjoy her help—and then his next shot would be worse.

He missed her.

He'd told himself at first that it was just the sex and easy companionship he missed. But now he admitted the truth.

It was she.

It was all of her, even the annoying parts. He missed how she rolled in bed taking all the covers with her. He missed how she refused to ever let him have the last word in an argument unless he actually left the room before she could get the words in. He even missed the way she refused to take him seriously, always assuming that he hadn't put any real thought into his words.

Maybe he'd have that drink after all. It was better than moping about a woman he couldn't have. A woman he should know better than to want. A woman who would never see him as more than a boy.

There was a sudden flurry of activity in the hall. The pounding of footsteps sounded, and he could hear the maids calling to one another. He dropped the stick on the table and went to see what was happening—maybe the vicar had braved the weather for a game of chess,

or perhaps the river had flooded and somebody was in
need of help.

Whatever the cause, it was bound to be better than
being alone with his thoughts.

She froze when she saw him. Violet felt the breath
leave her body and was fortunate that everybody else
was too busy to notice her shock—everybody except
him, of course. He saw her. She felt his eyes move over
her before his lips pursed in displeasure. He was not
happy to see her.

It hurt. It should not have, but it did. She forced herself to inhale, before pasting a smile on her face and
moving farther into the room.

Peter glared at her for another moment and then
turned and met his brother in a warm embrace. She
watched the two men, and something clenched in her
gut at the emotion flowing between them.

They looked so different, Peter, large and dark, and
Tristan, blond and elegant, if without his brother's
physical strength. At a glance, nobody would ever have
taken them for brothers, but together the filial love was
so strong it was unmistakable. She had never belonged
to anyone like that; even Isabella had never loved her
like that.

She turned away, pretending to shake the rain from
her hair.

She saw Marguerite watching the brothers also. Her face glowed with belonging. She too was part of the family. She moved eagerly into Peter's embrace when he finally released Wimberley.

Then it was her turn.

He moved toward her stiff and formal, taking her fingertips in his own, raising them almost to his lips, but not quite. "It is good of you to accompany Marguerite, Lady Carrington. Tristan tells me she is worried, and it is good of you to distract her from her cares."

"It is good to see you, Lord Peter. We have missed you in Town," she replied.

He nodded and turned back to his brother. He did not say that he had missed her or even that it was good to see her.

She stood for a moment, alone.

She could still feel the quiver of his touch in her fingertips, could still feel the heat of him, the scent of him.

But now he had moved away from her into another world, a world he had invited her into and she had refused.

So why was she so disconcerted now?

When Marguerite smiled and sent a maid to show her to her rooms, Violet went willingly, anything to be removed from the stage. She needed time to understand her own feelings before once again being on display.

* * *

"What on earth is she doing here?" Peter had not planned to phrase it in that manner, but the words had spilled from his lips the moment Violet was gone.

Marguerite looked up at him from where she had settled in a comfortable chair. She'd wanted to rest before climbing the stairs. There was a knowing glint in her eye. "I thought we'd explained that. I wanted a friend and she was good enough to accompany me."

Peter turned away so that they could not see his face. "But why her? I would have thought there'd be some-body more appropriate."

"I can't see who." It was Tristan who spoke now. "I would have asked Mother if she'd been in Town, but the physician stressed the importance of not delaying the travel. Most of our other friends had left for the summer, but I believe Violet would have been Marguerite's first choice anyway."

Peter clenched his teeth. His jaw muscles were so tight that he felt each individual tooth grind. He needed to get himself under control and fast. It wouldn't do for Marguerite or Tristan to understand how Violet's presence affected him.

"I don't see why you are so interested," Marguerite spoke. "I thought you liked Lady Carrington, and even if you do not care for her—which I cannot believe—why should it matter to you? She is here to keep me company, not you."

"You are correct. I am merely surprised." Peter forced his face to softness and turned. "I was not expecting to see any of you here, and now I am blessed not only by your company, but by that of an additional guest. That is all."

Marguerite did not look satisfied.

He wondered if she knew something. Surely Violet would not have told her. "Perhaps," Peter continued, wanting to get this over with, "I was surprised because she has no children of her own. I had always been under the impression that only women who had children of their own attended a lying-in."

"I believe that only applies to unmarried, impressionable girls—those who might be frightened or disturbed by what they will see." Marguerite looked up at him. "Do you see Lady Carrington becoming scared or upset?"

Peter had to admit that he could not picture Violet becoming disturbed by any situation. She was always in control.

Tristan walked over and clapped him on the back. "Then I take it having an additional guest will not trouble you?"

"Why no, I promise to be an exemplary host." He smiled back at his brother, and adopted an almost ducal manner. "She would be gone by now if I felt otherwise."

Tristan slapped him on the back. "I am not sure

she's the one who would be gone. So what are you doing here at this season? You spoke of your surprise at our arrival, but never explained why a young buck is alone in my house during a rainy summer. I would have thought you'd have found greater entertainment elsewhere."

Peter glanced at Marguerite. She was resting her head back and did not look healthy. "I suggest we save that tale for another time. I think your wife is ready to retire."

Tristan turned and without another word swept Marguerite in his arms and headed for the door. "I'll join you for a drink before dinner. You can tell me then."

Peter watched as Marguerite pretended to protest and then let her head fall against her husband's shoulder. It was good to see his brother so contented and relaxed, but Peter felt a tightening in his chest as he observed the close bond between the couple.

Then, he was left alone.

Dinner could not have been more awkward. Marguerite had chosen to take a plate in her room, pleading exhaustion, and Wimberley had decided to join her.

That left Violet alone with Peter. She could not imagine a more impossible situation. At least they had been seated with the length of the table between them. If they had been seated next to each other—it didn't even bear thinking about.

"Do you think it will ever stop raining?" Peter asked.

"I am sure it will have to at some time," she answered.

"The soup is really quite good."

"I've never been partial to onions, but combined with the beef broth it is delicious."

Silence.

Fish.

Silence.

Roast pheasant.

Silence.

"It sounds like the rain has slowed. Perhaps it will stop soon," Violet said. She wanted to pull her hair and scream. How would he react if she threw the baked peach the length of the table? Would some emotion show on his face then? Why wouldn't he even look at her?

Then he lifted his eyes to hers. "I met your sister at Summerton's. She is not much like you."

She didn't know why his words chilled her, but they did. "Isabella?"

"Do you have another sister? No? I didn't think so." He dabbed his lips with his napkin. "I was surprised by her attitudes."

"I don't know what you mean." But she was afraid she did. She had not forgotten how Isabella had admired Peter at Lady Smythe-Burke's.

"She is not as opposed to some things as you are. In fact she is more than enthusiastic."

"Some things?" She felt like a parrot mimicking his words.

"Yes, matrimony for one."

Violet closed her eyes. She had known what he was going to say before the words left his lips. She wanted to ask him for every detail of his interaction with her sister, but she knew that Isabella was not really what this was about.

She approached the real problem head-on. "I didn't mean to hurt you," she said.

"You didn't." He picked up a peach and examined it for bruises. "I am not sure why you mention that now. I thought we were talking of your sister." He cut a peach in half and brought it to his mouth.

She let her eyes follow the movement of the fork. She watched as it slid between his lips. She inhaled deeply, letting her breasts push at her tight bodice. "You know you only mention Isabella to hurt me. I don't want to play those games with you. If we're going to play, it is not Isabella I want to speak of."

She lifted her own fork and raised it to her lips. Her tongue darted out to lick at the heavy syrup. She savored the aromatic flavor.

He was focused on her lips now too.

She slowly, gently drew the peach fully into her mouth. She watched as he swallowed and shifted in his chair.

Then he shook his head and put down his fork.

"It won't work," he said.

"What won't?"

"We've played at this before. I know you love food and you know I love watching you eat. I don't care how many times we've ended in your bed before dinner was finished. This will not be one of them."

"But I wasn't—"

He cut her off. "Weren't you?"

She flushed under his gaze, but held firm. "Yes, Peter, I admit I was trying to get you to react, but, no, I was not trying to get you in my bed. If I had been, we would be there now. When have I ever failed?"

Peter rose and came around the table. He stopped several feet before her chair.

Her body quivered at the nearness of his. It was all she could do not to reach out and touch him. The connection sizzled between them. A physical thing.

"Did you ever consider that I chose to let you win?" His voice flattened again. "I wanted you and you let me have you. I've never denied that desire. I desire you even now, but I am not going to do this. You know my terms. They have not changed."

Violet lowered her eyes. She could take his anger, but there was an edge of pain in his voice that shook her. "I am sorry. I wish you could understand why we can't."

"And I wish you had the faith to see that we could." He turned and walked away from her toward the window. The rain started again and drummed heavily against the glass.

He placed his hand on the cold pane, resisting the desire to lay his head against it. He should have left the moment she arrived.

It was not a practical solution, but he should have done it anyway—what was a day or two of slogging through the rain compared to the torture of being here with her? He wanted to pound his hand on the window with the frustration of it all.

She knew him too well. Even his ploy in mentioning Isabella had not worked. There was no distracting her from the truth.

He wanted her. And she knew it.

When she'd first walked through the door behind Tristan and Marguerite, he felt as if his every prayer had been answered. For a brief second he'd believed she'd come for him, that she'd changed her mind.

Then he saw the shock on her face and realized the truth.

She wasn't even thinking about him.

He turned from the window and faced her.

She was so beautiful, full of color and life. Even after days of traveling through the rain in the carriage she was radiant. He wanted to sweep her in his arms, adore her as she deserved to be adored.

He took a step.

Her eyes dropped to his boots and traced his step.

When they slowly ran up the length of his body he felt himself tense and harden.

He took another step, then half a step back. He would not give her that power. He turned to his side and paced away from her toward the fire.

"Are you running from me?" Her voice was low and husky.

"Do I need to run?"

She paused at that.

He turned to look at her and saw the thoughts flickering across her face.

"I don't know," she answered finally. "Do you want to?"

"No."

She took a step toward him.

Then another.

His body shook with tension. Why not just give in? Tristan and Marguerite would not be down again and none of the servants would dare interrupt.

He moved toward her, stopping only when they were a hand's distance apart. He reached out and took her hand in his own. It was small and fragile. Normally he didn't think of her as dainty, but when they were this close he was aware of the vast difference in their sizes.

He lifted her hand and brought it before his face, examining it, the slender fingers, the pale skin, the single freckle at the base of her thumb.

She had a scar on the back of her ring finger. He remembered when she'd dropped a glass and cut herself the year before. He'd never realized that it scarred.

He brought her hand to his mouth and laid a gentle kiss on the scar. He could feel the slight roughness against his lips and placed another kiss upon it.

"I remember when you did this."

"I was careless. Who drinks wine in bed?" she answered.

"You do. We do," he said. "Or should I say we did." He placed another kiss on the back of her hand.

"We did have good times."

"The very best." He took her hand and placed it against his heart. "We could again if only you would let us."

She looked into his eyes.

He wondered what she saw.

She pulled her hand away and turned. "It is not me that has stopped things. If it were up to me we'd be making good use of that rug in front of the fire. It looks very thick and soft. Instead we are stuck sounding like the heroes of some tragic play three pages before the end. The rug would be much more fun."

He closed his eyes against the temptation. "You are a very selfish woman."

She stared at him, her face momentarily devoid of emotion. His words were unexpected. "I cannot see why you would say that. When have I ever been selfish with you?"

"When have you not?" There was an edge to his words, but he was learning that cruelty could be a champion defense.

She pulled herself together at that, then pulled away from him. "I gave you everything you wanted. I don't understand why you would complain now. You aren't even the jilted lover. I believe that would be my role."

"Aren't I?" He walked to the rug and with deliberation sank down before the fire. "We see the situation very differently. You have not even considered my point of view."

She stalked toward him and stood over him. "What you miss is that I am thinking about you, and that is why I answer the way I do."

He looked up at her, past the soft belly and lush breasts that he loved; it was her eyes that concerned him now. "Tell me how you have been thinking for me—as you must believe I cannot think for myself."

"I will not even dignify that last remark, but tell me, Peter, how would you react once we are wed, when I am your wife, and we walk into a room and more than one man looks at me with intimate knowledge? Can you face the fact that I have had other lovers?"

"I have survived it before, why should that change?"

"I was never yours before. Do you really want to take ownership of something so used?" She ran her hands down her body in mock seduction.

He followed her every move. The gesture was meant as both a taunt and a symbol of self-depreciation, but all he saw was her strength and beauty.

He said nothing, until she was forced to stand and watch him watching her. He started at her feet and let his eyes wander up her as he had on that first night they argued.

Tension sizzled in the air.

At last he spoke. "I have never wanted ownership."

Violet fought the urge to turn away. "Then why do you insist on marriage? What is marriage, but ownership?" Damn, she sounded like a hissing viper.

"Sharing. Companionship. A promise. Marriage is a promise." He accepted the vulnerability of his position lying below her on the rug. He leaned forward and kissed the top of her evening slipper. "Why do you have to see the dark side of everything?"

"Rubbish. I merely have a realistic viewpoint. Let us remember which one of us has been married."

"Yes, I know. You have been married three times and are therefore an expert on the subject. You know all there is to know."

She pursed her lips and did not answer.

He waited and then continued, "But you are not an expert on marriage between us. Am I the same as your husbands?"

"No." It came out grudgingly. "You know you are not. But neither were they like each other."

"Did you love them?" He knew the answer—no, no, not completely—but was still compelled to ask.

"Have I ever said I loved you?"

It hit him so hard he would have fallen if he had not already been down. She stepped back as she saw the expression on his face. He knew she would have taken the words back if she could, but it was too late.

He pushed to his feet and left the room.

He closed the door with the gentlest click.

He didn't even care that she'd had the last word.

Chapter 8

It wasn't raining. Somehow that seemed wrong. Violet had lain awake all night staring at the bed's canopy. It had stopped raining just before dawn.

The sun's rays lit the still cloudy sky, and she wanted to see it as a sign of new beginnings.

It should still have been raining.

She pushed back the covers and climbed out of the high bed. The floor was cold beneath her bare feet. She walked to the dresser and poured water into the bowl.

It was cold. The maid had not been in to freshen it.

She splashed her face.

She should have never said that to Peter.

The expression on his face.

She splashed again, wishing she could wash away the memory.

Have I ever said I loved you?

No, she hadn't. He knew she hadn't. She knew she hadn't, but the words had still been brutal. She didn't know why she said them.

Yes, she did. She'd needed him to stop.

He'd looked so delicious lying on the rug before the fire. She'd wanted to kneel beside him and kiss away the worry lines marring his brow. He was too young, too innocent to have so much worry spread across his face.

He'd looked so delicious—she'd been ready to say anything to be with him again.

He'd looked so delicious—they should have been entangled in each other's arms, damp and exhausted, utterly at peace with the world and with each other. They'd never fought in the past—well, that was an exaggeration—but they'd never actually been angry.

Not before he'd asked that bedeviled question. *Will you marry me?*

She realized she was holding the water pitcher between clenched fingers as if ready to toss it across the room, only toss was too gentle a term for what she wanted.

Will you marry me?

The words filled her with fury.

She hadn't meant to hurt him. She was working as hard as she could not to hurt him. Why couldn't he understand that?

She put the pitcher down.

Marguerite would need her soon. There was a purpose to her being here at Glynewolde.

Violet would ring for the maid and dress. Having

her hair brushed would ease the tension building in her temples. She would go down and eat a light breakfast and prepare to be delightful company to Marguerite.

And if she saw him—she would apologize.

He deserved that.

The bloody, bloody woman. Peter slathered butter on his toast and crunched down, hard. Nothing could be worse than last night. Nothing could be worse than having Violet make it clear she lacked all tender feeling for him.

She'd once admitted she married her last husband because she truly cared for him—even loved him in some way. The man had been eighty-two.

The idea was ridiculous.

The man had delighted in bringing her erotic tomes.

The man had slept in her bed every night until he died.

Violet's eyes watered sometimes when she spoke of him.

The man had been eighty-two.

And a twenty-year-old Violet had loved him, perhaps.

Violet did not love Peter.

He should have realized it before. He'd had blinders on for too long. It was time he accepted the truth.

Violet would never marry him.

He bit into the bread again and swallowed it with a large gulp of tea.

He had held out for too long believing she would change her mind and realize how right they were together. He would not do that any longer. He had pretended he was ready to move on before, but it had only been pretense.

He was through with that. Life would go on without Violet.

He need never see her again.

The door swung open and in she strode. She stopped when she saw him; her mouth opened, then closed, a fish blowing bubbles—only some beautiful exotic fish, something that existed only in fairy stories.

He pushed his chair back and stood, letting the half-finished bread fall to the table. He didn't say a word as he walked past her.

"I am sorry," she said.

He paused and looked at her. Violet did not apologize. She didn't make mistakes.

"For what?" he answered.

"For what I said last night." She placed a hand on his arm. "I should not have said it."

"So you do love me?"

"No—I just mean I shouldn't have—"

"To put it simply you are now apologizing for not loving me. I hadn't thought things could be worse." He stared at her for a moment, gave her the chance to refute his words. He pushed past her, but stopped in the doorway. "I was wrong."

For once he had the last word.

Violet had nothing to say. She had plenty to scream, but nothing to say. What was wrong with her? What was wrong with Peter? There were couples who thrived on argument, but she and Peter had never been one of them. Now arguing seemed to be all they could do.

Only she wasn't thriving. Every time they argued she felt diminished.

She walked into the dining room and sat down staring at her empty plate. The servants had vanished into the woodwork with her first words, and it would be a few moments before they deemed it safe to reappear.

She reached over and took the remaining slice of bread off Peter's plate. Judging by the number of crumbs spread across the table, he'd been at war with the previous one.

She nibbled at the edge and then placed it back on her plate. She wasn't hungry. She would go check on Marguerite. That was why she was there.

How long would it be before the birth? Did she need to stay until then? It seemed impossible that she could live alongside Peter in this state of hostility. Maybe he would leave. He seemed an expert at running, given the number of times he'd stormed out of the room.

That was not fair. He stormed out of the room be-

cause she gave him reason to. Apologize—how great
an idiot was she?

Marguerite. Birth. Babies. It somehow didn't seem
as fearful as it had yesterday. The thought of facing
Peter over dinner filled her with much greater terror
than the thought of a baby.

She would spend the day with Marguerite, and if
Marguerite and Wimberley chose to eat in their chamber then she would dine in hers. It could not be that
long before she could return to London. She could
always make an excuse that Isabella needed her if the
situation became impossible.

All she had to do was not be alone with the blasted
man.

Peter stared across the dinner table at Violet. How on
earth had he ended up alone at dinner with her again?
The facts were easy. Tristan and Marguerite had both
started the dinner with them. An urgent message from
a tenant had taken care of Tristan. And then the whole
fresh trout had vanquished Marguerite.

He should have left with his brother. A flooded cottage and the rising river could certainly have required
another pair of hands. He would have enjoyed a little
struggle against nature and helpless odds to even out
his mood. It might have put his life into perspective.
Only Tristan had asked him to stay and care for Marguerite, to make sure she didn't try anything foolish.

He could not refuse his brother or the hopeful smile of his sister-in-law.

It had been impossible to follow Marguerite when she went dashing from the table since there were some duties a man could not be expected to perform. He did hope she was not badly off. She had not looked good even before the fish had arrived.

He looked across the table at Violet, who was picking at the fillet, but not moving a single piece to her mouth. Her wineglass had been refilled several times. Normally she could make a single glass last the meal.

"Are you going to eat any of that?"

She started at his voice, glanced up, then looked back at her plate. "I am not sure."

"I thought you loved fish, and this is excellent."

"Do you think I should check on Marguerite? I should have gone with her, but she made it clear she wished to be alone."

"Perhaps you should," he answered.

She did not move, continuing to push bits of trout about her plate.

The plates were cleared and the next course brought in. Still she did not leave. Neither did she eat. She continued to stare sullenly down at her plate.

She didn't look good. Her skin was more pallid than usual and her eyes deeply shadowed. She must have lost weight over the past weeks since her dress hung slightly on her, and Violet had never been one for loose clothing.

"You really should eat." He sounded like a governess. Why did he even care? She was no concern of his.

She raised her eyes and looked at him. She placed her fork beside her plate.

Could they really be arguing without words? What right did she have to be angry?

She continued to stare at him.

Yes, it was definitely a fight.

He would not be baited. They could not fight if he didn't respond. He would just let her be, not say anything. "You don't have the right to be upset. I have done nothing to hurt you."

Her eyes flashed at that, but she did not answer. She took another swallow of wine.

"I should have known you would respond like this." He couldn't let it go. "It's always about you."

She leaned forward across the table. "I don't see how you can say that. I am not the one who keeps storming from the room like a spoiled child."

"No, you simply throw words like cannon shells and then wait for them to explode."

"Which is why I am choosing not to speak. Every time I try and answer you it comes out wrong. I want to explain, but you keep reacting badly and then I make it worse. I can't seem to say anything without hurting you further. Now I just want to eat my dinner in peace," she answered.

"Besides, it is not a crime to wish not to marry." She leaned further toward him. He could see the freckle that topped her left breast. He forced his eyes back to her face. She was breathing hard, her lips vibrating with emotion.

He leaned forward. "I am not sure it's even about that anymore. I thought I knew you and now I find I don't. You are not at all the woman I knew."

Violet glared back at him. That had been her point all along. Peter didn't know her. He knew her body, but not her mind. If he really knew her he would never have dreamed of marriage.

She sat back.

She should just tell him what she was thinking—tell him he was correct. How could he argue if she told him he was right? He would argue, though, and then she would need to defend herself.

She was tired. She didn't want to fight anymore.

There was only one way she knew not to fight. Leaving was the only option. She pushed back her chair and turned away from him.

"Who's the running child now? Aren't you even going to say good night?" His taunt froze her feet to the ground.

"I haven't been a child in many a year. I merely do not wish to continue this discussion. I do not care for argument. We are not getting anywhere. I never wanted to fight with you." Why did she sound so hoarse?

"Then come here and tell me that." He turned his chair from the table so that she could walk right up to him. She measured the space with her eyes. It was a dare.

She stepped forward. One step. Two.

She halted a few feet before him.

"I don't understand the reason for this exercise, but here I am. Do you wish me to try to explain? I would try, but I am afraid I will never make you understand."

He stood. She was left staring at the elaborate knot of his cravat. He reached out and placed a finger under her chin, raising her gaze to meet his.

"No, I don't think anything you can say, or perhaps I should say *will* say, can improve the situation," he said. "And I certainly have no wish to argue—it's why I always leave. I refuse to fight when there can be no winner, so why do we do it?"

She stared up at him, into those clear brown eyes that should be worshipping her, not dissecting her like the fillet of trout.

She took a half step forward. "I don't know. I think we have said all there is to say, and yet when we are near I cannot help myself."

He tilted her chin further, then splayed his fingers across her cheek, his thumb stroking her lower lip. His eyes were no longer harsh as they followed the pattern his thumb traced.

She parted her lips. It felt so good to be touched again. She leaned her cheek into his palm, his calluses rasping against her skin. She closed her mouth slightly, the soft inner skin rubbing against his palm.

She opened and closed again, nipping.

He did not move away.

She ran her tongue along the flesh pad at the base of his thumb. His whole body tensed.

He dropped his arm. Her face felt cold without his hand.

He did not move away.

Their gazes remained locked.

She placed a hand upon his chest and pushed. He held firm, then settled back into his chair. She stepped forward, coming to stand between his hard thighs.

Her hand trailed across his chest. He was so warm beneath the linen. She caught a button, rolling it between her fingers. She slipped it open, then another.

He did not protest.

One more button and she slipped her hand under his shirt, feeling the wiry hair of his chest. She swirled her fingers through it, loving the way it sprang beneath her fingers. She caught some and pulled lightly.

His breath caught and his eyes grew even darker, black pools shimmering. She inhaled, caught up in his desire.

She pulled again, then ran her hand fully across him, the nub of his nipple poking against her palm. She circled the nipple with a finger, watching him shiver at her every touch. She pushed his shirt open wider, so that her eager eyes could see the wonder of his chest, heavy muscles, smooth skin, and the tempting sprinkling of coarse hair leading downward.

She let her hand follow the path, moving her finger in ever shrinking circles down his belly. Just as she reached his navel, he caught her hand, held it tight, almost crushing.

She thought he would stop her, but instead he yanked her forward, bringing her fully against him. He grasped the back of her scalp, moving her face to his.

The kiss was devouring. Lips pressed. Mouths fully open. Tongues battling. She was both engulfed and engulfing.

Their teeth ground. She could taste the wine he'd had with dinner, smell the smoke of his cheroot still caught in his hair.

Then she could not think, only feel—his tongue circled her teeth, darted in, darted out, but always gaining ground.

She surrendered, let him take her where he would.

His hands came around her face, held her tighter then pushed her back.

She stared at him, chest heaving, trying to find a breath. She ran her tongue over her lips, over the taste of him.

"Damn." It sounded more a blessing than a curse as he spoke. He brought a hand to his own swollen lips. "I didn't mean for that to happen."

She could not move. He could not mean to stop.

"I—" She tried to speak.

"This can't happen, much as I want it to." His voice was gentle, more so than she would have expected under the circumstances. His brow was lined with strain.

She caught his hand and brought it her chest, held it there, making no demands. She brushed her other hand across his brow, easing the heavy furrows.

"Why?" she asked. "What difference does one more time make? We clearly both need it. Maybe that is why we keep fighting." She leaned forward, her thighs pressing hard against him. She ran her hand down his face, his chest, his stomach, down to the apex of his thighs. She caressed him through his trousers, loving the hard, heavy feel of him.

He sighed as her fingers closed about him, his head falling back revealing the long, lean lines of his throat above the edge of his cravat. It was still tied. With her other hand she grabbed an end and pulled till it trailed down his chest.

"It should matter." He sighed, but did not stop her. His legs sprawled further.

She knelt between his thighs, laying soft kisses across his chest, savoring the salty taste, then she moved lower. "Let me do this for you. It can mean whatever you want. I did not mean to hurt you. Let me do this."

* * *

He should stop her. Peter buried his hands in Violet's hair, ready to push her back and instead held her tighter to him. He had never been so aroused. He would die if she stopped touching him.

Her hands stopped and he heard himself moan in protest. He felt the fastenings on his trousers open and then her hands were on him, warm flesh to warm flesh, kneading, cupping, stretching.

God, he was purring. Helpless.

When her mouth moved lower he wanted to cry out his thanks. She ran her tongue along his straining arousal and his thighs clenched uncontrollably.

It was bliss. He closed his eyes and gave in, his hands still holding her head, guiding her. She circled the crown of his erection, again and again. His fingers tangled in her soft hair and he gasped as her hands cupped him from below, while her tongue worked its magic above.

He opened his eyes and looked down at her. She was fully engaged in her ministrations, but her eyes were on his face. When she saw him watching she circled him again with her tongue, her eyes full of power and mischief—and joy.

His eyes sank shut again from sheer pleasure, but the look on her face stayed with him. Joy. He'd never seen such a look of happiness and contentment about her before. It made no sense, but he was beyond thought.

Her lips closed about him, drew him deep. Warm.

Soft. Moist. This was heaven. Then deeper still. He must have died. She had never done this. She didn't do this.

She sucked harder, her intent unmistakable.

God.

Heaven.

His groans filled the room.

He gave himself over, and shattering orgasm overcame him. His mind screamed in ecstasy as he found his release.

Violet let her face fall against his thigh, wiping her damp cheek against the soft fabric of his trousers. Her body ached with unresolved passion, but she had never felt such satisfaction.

She ran a hand along his calf. His body was limp with pleasure. She laid a final soft kiss upon him and fastened his trousers. She sank back on her heels and watched.

His eyes were still closed, his breathing still uneven. It would be a few minutes before he came back to himself.

What would happen then?

Did this mean nothing? She didn't know. She dropped her face to stare at the crumpled folds of her skirt. She felt so vulnerable. A moment ago she had been filled with joy and power.

Now, she was lost.

She had done this for him, only for him. She'd felt his

need, his call, and been helpless to resist. But, now—now, she didn't know.

She sat between his legs feeling more a child than a woman.

He moved then, his fingers sliding through her hair, caressing softly. A thumb moved across her cheek and then again.

"Why?" His word was soft.

"You needed it."

"Yes, but why?" He would not let her evade his question.

She inhaled, trying to collect her thoughts. How could she answer when she didn't understand? "I've never been the one stopping us."

"That was not us, it was you."

She placed her hand over his, intertwining their fingers. "I didn't want to hurt you anymore."

He didn't answer, but sat up in his chair. She could see thoughts beginning to form behind his eyes. The lines of strain she had erased a moment before were deepening again on his brow.

He started to speak, but she leaned up and drew her finger across his lips, silencing him.

"Don't talk. Just take it as a gift, something to symbolize all we have meant to each other." She had meant to say a farewell gift, but the word had not come out.

She placed her hands upon his knees and pushed herself up. She bent and began to fasten the buttons on his shirt, retying his cravat as best as the limp linen would allow. She finger combed his hair, putting him to rights.

Then, shaking out her skirts, she leaned forward and placed a soft kiss on his lined brow.

She turned to leave, easing the door open.

Marguerite's maid stood on the other side, twisting her hands in clear indecision. What on earth had she heard? Or seen? The maid shuffled a bit from foot to foot. Her face flushed when she saw Violet.

"My lady, Lady Wimberley has requested your presence. I think the babe is coming. Her pain is ever increasing. I've sent for the physician in the village, but the rains have started again and the river . . ." The maid's voice trailed off.

"Has someone sent for Tristan? He should be here," Peter asked as he came to stand behind her.

Violet welcomed the authority of his tone and had to resist leaning back against him for support. "How is Marguerite? Does she have someone with her?"

She moved toward the stairs, fighting to overcome her own fears.

"No, my lady, I am sorry, but none of the maids know anything about confinement. They've mostly come from the city and Cook has several children of her own, but claims to remember little of the experience. The midwife was going to come, but it's still supposed to be a week or more."

Violet's nails bit into her palms. "How can there be nobody?"

"Cook will try to help," the maid answered. "She is a very reasonable woman and I am sure she'll figure something out."

Violet started up the stairs. She stopped when she realized nobody was following.

The maid stood wringing her hands; clearly she would be of no actual use. "Fetch hot water and plenty of clean sheets, also a sturdy crop—the softer the leather the better," Violet ordered. She ignored the gasp at the last item. She glared at the maid until the poor girl hurried off to do her bidding.

She turned to Peter. He stood in the hall, hesitating, but with distinct movement toward the front door.

"I thought I could ride out and find Wimberley. He is needed here." He stepped near to the door.

"Don't you dare. They've already sent riders out. I need you here. Come, let us check on Marguerite. That silly maid should never have left her alone."

As if echoing her sentiment, a loud a cry resounded down the stairs. Without another glance at Peter, Violet began to run.

She skidded through Marguerite's door and rushed to the side of the bed. Marguerite lay limply back on the bed, her hair hanging in strings around her face. Her belly rose high and hard from among the tousled sheets. Marguerite must have been tying knots in them to hide her pain.

"It was not the fish," she gasped.

Marguerite pushed her own fears aside and came to stand beside her friend. She stroked the damp hair back from her brow and smiled down at Marguerite. "Everything will be fine. You should have hours yet. The physician will come."

"Why isn't Tristan here? He should be here," Marguerite screamed the last as her belly caught and moved, squeezing tight in a contortion as old as time.

"Shhh, it will all be fine. Your husband will be here soon." Violet wished she could be as calm as she sounded. Her mind was filled with pictures of how badly this could end.

The maid came fluttering into the room past Peter, who stood beyond the door, undecided on taking the final step inside.

Violet grabbed the sheets and towels and gestured for the maid to set the water on the dresser. She clutched the towels tight, hoping they would hide how hard her hands were shaking.

Marguerite suddenly thrust forward on the bed, another contraction wracking her body. It should not have come again so quickly. They should start slow and then speed up. The midwife had explained to her all those years ago what should happen, what she should expect.

Marguerite should not be progressing so quickly. Violet didn't know what it meant.

Too early, too fast. *God, please don't let it happen again.* She sent her silent prayer up as she crossed back to Marguerite and offered her the crop that had been buried in the linens. "Bite down on it when the pains come. I know it sounds strange, but it helps."

"I still think I should try to help fetch Tristan or the physician." Peter had made it through the door, but his eyes were focused on the far wall.

"Don't you dare leave me alone." Her words sounded calm, but they reflected her inner fear. She was desperate, and it was only Peter's presence that gave her the strength to carry on, to maintain the façade of calmness.

"I'll wait in the hall then."

"No, you don't. Pull up a chair. I don't care where you look or don't look, but we are in this together." She wanted to threaten to leave with him, but as Marguerite began to shudder and cry again, she knew it would be an empty threat.

Peter was not yet convinced. "Maybe we should call for Cook. She's given birth, she surely must know what to do even if she claims not to remember."

Violet freshened the linen around Marguerite and then turned to face Peter. "That is the difference between Cook and me. I remember every moment of when my son was born. It will never fade from my memory."

Chapter 9

"**Y**our son?" Even the embarrassment of being in this room with Marguerite in . . . that . . . condition faded at Violet's words. "You don't have a son. You've never had a child."

Violet turned back to the straining Marguerite, smiling down at her even when it seemed her friend would crush the hand she had grasped so tightly. "I don't have time for this now. I had a son. He was born two days after Dratton died. I was only six months along. I labored for three days and can describe every moment of it."

She swallowed, trying hard to concentrate only on the problems before her now. "He lived one hour and seven minutes. It was the best and worst hour of my life.

"Now wet those towels and begin wiping her face. Be sure she can get the crop between her teeth when she needs it." She turned back to Marguerite, patting her cheek. "You don't mind if Peter holds your hand, do you, dear? Let him worry about the upper half and I'll worry about the lower." She draped the sheets about Marguerite's knees before pushing them up and apart. She could only pray she did not see a foot or shoulder. Her son had been born feetfirst.

"I really shouldn't be here—Tristan will—" Even as Peter spoke, he moved to take Marguerite's hand.

"Tristan will only thank you for helping his wife. He is not the man to be concerned about anything else. He will understand the priorities."

She saw hair. It must be too early to be able to see the head. Should she try to push it back? She remembered every moment of her own birthing, but this was clearly different.

Even as she debated what to do, Marguerite's back arched and she strained downward. The baby's head pushed against the opening, seeking freedom. It would arrive any second.

Only it didn't. Again and again, Marguerite strained and the baby eased closer, but never close enough.

Minutes passed.

An hour passed.

They fell into the rhythm of deep, relaxing breaths that lasted only seconds before they again were drawn in the strain—each one of them fighting in his own way.

"You're doing wonderfully." Peter's voice was soft and firm. He spoke to Marguerite, but it was Violet his eyes followed. His words kept her from giving up each time she wanted to run from the room and pronounce her ignorance.

Something had to change.

The physician should have been there, but was not.

Wimberley should have held his young wife's hand, but he could not.

There were only Peter and Violet.

Something had to change.

This time when Marguerite arched and strained, Violet breathed deep and slid her hands between Marguerite's legs. She ignored the blood and mess and focused on the baby—if she could just reach it, pull it.

Damn, she couldn't get hold. She wanted to swear, to curse, but could not risk upsetting Marguerite. "Everything is going well," was all she said.

"When she arches again push on her belly." She directed her comment to Peter in little more than a whisper. She didn't know where the words came from, but they felt right.

Marguerite strained, Peter pushed down, and she tried to pull.

Failure.

Again.

She felt her arms would break with strain and her heart with the worry.

Strain. Push.

Failure.

Breathe. Strain. Push.

She felt something move. "Don't ease up. Keep pushing, both of you." She felt it slip, and slip again, then in a sudden whoosh the baby sprang free. She almost dropped it, she was so shocked at the final ease.

A boy. A beautiful, screaming, healthy boy.

This child was ruddy and fat, his arms already flailing as he let his displeasure at the whole experience be known.

She suppressed the image of that other baby. The one who was not red and screaming, but blue and limp. Tears began to trail down her cheeks.

"Is there something wrong? You're crying." Marguerite could barely move, but her voice was wrought with worry.

Violet forced a smile through her tears. "No, they are tears of joy. Your son is beautiful. Let me clean him and I will give him to you. There is still some unpleasantness to be dealt with."

She worked methodically first on the baby and then on the mother. She could only cast a second prayer up to God that she had done everything close enough to right that the bleeding would stop and no infection would set in.

It would be so unfair to lose either one of them now.

She finished and turned, only to find herself brought full into Peter's embrace. "You are amazing. I don't know what would have happened if you hadn't been here. I always knew you could do anything." He turned to look at baby and mother, who had drifted off to sleep cuddled together.

"I don't know how I did it. You had more faith than I. I could not have done it without you. I would have gone running from the room at the first sign of difficulty. It was you who kept me here."

"That's nonsense, but I'll take all the credit if you want to give it to me." He placed an innocent kiss upon her brow and a not so innocent one upon her mouth. He gave her a last squeeze, then set her from him. "You must be exhausted. You should go and sleep now. Marguerite's maid can sit with her tonight, and I am sure in the morning all will be arranged. I'll go smoke one of Wimberley's cheroots, as a good uncle should, and await the proud papa and the physician. They cannot be long now."

Violet let out a hysterical laugh at that. How many times had each of them said that as the long hours of the night passed? She clamped her lips shut. She was exhausted. She'd take his advice.

She walked to the bed and kissed both sleeping mother and child. She nodded at Peter and turned toward her room.

Her mind was numb with exhaustion. Tomorrow would be soon enough to think about the events of this evening.

* * *

She slept like an angel, a very tired angel, but still an angel. Peter eased the door to Violet's room open and slipped in, shutting it soundlessly behind him. He'd introduced his brother to his child, kissed his sister-in-law, and finally snuck a bit of oatmeal from the kitchen.

Now he was ready for his reward.

He walked forward and watched her in the pale light of dawn. Her hair spread across the pillow more radiant than any sunrise. He grinned as he saw the pile of cast-off clothes beside the bed. She'd always been lazy when tired. He bet she was naked beneath the covers since getting a fresh chemise would have required too much effort.

All the better for him.

He scanned the room and took a chair from beside the small writing desk. He shoved it beneath the handle of the door. He'd have to talk to his brother about making sure all the guest rooms had keys.

He moved back across the room and shed his clothing, jacket, shirt, the boots with some effort, and finally his trousers and under linen. Naked as the day he was born, he slipped into the bed and cuddled up next to Violet.

Warmth and comfort welcomed him. He took her in his arms, and like a sleepy kitten, she curled into his chest. For the first time in weeks the world was at rights.

* * *

Hmmmm. Ahhhh. Violet stretched in absolute contentment. She was so toasty. She'd slept better than she had in weeks. She smiled without opening her eyes, enjoying that first perfect moment of awakening. The sheets were silky, almost velvet. They smelled of cinnamon. She couldn't remember anything ever feeling so good. Silk and velvet. And hair?

She opened one eye, afraid of what she'd see.

He'd splayed himself across the entire bed, yet again. She knew he was big, but did he need to have a foot off either side? At least this time he'd positioned her across his chest.

She rubbed her nose in the wiry fleece, resisting the urge to sneeze.

He had come to her. She had won.

She laid her head back against him, listening to the slow, steady beat of his heart. She closed her eyes and thought about the previous evening.

She'd delivered a baby. A beautiful, healthy baby. No other wonder could compare. She had done that. She had faced a great fear and survived. She would never have believed she could do it, but she had.

And the earlier part of the evening. What had that been about? She had no regrets, not a single one, but—
She looked at the man lying beside her. He'd been a man last night. She couldn't think of another man who'd have done that for a woman not his wife. She had

a hard time thinking of many who would have done it for their wives.

She ran her toes up his calf, tickling the back of his knee. He wiggled, as if shaking off a bug, and then shifted back to sleep. A great honking snore erupted from his mouth.

She suppressed a giggle.

She ran a finger down his chest. He quivered at her touch, but did not awake.

Her entire body hummed with his nearness. She turned her head and placed a kiss above his heart.

If he awoke they would have to face what was between them.

She wasn't sure she was ready.

She laid her ear back upon his heart and let him sleep.

He came awake slowly. First, he was aware of the weight, warm, soft, but not light. Second, he felt the breath feathering over his chest. Third, the hair rubbing against his nose tickled.

He opened one eye.

The hair shone russet in the morning light. It had not all been a dream.

He opened the other eye and found that clear orchid gaze staring back at him. A smile flittered across her face.

He grinned back. "Good morning."

"Is it?" There was a trace of uncertainty under her cheerfulness.

"The rain has stopped. I have a healthy nephew. Cook makes wonderful oatmeal. And I am in bed with the most amazing woman I have ever known. It seems pretty good to me."

"Why are you here?"

"I realized I belonged. It took me a while, but watching you last night I realized that, no matter what, I needed to be with you."

"Oh." A faint furrow appeared between her brows.

He ran a hand down her shoulder and lingered in the fold of her inner elbow. He'd always liked that spot.

"I don't understand. Does this mean you don't want to marry me any longer?"

He had to fight back a further grin at her petulant tone. "I am through with ultimatums, they never work anyway. I will take you any way I can get you."

"But—"

"Please don't tell me we're going to fight about this now." He trailed a finger back up her arm, across her collarbone. He stopped at the edge of the sheet she held clutched to her breasts. He ran the tip back and forth at the border of the fabric.

"Uhhh. No. Yes. Will you stop that?" She batted at his hand.

"Only if you promise not to argue. Discuss, yes. Argue, no. I am through with argument. If you start to fight I'll have to punish you." He nipped at her bare shoulder.

She pushed back and sat across from him, the sheet still tightly held to her chest. "Then let's talk. You are ready for things to be as they were before?"

"Yes, at least mostly." He slipped a leg between her silken thighs.

"I don't trust that mostly." She rolled away from him.

"I am not willing to be your secret anymore. I will not spread our relationship among society, but I refuse to hide it from my family."

"Marguerite knows anyway, and I suspect your brother and the whole house do too." She glanced across the room at the chair pressed tight against the door.

"Maybe they think I am so tired I wandered into the wrong room and didn't want to be disturbed while I slept. You, of course, were so shocked you fainted for hours."

She raised a single eyebrow.

He smiled back. "Otherwise, I am fine with continuing our past relationship."

"About marriage." She sat up straighter.

"Yes."

"I am not giving in and you will need to sometime."

"I can wait. Why worry about the future now?"

"The future has a habit of arriving faster than expected."

"Are you going to try and make me feel young in the face of your experience again? I won't stand for it any longer." He let his hands slide down her shoulders, enjoying the velvet of her skin.

"I just want you to be realistic. You will need to marry and have a family. I know you will want children?"

"Well, if you find yourself in an interesting condition, then I will insist on marriage, otherwise I am not even thinking about them yet."

"But you will someday," she stated, sitting up.

"Why bother with that now?"

She sat up straighter. "No, I need to know. Do you want children?"

"I always imagined that someday I'd have a large family. I always wanted another brother or two. Seeing my nephew born"—he remembered the magic of that moment—"well, I'd hate to miss that. You should have seen Tristan when he first saw his son. I can picture you with a whole passel of them. You'll be a great mother, Violet."

She pulled away suddenly. An unfamiliar expression crossed her face. "I think you should go."

"What? You're just acting contrary." He pushed the sheet down, revealing a tightly peaked nipple. He tapped a finger on the very tip, and a shiver ran though her entire body.

She yanked the sheet back up and tried to leave the bed.

He blocked her. "Why are you changing the rules, now?" he said. "I give you what you want and you decide it's not enough. Isn't that a woman?"

"Go away." There was steel in her tone.

He ran his finger across along the edge of the sheet again. "Don't play with me, Violet. I've met your conditions."

She tried to push away again. He'd never seen her like this. She seemed wounded and defensive. He moved toward her and she hit him hard. He grabbed her hand and held it tight. He leaned forward, forcing her backward on the bed. He saw her eyes darken with desire. He could have her flat beneath him in seconds if he wanted. And he did want. God, did he want. Just not yet.

"Don't pretend you don't want this. I know you too well."

"I don't want this." She twisted and tried to free herself.

He didn't understand her game, but he trusted his instincts. He ran a finger across her collarbone. She shuddered beneath him. "You don't want me, like you don't love me. You have to be careful or I won't believe anything you say."

She grabbed a pillow with her free hand. She battered him with it. He pulled it away.

She hit him with another. He pulled it away also. He placed it back on the bed behind her. She reached for it again and he took the chance to grab what he needed off the floor.

He turned, and the pillow pounded him hard in the side of the head. She reached back to swing again.

That was it.

He caught the pillow and pulled her toward him, grabbing first one wrist and then the other. He held them firmly in one hand. She struggled hard, trying to get away. Did she realize what a reward a lapful of warm, wiggling woman was? She froze. Ah yes, she had just discovered. He cocked his hips, rubbing hard against her soft behind. She tried to move to the side, but he lifted her arms high, forcing her to the center, his arousal tight in the cleft of her buttocks.

"You bastard."

"I did say you'd be punished if you fought—this might not be quite what I meant, but a promise is a promise." He took the cravat he'd taken from the floor and looped it tightly about her caught wrists.

A bend, a twist, more struggle, and he had her hands tightly fastened to the bedrail.

"I never took you for the type to beat a woman."

He smiled. "Does this feel like beating?" He ran a hand over her chest and down her bare belly. He let it rest there, fingers spread wide, a gesture of possession. "Would you like a spanking? That I could imagine."

He leaned forward and slipped his other hand beneath her, giving her buttock a firm squeeze. "God, you're perfect."

"You lily-livered, son of a—"

He cut off her curses with kisses. She tried to turn her head, but he pressed his lips tight, holding her still with the sweet pressure of his mouth, his tongue taking advantage of her still open mouth.

She bit at him, and not gently.

It was his turn to swear.

He did not surrender. He pressed the tenderest of kisses upon her face. He poured all that he felt into them, tons of tiny kisses.

He caught her lower lip between his teeth, not hard, just enough to pull. He licked the soft inner flesh of her mouth, flicking his tongue back and forth.

His hands were busy too. Nothing aggressive, just a long, slow massage of her neck and shoulders. He shut his eyes and allowed the physical sensations to overwhelm him, the suede of her skin, the womanly musk, the quiet but ever increasing moans. He savored each one.

Finally, with a sigh, she opened her mouth, welcoming him.

Still he kept the kiss soft.

She pushed forward, wanting more.

He refused. There was no hurry. Time was theirs to enjoy.

She pushed, again.

He pulled back. "Hush, relax, we'll get there."

"Let me go."

"No."

"I want to touch you." She tilted her pelvis up, rubbing against him.

"No, this is my chance to be in charge. I've never been the one in control." He ran a hand up her arms and over the tie, testing that it was not too tight, not too loose. He shifted his weight until he was kneeling over her. It was a heady experience to balance above her, so in control, able to fulfill his every fantasy.

"How can you say that? I've never told you what to do."

"But you have, not always with words. I've taken direction in the sway of a hip, the purr of pleasure you give when I do this . . ." His words faded as he buried his face in the crook of her neck, laving the indent at the center of her clavicle. He sucked. He bit. He savored.

He could feel her dissolve under him.

He licked some more, then worked his way up her neck, pausing to nip and then kiss each spot along the way. When he came to her mouth, it was a long, endless kiss. Sweet. Devouring. Loving. He couldn't say the word to her, but he could say it in his mind.

He lifted his head and looked down at her. Her lips were plump and swollen, her eyes so dark a purple as to appear black even in the bright morning light.

"Will you let me do what I want?" he asked. "Do you trust me?"

Her gaze focused slowly. She pulled at her bonds once. Looked him straight in the eye. He could feel the fight within her—and then the surrender. "I am yours."

"Really?"

"For now—for as long as this captive enchantment lasts."

Look out or that might be forever, he thought, but did not say. Instead he placed a soft kiss upon her mouth. He raised up on his knees, pushing the sheets aside so that he could admire her in the window's rosy glow.

She was perfect. He'd thought it before, but never had she been so incandescent, so soft, so woman. His woman.

He wanted to beat his chest like the gorilla he'd once seen at the zoological park. He didn't think Violet would appreciate that. He could almost see the pinched-lip look she'd give him, so different from her current soft surrender.

Gads, he felt like a king.

He bent forward and kissed the crinkles that formed at the corners of her eyes. He knew she hated them. "I adore you here."

He kissed the corner of her jaw. "And here."

The indent he'd loved so fondly earlier he revisited. "This is perfect." A spray of kisses down her arm, the soft fold of her elbow. "I can always taste you here. It makes the blood flow to my head—both of them." He leaned back and let her see. When her eyes ran over his length he thought he'd explode.

She licked her lips. Smiled. She parted her mouth, drew a breath in.

He moved forward and placed a quick kiss on her mouth. "No, this is my game and I am not done."

He moved to her breasts. What had man ever done to deserve such bounty? God was kind. Normally he moved right to the nipples, tugged and sucked the way he knew she liked. This was for him. He took them in his hands, enjoying their full weight, the overflow. He squeezed, massaged. Every schoolboy's fantasy.

He buried his face between them. He'd be content to die right now. She shifted beneath him, impatient. His cock came into full contact with her cleft, the curls urging him home.

He almost caved.

Control. He started to count the dogs he'd owned, named each one in his head, moved on to the horses.

He could do this.

He sat back on his heels.

She squirmed, tried to bring back the contact. "Please," she begged.

"Soon." But not too soon. He went back to her breasts.

* * *

She was in serious trouble. His lips closed about her nipple and she almost arched off the bed. She didn't know how long he'd been at it. He flicked his eyelashes over the sensitive peak and all she could do was beg. *Please, please, finish this now. Please, please, never stop.*

He was giving her everything she wanted—sex without marriage. Why did she resist?

She had never been one to dream of what she couldn't have. A flicker of her earlier anguish rose, and she forced it down.

She would live for this moment.

Her arms ached. She wanted them free, wanted to wrap them around him, wanted to draw him closer, wanted to push him down, to climb on top and see just how much control he had.

Her arms ached and all it did was sensitize every other inch of her body. She'd never felt so feminine.

She was tied to a bed.

She should be hating this.

His lips closed about her other nipple, while his fingers worked the first. It was wonderful. She should be hating this. She never liked giving up control.

He drew her nipple deep into his mouth, swirling about it with his tongue. She closed her eyes and fought the sensation.

Oh God. When had he learned to do that?

She never begged. She clamped her lips closed to hide her scream.

He knelt above her, all warm, hard muscle and velvet skin. She could feel the heat rising from his body. She strained up, lifting her head. He would not last much longer. She knew the signs, knew the quiver of his thighs, the drop of moisture at the crown of his arousal, even the dark glow of his eyes. He inhaled twice, before one long exhale. He couldn't hold out more than another few minutes.

She twisted to the side, trying to rub against him again. He pushed her back. Went back to work. She was going to die, die of pleasure, bliss.

His mouth and hands left her breasts, and for a moment, a fraction of a second, she felt relief and loss.

His mouth returned, but this time lower. He began a trail of kisses moving downward. When he reached her curls she knew he might not last minutes, but she'd be gone long before.

Children. She'd dreamed of children. She never dreamed of children. Violet sat up with a shudder. Her children. Her children and Peter's children. Children that would never exist.

She looked down at the man snoring softly next to her. She should have told him everything—told him what the doctors said after her poor son was ripped from her body, after the bleeding was finally stopped and infection set in—told him what they said when she survived the fever no woman should have lived through. She was barren. Had he never wondered at the lack of precautions she required before inviting him to her bed?

Damnation, but she should have told him.

He would not have told her she'd be a wonderful mother if she'd told him, would not have ripped the heart from her chest.

He'd understand why they couldn't marry if only she'd told him. She laid her head back down on his chest. She listened to the steady pound of his heart.

This was not a bad life to settle for. It was not the one she'd wanted, but it was better than most. She must remember to be grateful for all she had, not cry for what she couldn't have.

She closed her eyes and prayed for no more dreams.

Peter came awake with a start. Violet still slumbered next to him. A gentle tap sounded at the door. He wrapped a sheet around his hips and, slipping from the bed, answered the door, moving the chair. A maid stood there with a heavy tray.

"His Lordship suggested that Lady Carrington might require refreshment. He suggested she might be hungry enough for two. Should I bring it in?" the maid asked.

"I'll take care of it." He reached out and took the tray from her. The scent of warm beef met his nose, and he realized how hungry he was. It had been a hard-working morning.

He set the tray on the bed with care, and reached over to nudge Violet awake.

"No more, no more," she murmured.

"Wake up, sleepyhead," he answered.

She scrunched her face, wiggling her nose before opening her eyes. She was so cute. Finally she opened her eyes. She stared solemnly up at him. "I should be very mad at you. That was not playing fair."

"It was punishment, not fair play."

"I may not forgive you," she replied. She smiled, but it did not reach her eyes.

"I have food."

"Food. Food may make you victorious. Although we must not forget who the true winner is." She sat, pulling a sheet about her. She looked away from him.

He had thought she would be smug. He did not understand this quiet dignity. He pushed the tray forward, forking a bite of beef stew and holding it out to her.

She nipped the beef from the fork. "That's so good. I feel like I haven't eaten for a week."

"You're right." He took a bite himself. He waited until she'd had enough to slow the first rush. "Are you ready?"

"Ready for what? You can't want more."

"Ready to talk about your son."

Chapter 10

Violet had known it was coming; only the satisfaction of a night's pleasure had delayed it. She picked up the napkin and wiped her lips. She answered matter-of-factly. "You know I was seventeen when I married Dratton, two days past seventeen, to be exact. He was afraid that he would be laughed at for taking a child bride if I were any younger. My brother seemed not to care."

"Good God, the man was at least seventy. Did he think waiting a few days or a month would matter?"

"I do not know. It was never discussed with me. My brother told me what to do and I was obedient. For the first time in our lives he refused to talk to me. I did not understand it at the time. Perhaps neither did he, in retrospect. So I did as I was told. I did not realize there was another option."

"I cannot imagine that you were ever obedient."

"You didn't know me then. It is life that changed me." She picked up the fork and toyed with the food. "I only wanted a family of my own, a place where people loved me."

"And you thought marrying an old man would get you that?" Peter shifted toward her on the bed.

"I told you I was not consulted. And even if I had been I am not sure I would have understood the problem. My grandfather was the only kindly figure I remember from my early life. I pictured my husband like that."

"I take it he wasn't," Peter said.

"No, he was definitely not. I think he wanted to be a good husband, but he just didn't have the way of it," Violet answered. "Dratton was not a bad man, just one of little patience. He wanted a wife to warm his bed and manage his house. He wasn't really interested in knowing another person, a woman."

"I can't imagine you settling for that."

Violet dropped the fork back on the plate. "I did actually, and then I got pregnant and I thought everything would be fine."

Peter settled across the bed, lying on his stomach. "Ah, finally we get to your son."

"There is not much to say. It was a simple pregnancy. I felt well mostly, sick occasionally. Dratton was pleased, but not ecstatic. He had a grown nephew he had raised as his heir. He did not worry about succession. He was, however, proud to show he still could sire a child." Violet swung her legs off the bed. She needed to move. Her voice might still sound normal, but memories brought with them emotion. And she had decided to tell Peter the whole story. She would not awake ever again from a dream of their children.

"Any man would be." Peter rolled slightly so he could watch her as she went to the bureau and splashed her face with cold water.

"I did not mind his pride. He left me alone most often and so I was content. But then he died." Her voice stuck a little at the end. She splashed more water trying to cover.

"You make it sound so simple."

"It was, really. Dratton was there one morning and gone that afternoon. They said it was his heart." Violet moved to the wardrobe and pulled on a chemise. Her maid was conspicuously absent. "I never considered how quickly my life would change. I went from the security of being a wife to having my whole world hang on the baby still in my belly. If I delivered a boy everything would be mine to control. If I delivered a girl the nephew would inherit and I would have only a small portion, not enough to raise a child on without his benevolence."

"You must have prayed for a son."

"I should have, but I still did not realize how precarious life could be. I had always been somebody's responsibility, and it never occurred to me that I could manage my own life.

"Then," she continued, "my labor began early. All I wanted was a healthy child."

Peter sat up on the bed. "You don't have to continue if it pains you."

"It was a long time ago. I cannot deny there is still some pain when I remember how fragile he was, my baby. I had never seen anything so beautiful. He made all the pain worthwhile." Violet closed her eyes and remembered the wonder of that small, warm body. The whole world had stopped for a few minutes.

"I can't believe you never told me."

"I never had a reason to; very few people ever knew. I put much work into never thinking about it. Life is easier when I keep thoughts of my son tucked away in the back of my mind, wrapped carefully like a treasure." She chose a dress. She walked over to Peter and presented her back. "Our relationship was not about my past."

Peter paused at his task. "Then what was our relationship about? I thought we were getting to know each other and now I find you've hidden huge parts of yourself from me."

"Finish fastening my dress." She stayed perfectly still until he was done, then turned to him. "I am sorry. I thought we understood each other. All I wanted was fun and companionship. I don't have room in my life for more."

"And you complain of Dratton not being interested in knowing another person."

That cut. She had never considered it from that perspective. "You are right. I was not fair to you."

"You were not fair to either of us. It is your pain, not mine, that still stands between us. Is this why you won't marry me? Are you scared you will lose another child?"

"That thought does terrify me. I still remember the second that I realized he would not breathe again. I had already named him in my mind—Lyle, my grandfather's name." She turned from Peter and went to stand by the door. This was why she had dressed; she needed to know she could escape. She lifted the chair and moved it from beneath the handle. Her fingers wrapped around the handle and lingered for a moment.

Then she turned back, and sat in the chair facing Peter.

"That is not my real fear, however. I fear not having children more than I fear losing them."

His brow drew in, the lines heavy between his eyes. "Why would you fear such a thing? You are still young."

"I fear it because it is as much a truth as man can know. I was damaged internally during the birth and then caught a fever. I was not expected to survive. The physician said I would probably never be with child again. I did not believe him, but time has proved him right."

"Your husbands were all old; surely that could have been the problem." Peter leaned on his elbows and faced the blankets. She could not see his face.

"If it had only been my husbands you might have been right. But you forget that I have had lovers since then. At least one of them has fathered a child since. And us? Do you think that you cannot father a child?"

Peter blushed brighter than a peony. "I—I never thought about it—I assumed that you—that is, I know there are things—precautions you can take."

"Did you ever see me take precaution? Did we ever discuss them? I should assure you that most of the ones that work involve effort from both parties."

Peter's face was still red. He sat up on the bed and did not bother to pull the sheet across his lap. "I never even thought—"

Violet smiled in kind acceptance. "I realize that. We should have talked of it before."

"Yes, we should have." He sat up straighter, but let the words hang.

"I must be going now. I am sure there's something that I should be doing—Marguerite must need help." Violet rushed from the room before Peter could answer. She didn't want to see him once he'd had time to understand what she'd said.

She'd always known they could not marry.

She didn't need to see him accept that knowledge.

He should have realized what she planned. Peter cursed as he searched the floor for the trousers he'd discarded the night before. How had he let her get dressed without gathering his own clothes? Ah, there they were. He grabbed them and pulled them up his legs. Shirt. Shirt. He knew he'd had a shirt. He picked up the rumpled ball of linen. He could never be seen in this. Still swearing to himself, he pulled the shirt about his shoulders and went in search of his valet.

It was only as a fresh shirt was being smoothed over his shoulders that Violet's words began to fill him.

No children.

He'd never thought about wanting children, but he'd certainly assumed he would have them. Everybody had children. Well, perhaps not everybody, but they were definitely an established part of life.

No children.

The thought chilled him.

But then another thought froze him.

No Violet.

He'd realized over these last weeks how much he needed her. His life was not in any way as complete when she was away. He could imagine a life without children of his own. He already had a nephew and he imagined there would be more to come. Tristan and Marguerite were not the types to do things in a small way. He could be happy being an uncle.

He liked his current life. There would be far worse things than for it to continue as it was.

He could not imagine a life without Violet.

It was time he sought her out and persuaded her of that fact.

"Oh, just make it simple," he said to his valet. The man seemed to believe a full cascade of white froth was necessary for a day in the country. "I'll tie it in a bow myself if you don't finish up."

Where would Violet be? She'd said something about helping Marguerite, but after Violet's revelations of the morning he couldn't picture her cocooned with mother and baby.

Violet must be worn out by her revelations. In adjusting to his own loss he had not stopped to consider hers. He'd heard the pain echoing in her voice with each word she spoke. She'd tried to sound calm and reasonable, but there had always been that edge.

How had it felt to deliver Marguerite's baby knowing she would never have one of her own? She'd been so brave, so wonderful.

Violet pressed back against the door. Weren't new mothers supposed to lie abed for days? Violet had felt safe as she finished the plate of cold meats that had been left out in the dining room and prepared to hide in one of the library's large wing chairs, but there was Marguerite, and not just Marguerite, but Marguerite, Tristan, and the small swathed bundle. Even as she watched, a tiny hand wiggled free and batted back and forth in the air.

She should go in and congratulate Tristan. He was the father of a son. Such moments deserved hearty cheers.

She doubted Hannibal and all his elephants could have dragged her through the door.

It hurt. She'd managed to avoid these feelings for years and now they flooded through her. Last night she had been so caught up in the miracle of the birth and then, well, Peter had certainly provided a distraction.

Peter. It hurt to think of him as well.

A coo echoed from the library, followed by Marguerite's soft giggle.

Violet pulled away from the door and eased toward the drawing room on mouse feet. She would escape to the veranda from there, and then into the gardens. If she walked far enough she would be safe for hours. The center of the maze was always solitary.

"I wondered how long it would take for you to get here." Peter sat on the stone bench resting back on his elbows. His long legs sprawled in front of him. He kicked idly at the pebbles on the ground before him.

He'd watched Violet approach, her eyes fixed on the ground in front of her, her face solemn. He timed his words with care, waiting until she was too close to flee.

She looked up, startled. "I didn't expect to find anyone here."

"I know. It's why I came and waited." And she thought he didn't know her.

He edged to the side of the bench and patted the spot beside him. For a moment he thought she would not come, but then slowly she stepped forward and sat. She stared straight ahead. He turned his body to mirror hers.

"It was warm in the house," she said.

"Do you really wish to talk of the weather?" Peter answered. "I will, if that is what you want. It is amazing how quickly it has warmed after the days of rain. The fields should dry quickly for the harvest. I am sure the farmers are happy . . . Is this the conversation that you desire?"

She was quiet for a moment before speaking. "It is certainly the easiest and therefore I expect most acceptable."

"Do you want easy?"

"I have spent the last years of my life pursuing easy. Surely that should speak for itself?" She kept her eyes fastened straight ahead, as if not looking at him made it possible to talk.

"Have you really? I've never seen it in quite that fashion. I thought you wanted comfort and security. It is there in the perfection of your house, in the air of comfort that moves about with you. Perhaps you avoided risk, but is that the same as easy?"

"I had always thought so, but it certainly doesn't feel easy now."

"What do you want for the rest of your life? Have you thought of that?" he asked.

"You are correct that I do want comfort and security," she answered. "I had so little as a girl and young woman. I also want control. I never want another man to tell me what to do."

"Do you think I would order you about?" He worked to keep his voice level and carefree. He didn't want to reveal how much her answer mattered.

"I don't think you would mean to—but the man—be it father, brother, or husband—always comes first. If you wanted to go to the country, we would go to the country. If you wanted to go to your club and leave me home alone, you would. If you wanted to stay in, you would. A wife does not have the same freedom of decision."

He considered. He had never thought about the issue before. She was correct that the husband's wishes came first in all the couples he could think of. Even with Tristan and Marguerite it was Tristan who made the actual decisions—although he'd always suspected that Marguerite guided those decisions far more than his brother would ever admit.

Violet did not work that way. She said what she wanted. She did not hint and persuade.

"I would try to never override your desires," he finally answered.

"I do believe you, but it is too much to risk. And"— she finally turned to face him—"we are avoiding our conversation of this morning."

Yes, that was Violet, face the problem square on.

"I am not seeking to avoid it, merely trying to follow your wishes," he said.

"And how do you know my wishes if we do not talk?"

"I took your flight to the garden to be ample illustration of your desires." He reached over and took her hand, his thumb stroking the back of her palm.

She turned to face him. He could see the indecision in her eyes. "I fled more than words."

"I know. Does it hurt so much to see him, to see my nephew?"

"More than I expected," she replied. "But it is not so much him as them. I have seen many families over the years and after the first months the pain grew numb and then I started to ignore it. I was not prepared for how tightly it would twist my gut to see Marguerite so happy.

"I do feel joy for her. I really do. And your brother. He will treat them well and cherish them. He deserves all he has been blessed with, but—"

"It still cuts deeply," he finished her sentence. "I am sure that after last night you are more emotionally involved than you have ever been before."

"That is true," she said. "But I think you are as much at fault."

"I? I do not understand." His grip tightened about her fingers.

"You asked before how I pictured my future? I have avoided doing so before now. I chose to live in the moment and to make each moment as perfect as I could. You asked questions that made me look ahead."

"I should say I am sorry, but I cannot. I want you to think of the future, of a future with me."

She pulled her hand from his and pressed it with its mate upon her lap. "How can you still want that? It would be so unfair to you. You deserve everything that your brother has."

"We don't always get what we deserve, good or bad." He shifted sideways to face her more fully. "What is unfair to me is a life without you, Violet. I can accept a life without children. I cannot accept a life without you."

"And if you have to?" She stared fully into his eyes as she asked the question. "What will you do if you don't have me?"

"I will go on," he answered. "We both seem to be good at that, but there is a difference between going on and living."

She dropped her glance. "You are correct about that. You have never asked of my second husband. It's strange but nobody ever does. They talk of Dratton and Carrington, but never of Milber. Living with him was going on."

She tapped her fingers together. "I was still under-age when Dratton died. My brother told me he needed me to marry Milber. There were debts that had to be paid. My parents had apparently left the whole estate a mess.

"I did resist. I had not even finished my mourning. I had no desire to marry again and certainly not Milber. He did not remind me of my grandfather in the least."

"Even if you were not of age, surely your brother could not have forced you?" he asked.

"There are many types of force. I do not even know if Masters realized how much pressure he placed on me. He was only a couple years older than I, and I think even less experienced, for all his pretense of maturity. I knew that it was not only his well-being but Isabella's that hung in the balance. In the end I lacked the means to resist him. I had little money of my own and no other home to return to. In retrospect, I am sure Dratton's nephew would have taken me in, and perhaps he would even have taken in Isabella, but at the time I felt so alone."

Peter began to understand her deep need for control. It was easy to imagine Violet at eighteen, still grief-stricken from the loss of her son, feeling forced into another loveless marriage. "I wish I could have been there for you."

"I believe you were eleven at the time," she said. "I doubt you could have been of assistance."

"I would have offered you my allowance and snuck you into the nursery."

She smiled at that and answered seriously. "You probably would have. I am not sure I would have cared for survival on milk toast and biscuits."

"You never tasted Cook's biscuits."

They were both quiet then for a while. Violet's hand snuck out and found Peter's again. They sat, their faces turned up to the sun.

"Is there more? I did not mean to change the subject," Peter asked when enough time had passed.

"Not really. I will say only that I was glad when he died, very glad. It was my marriage to him that made me value Carrington's warmth and friendship so greatly. I know that society thought it odd, to put it in the best light possible, when I chose to marry another much older man, but it was one of the best things I have done. He gave me safety and security and I gave him joy."

"I have never doubted that you cared for each other."

"You mean you never thought I married him for the tidy fortune he left me?" she asked.

"No, I certainly never—"

"Well, I did. It was actually part of our agreement. He understood what the money would do for me far better than I did. It gave me the freedom to become myself."

Peter brought her hands to his lips and kissed them gently. "Then I cannot blame you for it. I rather like who you have become."

She batted her lashes at him and smiled coquettishly. "Do you, now?"

It was amazing how swiftly a mood could shift. In the time it took to draw a breath, seriousness was gone and play and passion moved in.

"You know I do." He drew her thumb into his mouth and sucked.

"I have always enjoyed a good garden."

He ran a finger across her cheek, down her neck, and along the edging of her bodice. "Let's see if I can make you enjoy it even more."

Sex certainly helped make things better. Violet brushed leaves from her hair and shook the dirt and wrinkles from her skirt. She turned and smiled at her lover.

Peter was that again. Her lover.

"It is time we went back to the house," she supposed.

"Unfortunately, I am sure you are right." He kissed her hand again.

"Stop that. Look what happened the last time you did that."

He drew her thumb into his mouth.

She pulled her hand away and slapped at his chest. "I am hungry and your brother will wonder at us."

"I doubt he will wonder much. I am sure he will guess, and guess right."

She smiled at him again. "You are so bad."

Hand-in-hand they walked out of the maze. When the house came into sight they stopped and glanced at each other and then, hands still clasped tight, continued to walk.

It should have gotten easier. Violet sat across from Marguerite—and the baby. After three days it should be easier. Even the readiness with which Tristan had accepted her relationship with Peter had not alleviated the situation.

She had known for more than ten years that it was unlikely she would ever have children.

It should not still hurt.

It did.

She smiled at Marguerite. She said all the right things. She'd even held the baby, twice. It had been soft and sweet and so dreadfully wonderful.

Peter came up behind her and began softly kneading her shoulders. She could remember Tristan doing the same thing to Marguerite. She rolled her head back into his touch. It felt so good.

"I was hoping you'd agree to be little William's godmother," Marguerite said, drawing Violet's attention. "I know, forgive me for telling you this, that Tristan intends to ask Peter, and I thought it would be perfect to have both of you stand up for him." She smiled at them knowingly as she gently bounced the baby against her breast.

"I—I—I need to get back to Town. I have business." Violet had never stammered before and now it felt that each word must be pushed out of her.

"Oh well, the christening won't be for at least a month, probably more," Marguerite answered back. "And we will hold it in London. I was thinking about sometime in the fall when we can share our blessings with all our friends."

Peter's grip had become stronger. She could feel him trying to give her strength. "I'll have to see. I am not sure what my plans will be."

Marguerite had stopped smiling, and Violet could sense her confusion and disappointment. "If you don't want to—"

"Of course I want to." What else could she say? She had helped deliver her best friend's child. It would be impossible to say no and equally impossible to take on the responsibility.

"I had talked of taking Violet to the continent in the fall. She's never been away," Peter spoke up. His grip was almost painful.

Violet shrugged her shoulders and he loosened his grasp.

"You make it sound like not leaving England is a sickness. I've certainly never gone abroad." Marguerite was not to be deterred. "And we could always hold the christening earlier or later if necessary. Christmas might be nice. It is always a good time for family."

How could Marguerite speak of family with such warmth? Violet knew her childhood had not been easy. Marguerite had a mother who sent children, and many adults, fleeing in terror.

"I am not sure when we would be back." Peter was still trying to be her protector. Surely after their conversation he realized she might not want him planning her life. Only it did feel nice. It made her warm and safe in a moment when she wanted to run.

She reached up and squeezed his hand. "I think Christmas would be wonderful." She looked up and met Peter's gaze. "I am sure by then we will be back." *And I'll be ready.* Violet hoped Peter could read the second thought in her eyes.

"If that's what you want we will certainly be home for Christmas." Peter's eyes crinkled in reassurance.

"It's settled then." Marguerite was all grins. "Now I just have to let Tristan know what he's decided."

"What he's decided?" Violet asked, knowing confusion sounded in her voice.

"Yes. He doesn't always understand what decisions he's made until we talk." Marguerite added a giggle to the grin. She bent over and kissed the baby on his head.

Violet closed her eyes. "I am feeling a little tired.

Perhaps I should rest. And, Marguerite, I did mean what I said about needing to return to Town. I've delayed too long already. I left several matters undecided when I received your urgent message." She pushed up from her chair.

"I would hate to hold you back if there are matters that need your attention. I do appreciate all you have done for me, for us." She kissed the baby again.

"May I walk you to your chamber?" Peter took Violet's arm and threaded it through his own.

"Certainly." Violet followed him from the room.

Once they were in the hall he turned to her and asked, "Do you really need to go?"

"Yes, I think I do." She placed her hand over his and squeezed it softly.

"I do understand."

When they reached her door he brought her hand to his lips and placed a sweet kiss upon her palm.

"Peter," she said as she eased through the door. "I do want you to know that I am thinking about what I want for the rest of my life, and I am considering you and what you want. I am making no promises, but I did want you to know that I am thinking." She closed the door behind her.

Chapter 11

Her staff had taken the knocker off the door. Violet considered this subtle signal of her absence and smiled. It was wonderful to be home, wonderful to be returning to a place that ran the way she wanted without her ever even having to express a single desire.

She sighed. It was even more wonderful that if she left the knocker down for a day or two nobody would know. She could have time to consider how to manage Ian and Struthers—and Peter. The first two should not be difficult; neither one seemed the type to continue a lost battle.

With Peter, however, she still didn't know what she wanted, which made it difficult to decide how to proceed.

At least she would have time and space. She said a small thank-you prayer for her porter who had undoubtedly removed the knocker himself.

Peace and quiet. She needed them.

She hummed softly to herself as she entered the

house. It was good to be home. She breathed deeply, lemon oil, beeswax, fresh flowers—perhaps the scent of fresh bread from the kitchen.

She'd left orders that her home was always to be kept as if she might be arriving at any moment. Extravagant, yes, but there was nothing more wonderful than arriving home from a trip and instantly being surrounded by comfort.

Lazily, she stretched and headed for the stairs. She might even take a nap. What could be more delicious than a nap in her own bed on a sunny afternoon, safe in the knowledge that she wouldn't be disturbed?

There was a clatter at the top of the stairs.

She glanced up.

Isabella. What was her sister doing here? And why did she suddenly look so relieved?

"Violet, I am so glad you're home. I almost came after you. You won't believe what has happened." Isabella scurried down the steps and threw herself into Violet's arms.

"Calm down, dearest." Violet caught hold of the flurry that was her sister. "What is it? Has the dressmaker said your new gowns won't be ready in time? Or perhaps you have a new beau and he forgot to send you flowers? I am sure it can't be that bad."

Isabella pulled away and began to pace, her movements sharp and abrupt. "No, you are wrong. It could not be worse. Masters has found me a husband."

"I thought that was what you wanted," Violet soothed.

"But you should see who he's chosen. It really could not be worse." A hysterical edge had crept into Isabella's voice.

A knot formed in Violet's belly. For a moment she felt she had stepped back in time. Masters could not have done it again. Her brother could not be so misguided. "Tell me who."

"Foxworthy. Colonel Foxworthy," Isabella moaned. "He should be named Toadworthy. He is nothing but a big, fat toad."

Violet wanted to contradict her sister, to tell her it was rude to make such comments. But, unfortunately, her sister was correct. Foxworthy was a big, fat toad, in action as well as appearance. Violet shuddered as she remembered the lascivious comments he had made to her after Carrington's death. He'd seemed to believe she'd consider herself blessed to welcome him into her bed.

She drew a deep breath. She must be calm. Isabella was not she. Isabella was not without defenders. Violet would never permit her to marry somebody like Foxworthy. She had been ready to protect Isabella from choosing an unworthy husband on her own, could Violet do any less now that Masters was attempting to make the decision?

She needed more information. Masters never acted without reason. He would have thought carefully before reaching such a decision. She needed to understand what had driven him to such a choice.

She took a second breath. "Come into the parlor and I'll call for tea. You look in need of sustenance."

Violet moved ahead of her sister and led her into the bright, sunny room. It was not Isabella who needed the tea. A slow, deep pain had taken residence in Violet's temple. She closed her eyes for a moment and imagined herself curled in her bed, lavender-scented sheets drawn tightly about her.

She allowed herself one moment to dream.

Then she opened her eyes and stared at her sister. "Tell me everything. Begin with why you seem to be hiding in my house. I know Masters would never have allowed you to come to me. He knows too well what my opinion of this matter would be."

"He thinks I am at Annie's, or at least he did," Isabella replied. "When I indicated I would agree to marry Foxworthy he agreed I could spend a few days with my best friend to begin planning the wedding. He went to check on me two days ago. Annie said I was not feeling well and could not see him."

"You agreed to the wedding?" Violet asked, skipping to the most important fact.

"Not quite. That was the mastery of my plan, I even discussed it with Lady Smythe-Burke. She thought it a most masterful idea." Isabella's fingers twisted in intricate patterns betraying the pretend calm of her voice.

"If Masters thought I would agree he would let me go, and then if he couldn't find me I could not actually agree. Until I say I'll marry Foxworthy it can't actually be binding."

Violet had her own suspicions of just how binding Masters and Foxworthy would find any agreement. What was Lady Smythe-Burke thinking, advising Isabella to continue with this foolishness? Violet didn't know Foxworthy well, but once Masters made a decision he became immovable.

If he found Isabella now, she'd be wed as soon as the license could be produced. Masters would not trust any delay now he had suspicions that Isabella had escaped him once.

Violet arranged her skirts carefully and sat. Calm. She must stay calm. "Does he know you are actually missing? If so, I am surprised Masters hasn't found you here. I would have thought it the first place he'd look."

"He did come, right after talking to Annie." Isabella threw herself into the facing chair, her foot beating a rapid rhythm on the floor. "He demanded to see you, but when you weren't here it didn't occur to him to ask for me. I don't know if your servants would have hidden me or not, but he never asked. At first I thought I was lucky you were out, but then I didn't know what to do. I'll die if I have to marry Foxworthy."

"I am still not clear on what he knows."

"He doesn't know anything. Annie keeps saying I am with her. She says he doesn't believe her, but he can't prove anything."

Violet wondered how long it would be before Masters arrived at Annie's with a physician in tow. It was surprising it had not happened already.

How bad would it be if Isabella was forced to marry Foxworthy? Violet knew her sister would not die. Isabella might be flighty and far more calculating than she had ever guessed, but, like Violet, she was a survivor.

No, she would not think like that. Violet knew how many things were worse than death. "Tell me the whole story, Isabella. Why is Masters so intent on Foxworthy? He is rich, but there are other wealthy men."

"I don't know if it has to be Foxworthy," Isabella answered. "I do know it has to be soon, very soon. I overheard Masters talking before we came to Town. He mentioned Foxworthy then. He owes Foxworthy money—it was clear what Foxworthy wanted in return."

Violet straightened her back. She closed her eyes and imagined a steel rod ran straight up her spine. She had often sat thus when entertaining Dratton. She pictured each bone perfectly aligned, one upon the other. If she concentrated hard enough she could almost ignore the choices she felt coming.

She moved her feet evenly in front of her, lining up her toes, hips perfectly straight. "Is that why you were so intent on finding a husband? Did you hope that you could prevent Masters from choosing Foxworthy?"

"Yes, exactly. Anybody would be better than he."

"I am not quite sure that is true," Violet responded.

"You know it is. He's not only ugly, he smells if you get too close." Isabella jumped to her feet, unable to contain her restless energy.

"There are worse things than either smell or appearance."

"I can't imagine what." The hysteria was back. Violet was reminded of how young her sister was.

For a moment Violet considered telling her of Milber. There were so many forms of cruelty. No, Isabella did not need to know just how bad things could be.

Isabella stopped pacing and turned to her. Violet could see the edge of panic that brushed across her sister's face.

"It doesn't matter, Isabella," she said. "What matters is that we decide what to do now. You are sure that it is only money? That is the only hold Foxworthy has on our brother?"

"I don't know. It could be something else." Isabella's hands flapped like a small child on the edge of a tantrum. "I only know that Masters does owe him money."

"How can Masters be out of funds? I know he was well settled when I married Carrington. I made sure of it."

Isabella started to pace again. "I don't know. I know that Masters was involved in some speculation. He invested in some Dutch company that recently closed its doors. Maybe that has something to do with it."

That might have quite a lot to do with it. Their brother had never seemed lucky with investments. "Still, the estate should bring in enough to cover his expenses. Does he gamble?"

"I don't think so," Isabella said. "He always talks of how foolish it is to risk money on dice and cards. He sees it as a real vice."

That had not changed, then. "I still suspect there is something more. Why Foxworthy? That is what we must find out."

"I don't see how." Isabella's tone was shrill. "Masters will tell never tell us."

Isabella was wrong about that. While their brother had never felt the need to share his counsel with her in the past, he was about to find out just how much she had changed. "Leave that to me. Why don't you go and rest now—this anxiety cannot be good for you. Stay out of sight. I'll try to delay knowledge of my arrival from spreading. That will hopefully delay Masters until I am ready. He won't believe you have anyplace to go. The longer we can keep him from being sure you have fled, the safer you are."

Isabella leaned over and kissed Violet on the cheek. "I knew you'd keep me safe. Even if Masters does find me you mustn't let me go with him. Thank you. Thank you." Isabella scampered out.

Violet continued to sit. She doubted very much that she could keep Masters from taking Isabella if he demanded she be returned to him. She really had only one choice.

She would confront her brother for Isabella as she never had for herself.

"What do you mean you don't have a choice?" Violet kept her voice low, although she had a desire to scream. She stared across the carriage at the brother she had never understood.

"It means exactly what it sounds like. Isabella must marry Foxworthy." Masters stared out the window at the dark street. He did not meet her gaze.

Violet drew in a deep breath and held it. Accosting her brother outside his club had seemed like such a brilliant idea when she'd thought of it. If she invited him to her home, that would put him too near Isabella, and if Violet met him at his home, that would give him too much power.

Drawing up beside him as he left his club had been a stroke of genius. A carriage was neutral territory.

Only she'd forgotten how large and overpowering he could be. He was several inches shorter than Peter, but that didn't matter when crowded in a carriage.

She'd also forgotten how skilled he was at simply

not answering questions. He didn't avoid them; he just didn't answer them.

"Besides," he continued, still not looking at her, "Isabella has not indicated that she will not marry Foxworthy. Indeed, everything she has said has indicated her willingness."

"And that is why she has fled?" She knew she sounded too sarcastic. She didn't want to antagonize her brother, but it was hard to hold back her feelings.

"And how do you know all this? I believe she is staying at friends'. Do you know differently?" Masters finally turned to face her, and for the first time she remembered how he'd always made her feel like she still belonged in the schoolroom. He was always so proper, never a single hair out of place.

"How I know doesn't matter," she replied, fighting for calm. "Do you deny it?"

"How can I deny anything when I do not understand the question?" His voice was flat. For the briefest of moments she thought she saw emotion flicker behind his eyes, but then it was gone.

It was time to cut to the center of the matter. "You are forcing Isabella to wed just as you forced me."

"When did I force you? It is true I arranged your first two matches, but the choice was always yours." He turned back to the window and stared out as if bored with her.

"I remember the situation differently."

"It is no use arguing with memory. We each have our own." Masters's voice was almost a whisper, and she almost had to strain to hear it.

"Then you will not relent." She didn't know why she had expected more.

"As I said. Your sister has not given me any indication that she is unwilling, just as you never said no. If she has a difficulty with the match she should inform me. I sign the marriage contracts tomorrow."

"Tomorrow. Surely there is no such urgency."

"That is not your affair." He sounded so detached.

"What are you not telling me?" If only she could understand the situation.

"Nothing that would make a difference. If you should happen to see your sister, I suggest you tell her it is time to come home." He faced her one last time. If she hadn't known better she would have thought there was a certain sadness about him, but she did know better.

"I'll let Isabella know your feelings—if I should happen to see her. And perhaps I'll visit Foxworthy myself."

"Do that." He knocked on the roof of the carriage. "I'll get off here. And Violet, remember things have not turned out so badly for you. Perhaps you could have some faith that I am older and do know what is best."

The carriage stopped and he swung out. He paused for a moment, staring out into the night. "He has promised to do well by her, Violet, to give her whatever she needs. Foxworthy will not be as bad a husband as you fear." Then he strode off into the darkness, not looking back.

She squared her shoulders and sat without touching the back of the bench. She could sit like this for hours.

But she didn't know if she had hours.

It took less than a minute for different possibilities to run through her mind.

She could flee with her sister, but what then? She knew how few possibilities there were for a woman without connections. Money could accomplish only so much. She did not wish that life for her sister.

Another husband? Not a bad idea, but impossible to acquire on such short notice.

Just refusing Masters? No, the law was on his side. To all practical purposes, Isabella belonged to Masters.

Should she face her brother again, try one more time to talk to him? Even the thought of it caused bitter acid to rise in her stomach. This encounter had demonstrated how hopeless that was. She had not moved him this time. Why did she think another try would change anything?

There was really only one choice.

This time she rapped the roof of the carriage and directed her driver home. It was time to dress, time to play another part.

The room reeked of stale cigar smoke and sweat. Violet stared at the short, heavyset man. Foxworthy. It had been easier than she'd thought. She sent a note and he replied. She suggested a time and he supplied the meeting place.

She'd hoped to be done with gambling hells. She didn't even want to imagine meeting Ian or Struthers. With everything else, she still hadn't decided what to say to them.

At least Foxworthy had provided for a private room.

"You look lost in your thoughts, my dear. Surely my words have not surprised you?" Foxworthy asked, his sentence ending in a hacking cough. He looked ill.

Maybe he would die before a wedding could take place, and if he didn't, Isabella would not have long to— She mustn't think like that. Violet knew how quickly damage could be done. She would not wish such a husband on anyone, no matter for how little time.

She turned toward him with a smile. "It's not every day one finds out one's brother is a traitor." She shifted forward and watched how his eyes trailed over her body. She resisted the urge to shudder when he licked his lips.

"Not a traitor precisely." He coughed again.

"But you said—"

"He made some unwise investments, wasn't always careful where the money ended up. If some landed in French pockets at crucial moments . . ." He let the sentence hang.

"So Masters didn't know that—" Violet couldn't

even say the words. She'd never had a false image of her brother, but neither had she imagined he could betray his country. If Foxworthy had proof, there would be no choice; nothing she could do would persuade Masters to change his mind. He'd have no more choice than she did. It would explain his coldness to her approach. Her belly felt full of lead shot.

"It doesn't really matter what he knew or didn't know." Foxworthy pushed to his feet and came toward her. "I kept the records and they clearly show that several thousand pounds of your brother's money ended up in French pockets during the wrong years."

"Why would you keep such records? What could you possibly hope to gain?" Violet stepped back as he approached. The blasted man did have proof. What could be done now?

"I've never heard you were a shrinking violet." He laughed at his own joke and stepped forward again, catching her arm in his grip. "I keep many such records. Most of the time they have no use. I never expected I'd use these beyond being sure I was the first in line when Masters paid his debts, but then I saw your sister. Such a pretty thing. Almost as pretty as you were." His fingers tightened and his thumb stroked down her arm.

She wanted to pull away. It was hard to stand too close to him, but she had done many hard things. This was trivial. "Why her? You have money. You evidently have power."

He licked his lip again. "I do like the power. I considered a mistress but they are always wanting more. And, I haven't seen one that interested me." He stepped even closer. She could feel his body press against her, his heavy round belly and thighs. The buttons of his waistcoat caught in the soft fabric of her dress.

He coughed again.

Spine straight. Vertebra lined up. She turned toward him, her breasts even with his chin. If he drooled on her she was done. "Not a one that you liked?"

"I might be persuaded." He reached around and squeezed her bottom, drawing her more tightly against him.

She could only be grateful that his belly kept them from more intimate contact. "What would it take to persuade you that you were no longer interested in Isabella?" She dropped her gaze to his lips, lowered her voice. "I also have money. I could give you—"

"Money is not what I seek." He squeezed harder. "Why should I give her up? I think perhaps I could have both of you."

His fingers stung. She was going to have the imprint of his hand spread across her behind in the morning. She pulled back, spinning out of his grasp. She strode across the room and sat on the couch, only at the last remembering to bend forward and flash her breasts at him.

"Don't mistake me." Her voice was cold, but she

smiled sweetly. "I couldn't care less what people say about my brother. I don't even care if you send the authorities after him. He is responsible for his own actions." That was not quite true. He was her brother, despite everything. She did not wish him ill, not even now. She could not, however, let Foxworthy sense any weakness. "My only concern is my sister."

He walked toward her and stopped a foot in front of her. She could feel his gaze as he considered her and weighed his options. Her eyes were level with the front of his trousers. His belly might have prevented her from feeling his arousal, but it was clearly there. "Why should I take you instead of her? She is young and innocent and you are not."

"Why do you want a wife? I understand you have a son from your first marriage and so have no need of an heir. Are you in need of a woman to keep your house orderly, clean, and peaceful? If so I can recommend a reliable housekeeper at much less expense than keeping a young wife. I promise you that my sister's dressmaker's bills would make you shudder. I understand from Masters that you have promised to keep her well. And should you think of depriving her of her frivolities, you cannot even begin to imagine the tears and pouting that will result.

"As for innocence and youth, are they really what you want?" Violet picked up her glass and let her tongue trail around the rim. She took a small swallow and relished the flavor before letting it slide down her throat.

His eyes followed the motion as she had known they would. She dipped a finger in the strong liquor and then trailed it across her mouth. "I promise you that experience has much to recommend it," she said.

She sucked the finger hard into her mouth.

Foxworthy swallowed hard, his Adam's apple bobbing like a ball on a string. He stepped closer, his shins brushing the couch between her legs.

This was going much faster than she had planned. Tonight was only for talk. She needed longer to prepare herself for more.

She took a rapid swig of her drink, draining it to the bottom. She held out her glass. "Could you please fetch me another? I find myself quite thirsty."

He hesitated and she licked her lips again. "Very thirsty." She fastened her eyes on the fall of his trousers.

He turned and strode over to the decanter on the far table.

Violet rose quickly to her feet. Where could she stand that would prevent his maneuvering, while still continuing her play at seduction?

It was too warm for a fire or she would have positioned herself in front of it. A body silhouetted through fine silk was always alluring, and a woman could only be pressed so far back toward it. A sunny window could have served the same purpose—she doubted Foxworthy was eager to show the family jewels to the street below.

The thick curtains provided no such safety.

He walked back toward her, drink in hand.

She stepped away from the couch and into the middle of the room. She had space to maneuver if not to outright flee.

"Will this satisfy your appetites, my dear?" He held the glass out to her. The liquid was a more golden shade than before.

She raised the glass to her nose. She hated whiskey.

"Perhaps a few of them." She smiled and sipped, hiding the rough burn on her throat.

"Then let's try and fulfill some of the others." He stepped forward.

She stepped to the side.

"Now, my dear, I thought we were done with games," he said, stepping toward her.

"And I thought we had just begun to play." She stepped aside with a girlish giggle.

"As long as I know who will win." He lunged.

She avoided him at the last moment. A table stood to the side and she slid behind it. "We have not finished the other matter yet. Will you speak to my brother and tell him you are no longer interested in Isabella? And will you also agree to destroy the papers that give you power over him?"

"If my own appetites are well satisfied I might." He

tried to reach her around the table, but it was too wide. He eyed it, clearly trying to decide which way to go.

"I never give in too easily. I like anticipation." She leaned across the table toward him. "It makes the ending so much more enjoyable." She leaned back and turned a colder eye upon him. "Besides, I need some assurances before we proceed. I believe you should talk to my brother first."

"What about my assurances?" he asked.

"I am a woman of my word."

He coughed and walked from the table. "I've never found women particularly trustworthy. I want to be sure what I am buying before I proceed."

What did he expect her to do, strip naked and display herself like a cart of melons for sale? Maybe she should be glad he was not more attractive. It would certainly help keep this whole distasteful matter a more businesslike proceeding.

"No." The single word was succinct. "If I am to barter myself—and we have evidently dropped any pretense that this is anything but a barter—I will not risk being cheated. Isabella must be safe."

"Do you really believe I would be such a bad lot as a husband?" He spread his arms. "I would be properly indulgent to a deserving bride."

Violet turned and walked to the window and pushed aside the drapes. Was she really going to do this? He would not be a pleasant husband for her sister, but he probably was also not the worst. Violet had seen many women marry a handsome man for love only to find they had not gotten quite what they bargained for. With Foxworthy at least Isabella would know what she was getting.

Violet leaned her face against the cool glass. She had paid her dues already—why should she welcome another old man to her bed, pretend again that she was willing when her entire being cried otherwise?

She turned back toward Foxworthy, ready to tell him the deal was null. He was right behind her. For such a large man he moved on mouse feet. She could smell dinner on his breath, feel the heavy heat of his body.

She could not do this to her sister. Violet knew how to survive. Her sister should not have to learn.

She drew a breath in, filling her lungs to their full capacity. "You will tell Masters you have changed your mind." She placed a hand on his chest, let her hands trail across it. "That you've decided a bride is more of an inconvenience than you desire."

"I still don't see why I should trust you," he said.

Violet let her fingers slip between the buttons to play with the heavy mat of hair. "You don't have a reason. Consider it a gamble, one with rich rewards." She leaned forward and blew softly at his collar. "Very rich rewards. And I am a woman of my word. I shall not betray you."

Foxworthy pulled away and stomped toward the couch. "I will send for your brother, tell him to delay posting an announcement of the engagement in the papers. I will decide upon another way to seek repayment from him. I will expect you to accompany me someplace public. I want all London to know that you are mine. I give you one week." He sank back into the cushions.

Violet walked halfway across the room toward him. A week was more than she had bargained for. "For how long will our arrangement last?"

"A wife I would have had until death."

"Isn't that one of the advantages of not having one? You are free to seek other pastures."

"Who says I wouldn't anyway?"

"I'll give you one year."

"You'll give me as long as I want."

Violet nodded. What did it matter anyway? She had thought she was free of that life, and now she was willing to put herself back in the cage. She walked to the door. She did not turn as she spoke. "I'll send a note saying when I am available. Let me know where you wish to go so that I can dress appropriately."

She walked through the door and into the hallway.

She felt as if her knees would fail at any moment.

The hallway was dark, the few sconces on the corner giving little light. She leaned back against the wall, hoping that Foxworthy would not follow.

It sucked the breath out of her to realize she was going to do this.

Peter. She had not thought of him at all this night. For the briefest of moments she wondered why—then she knew. He did not belong here in this sordid place. He did not belong in what she was going to do. If she thought of him she would not be able to do what was needed. It would hurt too much.

"I didn't realize you were back. Were you going to inform me?" Ian's low tone slid around her like a noose.

Violet raised her head and stared at him. He was shadowed in the dim light, but his eyes gleamed fierce. She pulled her shoulders back with effort. She was so tired of performing. "I only arrived in Town yesterday."

"And, of course, you came here as soon as you were rested, searching for me," Ian replied. "I am sure that when I return home I will find your card awaiting me along with a note describing just how eager you are to renew our acquaintance."

Despite the heavy tone of sarcasm in his voice, Violet could sense the underlying hope. He really was a boy no matter how thick his pretense of sophistication. She allowed herself to lean back against the wall again. "I had matters I needed to attend to tonight. I would have sent for you within a day or so. I know there is much to be resolved between us."

"And Struthers?"

"I would have sent for him too."

Ian turned away from her and went to stand at the top of the stairs, heading down to the main hall. "I may be young, but I am not a fool."

Why did she have to hear Peter echoing in his words? She was done thinking of Peter, of what could never be. "I never took you for a fool."

"Then pray do not treat me like one. I know that you have no real interest. It was there briefly, but it has passed."

"I never—"

"Oh yes, you did." Ian turned back to face her, his face lit with his beautiful grin. "Don't worry. I am sure I shall recover. You are not the only beautiful widow in London."

"No, I am not." Perhaps he had meant his words to sting, but she could find only relief. He was one less matter she needed to deal with.

He smiled again. He truly was beautiful, each line perfectly drawn and executed. "Do me one favor," he asked. "Don't choose Struthers. I don't think I could face that loss."

She wanted to laugh. She began to stroll down the stairs. "Don't worry. I promise when I appear with a new escort it will be someone rather more unexpected."

Chapter 12

Peter didn't know whether to whistle or dance. Well, considering he was on horseback, whistling seemed the safer option. He was surprised he didn't burst into song.

The sun shone. He was back in London. Tristan and Marguerite were safe and happy with their new son. Violet had hinted she would consider marriage. He would see her soon.

A few weeks ago he would never have expected to be so happy again. He should return to his apartments and change before calling on his love. His love. He'd enjoy seeing Violet's face if he ever called her that— perhaps on their wedding night when she was truly his and could not escape.

He stopped himself at the thought. That was what she was frightened of—the inability to escape. Didn't she know he would always give her what she wanted, even freedom?

He glanced down at his travel-worn pants. A quick

brushing released a cloud of dust. He could change quickly and be fresh and ready when he called on her— only the sun was sinking low in the sky and she might have plans for the evening. He would hate to arrive and find her already gone. He would chase her all over the city if he must, but it was not a thought he relished.

No, it was better to go straight to her home. Her housekeeper had a way with clothing. He could settle in with Violet, and his clothing would magically disappear and reappear in pristine condition. That was a fine plan.

He began to whistle.

Violet smoothed her gown over her hips. It was the same gold gown she had worn on the evening she first met Ian and Struthers. Tonight, though, it failed to make her feel radiant or seductive.

Instead, when she looked in the mirror all she saw was an aging woman who had given up. She brushed the fabric again, praying for the earlier enchantment. She needed to believe she could survive this.

She pinched her cheeks trying to bring color to them. She didn't trust Foxworthy. He would only stay away from Isabella as long as he believed he was getting the better part of the deal. The moment he tired of Violet he would have no compunction at beginning his bargaining with Masters again. She needed to hold his interest until Isabella could find safety of her own.

Again she looked in the mirror and this time she saw it, not enchantment: strength.

Pulling back her shoulders, she pushed out her breasts and smiled at her reflection.

She glanced at clock on the mantel. Foxworthy would be here any moment. She would go with him and she would shine. He was taking her to small dinner party—no more public spectacle had been available this late in the summer—and she would bring every man there to his knees. By the end of the night she would leave Foxworthy with no doubt that he had made the right choice.

If she was going to do this she would do it with style.

There was knock on the door below.

She took one last glance in the mirror, bit hard at her lips until they pulsed with color, and headed to the stairs.

She did not look back. There was no going back.

She paused at the top of the stairs, eyes fixed straight ahead, not looking down. A small secret smile played about her lips.

She was strong.

He had never seen her look so beautiful. Peter stood at the bottom of the stairs and looked up at his goddess. She stood so proud and serene, filled with glory and strength. What more could a man ever want?

He was glad he had come straight here. He would have hated to miss this moment. He couldn't wait for her happiness when she saw him.

"What are you thinking?" he asked. "I've never seen quite that look of determination about you before."

Violet's face turned down toward him. That was not happiness. Her whole body stiffened and froze. For a moment her eyes flashed with despair before they too iced over.

"What are you doing here?" Her tone was colder than her look.

"I came to see you. Is there another reason I would come?"

"I meant, why have you returned to London? I thought you well contented with your brother." She descended a single step.

"Tristan is completely lost in Marguerite and the new baby. My attendance was superfluous. I thought my time would be better spent here with you."

"As you can see I am going out. I thought you were my escort." Violet strolled the rest of the way down the stairs. Her dress was amazing. It hugged and hid her figure at the same time. It seemed a continuous flow of liquid gold whirling about her in endless froth. He couldn't wait to take it off.

"I was afraid that would be the case. I came directly from the road to be sure I didn't miss you. I wanted a chance to persuade you to stay in with me." He grinned at her. "Won't you stay? Nothing can be so important that you cannot tarry."

She paled at his words and turned away. Something was very wrong. They had been at peace when she left. What could have happened in the few days she'd been home? It must have been bad—she wasn't even fighting with him.

Peter walked to her and placed a soft hand upon her shoulder. "What is wrong? You do not seem yourself."

She shook off his touch, refusing to look at him. "I am fine. I merely would not wish my escort to find you here."

That stopped him. She was trying to hide him; had they not agreed that the time for subterfuge was past? "Who is coming?"

"Oh, it doesn't matter. The point is that you cannot be here." He had never seen her so flustered. She fluttered her hands. Violet never fluttered.

"Well, I have no intention of leaving. We have an agreement."

"Agreement? I remember no such thing." Her normally smooth skin was blotchy with emotion.

"We agreed not to hide what we are to each other."

He saw her pull in a deep breath, could almost see her counting the seconds as she held it. "I remember no such agreement." She looked away from him as she spoke. "And even if we'd had an agreement, what is important is that this is my house and I want you to leave."

"No." He was angry now. She had never treated him like this before. Even when they fought, she had never ordered him gone. If he left, it was because he wanted to, not because he was commanded like some errant puppy.

There was a clatter of wheels and hooves out front. Violet moved to the window and peered out. She relaxed again as the noise moved on.

"Come into the parlor," she said. "If we're going to talk, it will have to be fast. I cannot be late."

He followed her from the room, determined to learn what was happening.

She shut the door firmly behind them and began to pace. "Is there anything I can say to make you leave without a fuss? I promise to explain all later."

He considered for a moment. He did not like to upset her, but— "Tell me now. It's only been a few days since we last were together. How much can have changed?"

"You can be so young sometimes, not to realize that the whole world can change in a moment."

"Then tell me. We can get through anything together."

She sat then, a hand rising to contain the bitter laughter that flowed from her mouth. "Together? I don't think so. This is a situation where you are definitely of no help."

"I don't believe that," he said.

She brushed back the bright fringe of hair that had

fallen in her face, then dropped her hands into her lap. Her fingers clenched once and then relaxed. She looked up at him, solemn. "You should. I have realized I really don't need you or your help at all."

"I don't understand."

"During the carriage ride back from Glynewolde I did consider your proposal. I considered it very seriously and realized it was not what I wanted. I want to be free, able to make my own choices, not tied to you or any man."

He suppressed the urge to argue. They had fought this out already. If she was unwilling to consider his proposal he would do what he must to keep her anyway. "I have already said I will not insist on marriage. I am contented to continue our relationship as it has been."

"And yet you arrive at my house and begin making demands. That is surely not as it has been. You seek more."

He felt like a leaf tossed by the wind. He could not move in one direction without being blown in another. "I only seek what I have always sought—to make you happy."

"If you wished to make me happy you would depart and leave this discussion for another day. It is not my happiness that is your concern. It is your own."

He turned and walked to the door, placed his hand upon the lintel. Then he turned back. "No, I may seek your pleasure, but I am not a schoolboy and I will not be treated as such. We made promises in the maze even if no words were spoken. If something has changed you must tell me."

She bowed her head for a moment and then sat up straight, her back so firmly fixed there could have been a heavy stick straight through it. "I merely wish to avoid unpleasantness, but if you insist—I am awaiting another lover. We are going to spend the evening with friends and then retire either here or at his residence. Your presence is a complication."

It was all he could do to continue standing. He knew he was not her first lover, but to the best of his knowledge Violet had never taken more than one lover at a time. He felt his heart tighten and shrink in his breast. "Why do you say this to me? It cannot be true."

She stood and ran her hands down the length of her magnificent body. "I don't see why not. I've never had trouble finding a new lover before, why should you doubt me now?"

"But you've always been faithful."

"How would you—?" She looked disconcerted for a moment, but recovered quickly. "You looked into my past. How sweet."

She was treating him like a boy again, smiling at him like a child who had misbehaved and now sought approval. "It was not sweet. I like to know what I am buying."

Her lips quivered and then relaxed into a smile. "Ah,

you're going to hit back. I should have anticipated. I hurt your feelings and you try to hurt mine. You should know by now that I am very aware of all that I am."

She walked toward him, hips swaying, breasts thrust forward. "I bought this dress for you. Do you like it? I hoped it made me look younger. And if it didn't, I at least hoped it proved distracting."

She was close enough to him that a quick glance down revealed all her hidden treasures. The soft lace at the neckline only pretended to disguise what was below when looked at from this angle. For a moment he was caught up in the image of soft white skin sloping into dark valleys and the barest hint of rosy nipples pulling tight against the incandescent fabric. His hand rose to touch.

She stepped back with a laugh. "Aren't you beginning to understand yet? We are finished. You say I am always faithful—well, if that is true and I have another lover it must mean—"

"You said you bought the dress with me in mind."

"Ah, but that was weeks ago."

He grabbed her then and pulled her fast against him. He could feel the beat of her heart rising to meet his own. He held her there, so close their bodies were almost one. His fingers bit into the flesh of her arm. He was sure to leave bruises and he didn't care. She was his. How dare she say otherwise?

He stared down at her lips. Almost on cue her tongue

came out to wet them, leaving them glistening, beckoning. He bent forward, felt the intake of her breath, her anticipation. He brushed his mouth across hers. She tried to nip at him but he was too fast.

He let his hands slide across her back, down to her waist and below. He cupped her full buttocks tightly, pressing her firmly into his arousal. And he was aroused. He held her there, grinding forward with his hips.

He expected her to fight. She did not, but neither did she surrender. She stayed still within his arms, not granting him a single inch of softness.

If she would not grant, he would take. He bent forward again, letting his lips settle against hers. This time she did not bite, but stayed stiff, unwelcoming.

That was her game. It was one she could not win. He caressed her lips softly with his own, not seeking entrance. He pressed against her mouth again and again, letting her feel his determination, his patience. He ran feathered kisses up her face, around her eyes, across the lids.

He found her ear and let his tongue trail around it. He caught his teeth at the outer rim, pulling, teasing. She moaned, and then contained herself, trying to deny the sound.

He squeezed her buttocks with his fingers, gently separating the globes. She squirmed, but gave no other indication of her desire. He pushed his erection against her. Even through the skirts of her dress he could feel her. Her legs slipped open, granting him room between. He moved forward, settling himself firmly while lifting her hips to bring her more tightly against him.

Then he went back to her face, a rain of kisses, a flock of caresses, each one softer, but more daring than the one before. He found the corner of her jaw, a large kiss. He moved lower, nuzzling the soft spaces of her neck. He moved his mouth until he found the hard beating of her pulse and he settled there, sucking, kissing, marking. She was his. He shifted his hips again and felt the flurry of her heart beneath his lips. She was his.

He leaned back against the wall to better take her weight. He was supporting her fully now, their cores pressed together despite the layers of clothing between them.

He moved back to her mouth, and this time there was no question of denial. She opened beneath the onslaught of his lips. The kiss no longer gentle, but all fire. Tongues fought and danced—parting only to rejoin. She bit at him. There was still anger mixed in the passion. He tasted the salt of his own blood and it only drove him higher.

He turned, pressing her into the wall, lifting her knees to straddle him. And still he kissed her. She twisted and turned, but each struggle only brought them closer.

He pulled back for a moment, panting. He needed

breath, breath and sanity. He could take her here, pressed against the wall, awaiting his replacement. There was no doubt of that.

He looked down upon her upturned face. Her eyes were half closed, almost black with passion. Only the outer rim of the irises still gleamed the deep purple of a pansy. Her lips were red and swollen, her breath rapid and shallow between them. Her skin was flushed and warm. She would taste sweet and salty if he licked her.

She was his. Only she denied that.

He let his hands open, let her legs slide to the floor. He waited until he felt her steady herself and then stepped away. He turned to face the mirror that hung over the corner table. He walked closer, caught by his own reflection.

His face matched hers, darkened eyes, swollen lips, sweaty flush—but in it he saw something else. Control.

If she wanted freedom he would give it to her. He had promised not to tie her to him against her will and he would not.

Not with marriage.

Not with sex.

If they were together it must be because both of them wanted it. He looked at her over his shoulder in the glass. She still leaned against the wall, her breathing heavy and her eyes glazed. She did want it. But that was only her body. He might love her body, but it was not her body he wanted, needed.

"You say you want me to go. Do you mean for now or forever?" He spoke softly; passion had stolen all his fire.

She pulled herself up, pushing off the wall. The heavy stick was back in her spine. She shook her skirts, brushed back her hair with her fingers, squared her shoulders. She walked toward him more steadily than he would have thought possible.

She stopped a few feet before him. "Why did you desist? You knew my resistance was only token by the end."

He looked straight into her eyes. He felt an equality between them. "You did not want this, for me to take you against the wall—you said as much. I could have persuaded you. I did persuade you. But I want more than for your body to be willing. Did you wish me to continue?"

"Yes. No. I don't know—no, that is not true. It is best that you stopped."

They still looked at each other. He felt so much beyond the words that were said. "That is what I thought. If what you want is for me to let you go, then that is what I must do. Just tell me that it is what you want."

She turned from him then, breaking the connection. He thought he saw despair in her glance, but the contact was gone. She walked to the door and held it open for him. "I am sorry, but it is what I want, what I need."

He willed himself not to feel. That would come later. Now all he could think was that it must be the world's greatest irony that the only way he could prove his love and commitment to Violet was to leave her.

He moved toward the door.

The sound of a carriage pulling to a halt echoed through the room. There was a hard rap on the door.

Violet turned to face him. He had never seen her look so dead, so bleak. Her lips curved up into a smile, but it reached no other part of her face. "I am afraid I must ask you to stay after all. Please do not cause a scene, Peter. Do this one last thing for me. Just stay in this room and don't come out until I am gone."

She stepped through the door and prepared to shut it, halting only when an inch of space remained. "This is not how I wanted it to end. I truly am sorry for any pain I have caused you." She let the door click behind her.

He heard her heels tap as she crossed the marble floor of the hall. There was a brief exchange of voices and then the heavy slam of the front door.

Against his will he moved to the window, keeping himself sheltered from view by the heavy drapes. He saw a footman helping Violet into a carriage. Whoever her caller had been, he had not even come to the door for her himself.

The back of the carriage was black, unmarked. Peter could not make out the crest on the side as it slid back into traffic and rambled off down the street.

"You look ravishing, or should I say ready to be ravished." Foxworthy laughed at his own joke as he was prone to do. "You make me want to forget dinner and head straight home."

"If you like, we can return to my house. There is no need to pretend seduction," Violet answered. She prayed Peter was gone. He would be gone. No man would stay after the scene they had just played out.

She knew now why she had not considered him in these last days of planning. The pain of seeing him, of being forced to push him aside, to drive him away, was unbearable. She could never have imagined that last look of loss on his face.

"No," Foxworthy began again. "We will go to dinner as planned. I want all my friends to see you, to know what I have won. I do hope you will be properly adoring." He placed a firm hand on her knee and slid across the carriage bench toward her.

He had not bathed that day. What man intent on acquiring a new mistress would not bathe? He squeezed her knee tightly, the fingers biting through the fabric of her skirts and into her skin. He was confident of his victory.

But then he should be—he had bought it, bought her.

She should feel a whore.

But she had not put herself up for sale any more this time than she had the two times her brother had sold her to the highest bidder. She refused to name herself a slut because of what men forced her to.

"You're being silent, my dear. I hope it's because you're imagining other things to do with those fine lips." Foxworthy laughed again. "Just be sure you're not quiet at dinner. I want it clear that you wish to be with me. Remember what rides on my satisfaction."

"Have you spoken to my brother?" She must remember Isabella. She would not think of Peter. Not now. Not ever.

"We talked this morning. He was very concerned that I was reconsidering the terms of our deal. He tried hard to persuade me of Isabella's delights."

Violet turned her face to the wall. She would not let Foxworthy see her distress. It did not sound quite like the brother she had always known, but she had never understood her brother. "You held strong, though, and convinced him that he would have to make other arrangements regarding . . . your knowledge. If you ruin my brother, my family name, it will change our agreement as well."

"Yes, I made it clear that we will come to some other arrangement, and now I want some reward." Foxworthy reached over and took her hand. He brought it first to his lips and then placed it squarely in his lap. "It's a good ten minutes until we arrive. I am sure you know some trick to pass the time."

She wanted to slap him across the face. Tricks. She knew tricks, all right. She'd—

No, she could not afford to anger him, not until she truly knew that Isabella was safe. She'd assured her sister that everything would be fine and Isabella was planning on returning to her home that very night. She could not let Isabella down.

She ran her fingers down Foxworthy's thigh to the knee and then back up, circling around to do the same on the other side. He tried to twist, to bring her fingers in more direct contact, but she smiled and avoided him. She leaned forward so that her breasts were displayed before him.

"Do you like my dress? I wore it just for you." She licked her lower lip.

His eyes fastened on her breasts. Was that drool? When Peter had glanced down her gown earlier her toes had curled with desire. She'd wanted to undo her ties and let him examine everything in much more detail.

Now she had to fight not to grab the coach blanket and cover herself up to her eyes. She'd have covered them too, but she didn't trust Foxworthy. She wanted to keep him under close observation.

Fighting her impulse, she leaned farther forward, placing a hand on each of his plump thighs. "I do know tricks, many of them. Carrington brought me beautiful books from the Orient, books with beautiful pictures. I'd be pleased to show them to you."

"Pictures, never cared for art."

"I think you'd care for these. They are quite detailed."

"Don't see what difference detail should make." Foxworthy was trying to maneuver her hands into direct contact with his—she couldn't think of a word to describe it, she'd used them all with Peter, and what was contained in Foxworthy's breeches bore no relation to Peter.

For a moment she was there in bed with Peter, lying back, sated. She could see him grin as he looked down at himself. "It doesn't look like a mighty man-o'-war now."

"I believe I said a cannon, an eighteen-pounder. I don't remember ship references," she'd replied.

They'd moved from reference to reference, each more exaggerated than the last. She smiled to herself at the memory.

"Oh, you like that do you?" Foxworthy had reached into her bodice and actually buried his hand there, his fingers twitching like a lost spider. "You're not the only one with tricks."

She held her smile, sighed softly. "We must be getting near. I am afraid I won't have time to demonstrate more."

He jerked back, looked for a moment like he would

take a swing at her. "You women are all the same. You get a man all hot and bothered and then leave him with a cockstand in company. You can be sure I'll make you sorry later."

"Oh, you'll punish me, will you? I should warn you I might like that." She stretched her smile further, then plucked his hand from her bodice. "I'd have thought you'd enjoy showing off your prowess to your friends— they'll spend the evening imagining what you're going to do with that fine . . . cockstand, did you call it?" Pleasure pencil was more like it. Her delight was almost genuine as she imagined Peter's response to the term.

But he was not here. He would never be here again.

She stiffened as the realization swept through her. She was done with him, done with Peter.

Driving him away had been the hardest thing she'd ever done, harder even than what was still to come this night.

And he'd let her go. It was what she'd wanted, needed, what she'd forced him to, but she'd never expected him to give in, to leave her the choice. She realized now that when she'd seen him at the bottom of the stairs she'd hoped for rescue. Instead, the man finally proved he really would grant her the choice to live her life as she wanted.

He finally proved that she could trust him to put her first, finally proved that she could trust herself to him—and this was the result.

She had known the choice she made, but not how barren it would leave her.

She forcefully held the look of delight as she allowed Foxworthy to hand her from the carriage.

Barren. She'd been barren for years. She'd just never felt it quite so deeply, so hopelessly.

Peter swung his legs up on Violet's dainty writing desk. Ridiculous how delicate they made things for women. Yes, women were smaller than men, but not that much so.

His heels almost covered the surface. They'd probably leave scuffs. He hoped so, a mark that he'd been here.

He poured another glass of Violet's finest brandy. The servants had tried to avoid bringing it to him, but in the end they knew their place. He swallowed. Felt the burn. Felt the warmth trace through his chilled limbs.

It was August and he was freezing. Ice filled him. He was frozen from the heart out.

He swallowed again. Ah, melodrama. At moments like this a man could almost become a poet.

He stared blurrily at the clock. She'd been gone two hours and fifteen minutes. If they were returning here after dinner it was possible they'd arrive soon. Not likely, but possible. He knew dinner could last for hours and hours, but if he were taking Violet home, he'd cut the evening short.

He wondered what her new beau would say to finding him here. He might have promised the woman her freedom, but that didn't mean he couldn't put up one last fight.

If he'd lost already there was nothing else to lose, and if he hadn't, well—he'd never know if he didn't try.

He dropped his feet to the floor and rose, swaying only slightly. He raised the glass to his lips and then placed it on the desk without taking a swallow.

If he was going to fight, he'd better be sober. He didn't know who Violet was with and whether the whole affair might turn physical.

He'd fight a bloody duel for the woman if necessary. He wondered if she'd like that—two men bleeding and dying for her. If he was going to die for love he'd certainly make sure the other fellow did too.

He walked to the door and peered out into the dark hall.

How much longer would they be?

What if they didn't return here? He hadn't considered that. Violet always brought him home, but what if she had other arrangements with this new gent? She'd mentioned she wasn't sure where they would spend the night.

Damnation. He didn't even know who the competition was. If he was going to stop her, he'd need to know that. Somebody must know. Her staff would never tell him.

He shook his head trying to clear it. If he couldn't find out here, he'd have to go someplace else. His club. If there was talk, somebody there would know it.

He slammed the door behind him.

She was his. It was time to persuade her of that fact.

He paused halfway down the walk.

What if he was too late? What if they'd already done the deed?

Oh, how could it possibly matter? All that mattered was that he got her back.

Chapter 13

This was it. Violet looked around the dark chamber. The time for reprieve was past. Foxworthy was consulting with his porter, making certain the house was locked for the night. She wasn't sure if that showed true diligence or a lack of trust in his servants. She had complete confidence that her own windows and doors were open or locked with exact timing and precision, and she never checked that the doors had been locked for the night. But she had faith that if she ever did, each and every lock would be fastened tight.

Why was she thinking of locks? She should be preparing herself for Foxworthy. The room was not designed for seduction. The bed was large, but rather lacking in pillows. There was no chaise that a woman could display herself upon. The fire was unlit. She walked to stand before it, staring into the clean-swept hearth. Despite the warmth of the day, the night had grown chilled, and she would have welcomed the warmth. She considered calling for a maid, then rejected the thought. She had no position here, and she doubted that Foxworthy would welcome the presence of a maid when he arrived.

She began to pull pins from her hair, letting the cascade of auburn curls fall about her shoulders. In her experience, men liked loose hair.

It was only as she stood there, alone, that she realized how little she actually knew. Her first husband had never demanded or wanted anything but her presence, flat in his bed. Milber, she would not even think about what he had liked. Even for Isabella she didn't know if she could go through that again. She'd never heard any such nasty rumors about Foxworthy. And there were always rumors.

She fluffed her hair with her fingers, bit at her lips. She had played at seduction with Carrington and the lovers she'd had since, but never had it been so cold-blooded and lacking in emotion.

She'd never pretended desire she did not feel—no, that was not true either, she had used every wile and advantage at her disposal to maneuver men like players on a chessboard, but she'd always been clear where the boundary was.

She shivered and wrapped her arms about her shoulders. The air felt positively frigid. She should have called for a maid. No man wanted a woman huddled and frozen.

She forced her arms back to her sides. It couldn't be that cold. Perhaps she was growing ill. Should she tell Foxworthy that—

She was acting like a scared child instead of a woman. She was strong and would remain so. She walked over to the window and peered momentarily out into the darkness before turning back to the room.

Her task tonight was not hard. Two bodies met, two bodies touched. The end. It was almost mechanical, like windup figurines.

The door opened and Foxworthy marched in.

He peered about the room for a moment before seeing her standing by the window. "I thought you'd be in the bed."

She walked forward. "Do you wish to hurry things along? I've always enjoyed anticipation."

"Six days was enough anticipation. Get in the bed." He did not sound cruel, just demanding. It might have been easier if he'd sounded cruel.

"I thought we'd have a drink first." She needed a little liquid courage. Think mechanical. Her body could do this, her mind did not need to. She had left her mind behind before.

"Are you having second thoughts, my dear?" He walked toward her. "I have decided that I prefer you to your sister and that a wife would perhaps present more complications than I need, but I will not force you. I only like willing women."

"Do I seem less than willing?" She moved forward, legs stiff.

"A willing woman would have been in bed naked."

He began to remove his cravat and then his waistcoat. When he pulled the shirt over his head she almost giggled at the mass of corsetry that resided under it. Corsets were fashionable for men, but she'd never actually known a man to wear one—not even Dratton.

She had to get her nerves under control. "I couldn't unfasten my gown."

"You should have sent for a maid."

"I thought perhaps you would enjoy undoing it, releasing me. Many men do." She smiled at him with all the coyness she could muster.

"I am not one of them. I am not a maid." He walked over and rang for a servant. "I need my valet in any case. Never can manage to unhook this blasted thing." He gestured to the corset. "Should have thought of that. The man can do your dress as well."

With the lightest rap on the door the valet entered and, without looking at Violet, proceeded to unhook Foxworthy. His belly fell forward, well marked with the red lines such a contraption produced. Violet looked away.

The valet moved toward her. She turned away and felt cold but proficient fingers move down her back. The dress loosened and fell forward. She caught it in her arms. She was not prepared to be naked before another man this night.

"Do you need help with your underthings, my lady?" the valet asked.

Violet shook her head. With another man she might have thought this scenario designed for humiliation, but, despite his political intrigues, she doubted Foxworthy had that subtlety.

She turned to Foxworthy, her dress still clutched about her bosom.

The man was naked. Despite his belly and lack of height, he was not hideous, not even particularly bad. His skin, while white and unmarked by the sun, was not sallow. It was tight and smooth, not sagging and wrinkled. He was quite hairy.

She stepped toward him.

He leaned back on the high bed. "Drop the dress. Let me see what I've bargained for."

She let the dress fall. Only a thin chemise and light corset still clothed her. She was thankful for the newer corsets that allowed her to unfasten herself. She could not have borne the presence of the valet.

Her fingers made quick work of the hooks. She met Foxworthy's glance and eased the chemise off one shoulder and then the other. It caught and held for a moment on her nipples and then dropped.

He appraised her naked body. "You are all that you promised. It's a pity my friends can't see you now. I'd love for them to know what I am getting." His pleasure pencil jerked at the thought.

She would not take this seriously. "Do you want me on the bed now?"

He considered. "No, if I'm going for experience I might as well enjoy it."

"What would you like then?"

He paused for a moment, flummoxed.

She saw him clearly then. The older man who'd probably never had more than the most cursory experiences. She didn't doubt he'd had sex aplenty, but she felt sure it had all taken place flat in a bed.

She had painted him as a villain in her mind, and now was forced to see his humanity. It might not make him a better man, but it did make him a man, a man who used the tools at his disposal just as she used hers.

She looked away, feeling exposed and naked in a way she had not a moment before. If she had painted him the villain, she had let herself be the victim.

If he was human, then so was she.

She didn't want to be. She wanted, needed to be a body, only a body.

"Well, what are you waiting for? Do something." He might be a human, he was not a nice one.

She moved toward him, resting a hand on each shoulder and bending forward to kiss his chest. She ignored the hair, the smell, and concentrated only on her own motions. She prayed for the moment when she would not feel.

She rubbed him, caressed him. She could feel his response against her belly.

He pulled her face toward him, planting a damp kiss

over her lips. She closed her eyes and tried to imagine she was somewhere else. His hands clamped over her nipples, pulling them hard.

Her eyes opened. She could see the pores on his nose. His fingers pulled again. She fought the urge to push him away.

She needed to take control so she would not feel so helpless. She pressed his face away. "Slow down. Remember what I said about anticipation."

She looked about the room. There was a simple hardwood chair in one corner. She led him toward it. "Sit."

"Don't see what can happen in a chair."

She closed her eyes at his lack of imagination, trying to imagine it was Peter there with her. He had always believed a chair could serve many purposes.

The image would not come. Her mind would not bring Peter there, into that room.

She tried again. Failed again.

She truly was alone.

Foxworthy sat in the chair, legs splayed, massive thighs hip-distance apart. He smiled at her.

She walked behind him.

"I don't see what you're going to do back there," he said.

"Back is the key word. A good rub can serve to inflame at the same time it relaxes." She dug her fingers into the muscles of his shoulders, kneading, pressing.

Gads, the man was hairy. She must quit thinking that. Must quit thinking at all.

"It does feel good, but I am ready to get down to business. I've got a good hard one and I am ready to use it. Come around front and let me suck on your titties a minute. You do have nice ones. Bigger than your sister's."

"I thought you wanted my experience. Won't you give me a chance to show you how good things can be?"

"Maybe later, my dear. If I wait too long I might not last. It's been a long time since I've been this hard. Now get over here."

Violet moved around him, resisting the urge to cover herself with her hands. She had never been a shy woman, but now she felt exposed and vulnerable.

She stood in front of him, hands by her sides, a tight smile on her face. "What did you want?"

"Leave it to a woman to ask a stupid question. I want you, of course, but I think the bed will do. This hard chair is not good for my back." He pushed himself up from the chair with a creak. "Come. Let's go to bed and begin. I've had enough of this anticipation."

Violet followed him to the bed and slid in beside him. She had lost track of what he wanted. Did he want her flat on her back or taking a more active, experienced role?

He patted the space beside him. The back it was.

She lay there, staring up at the canopy over the bed. She was reminded of all the whispered references to what mothers told their daughters on their wedding nights to help them get through it. She wished she'd paid more attention.

Foxworthy leaned over and fastened his lips about one breast. He sucked hard and placed a large hand over the other breast, kneading her like a mound of dough.

"Bet you didn't think I'd be so good at this, did you? I may not have been around as much as some of your fancy boys, but I've had my share of women. Maybe next time you can use your mouth, I've only had whores do that and I've always fancied a lady."

She could do this. She could do this. It became a mantra in her head. It was her choice. There was nothing he could ask for that she would not do. Isabella. Isabella.

If she was not here her sister would be. No matter how she looked at it she was trapped, trapped by doing the right thing.

Maybe he should just return to Violet's house. Peter kicked at the step of the club he was about to enter. After two hours of searching he was no closer to finding Violet than he had been when he left her house.

He kicked again.

He'd heard a rumor that she'd been seen about Town

with Struthers and young Winchester, he couldn't remember the boy's given name. He'd heard that they visited museums and parks with Violet and had on numerous occasions been seen entering Violet's home.

He wanted to pound something. They'd been seen with Violet weeks ago and on numerous occasions. She hadn't even bothered to tell him she was looking for another lover. He didn't care that he'd walked out on her and been avoiding her at the time. She should have known that he would come back to her. That he would forgive her anything.

Only she didn't want him back.

He shouldn't have had so much to drink during his search. It was hard to be mad when inebriated. He was more prone to melancholy. He wiped at a moist eye. Men did not cry, and despite Violet's frequent comments, he was a man.

Why had she never seen that?

He pulled back his leg to kick again and noticed the large scuff running along the toe of his boot. Now he'd have to deal with his valet as well.

He slammed his toe into the stones so hard the impact reverberated up his leg. Maybe he could find somebody to punch. A good fisticuffs might not solve his problems, but it would certainly make him feel better.

He should go back and pound Struthers. He'd seen him in the last club, sitting in a corner, shuffling cards and pouring whiskey. He'd been tempted to walk up and demand to know where Violet was—only Violet clearly hadn't been with him.

Winchester. Ian Winchester. That was the name.

He must be whom Violet was with. He knew the lad had kept apartments near the Albany. That would be where Violet was.

He turned on his heels, managed not to fall flat on his face, and set off with only a slight limp. Perhaps he should not have tried to drive his foot straight through the stone.

Winchester, if he remembered right, was a pretty boy. Violet liked pretty boys.

He wouldn't be so pretty in an hour or two.

Violet lay there flat. Back flat. Emotions flat. She had finally found that spot where her mind and her body were separate. She was not her body; it was only a body.

"God, you've got good tits, my dear. A man would be happy to die between them." Foxworthy was a talker. He couldn't seem to make a single move without describing it.

At least he wasn't expecting much participation from her.

"Such big tits. I never liked small tits—might as well fuck a boy—not that I ever."

Look at the canopy. Look around the room. It was better here than in her own rooms. Here she could focus on new things. Was that Foxworthy's father hanging over the dresser? There was a similarity, and the cut of his coat placed him only twenty or so years back. Who would want a parent staring at his bed during intimate moments? Did Foxworthy ever consider his proud papa as his buttocks rose and fell in the age-old motion?

It was coming to that soon. She'd been amazed that Foxworthy had not plunged in the moment he had her flat on the bed. He'd seemed the hurried type a few moments ago, but now he seemed eager to examine every inch of her chest—examine and pinch. She would have bruises in the morning.

She would not think of morning.

"Open your legs, my dear. I always do enjoy a good look first. You're much cleaner than the girls I normally take. Never thought it mattered much, but it does seem to add to the whole thing. I'll have to insist on baths in the future."

She wondered if he'd make that connection to himself. If she'd been more involved, she wasn't sure she could have taken the odor of stale sweat. She'd always adored it when Peter came to her bed still damp from an afternoon of riding. The smell of leather and horses had made her positively— No, Peter did not belong in this bed.

She stared at the picture of Foxworthy's father again. Was he grinning? She'd shut her eyes, but then she would have to feel.

"Come on, spread them further. I bet your sister is more obedient. She doesn't have your tits, though. Maybe she would after a brat or two. I'll have to ask whoever Masters finally unloads her on.

"Oh, you've a nice cuny too. It looks like it's just waiting for me. I've seen those boys you normally share yourself with. You must be pleased to finally have a man. I can't wait to tell everyone how much you prefer me to them."

He positioned himself between her legs.

It would be now.

And just like that, she couldn't.

Her knees slammed shut, knocking him to the side, and giving him an unintentional ram in the ballocks.

She lay there a moment, while he moaned beside her.

She couldn't. She should be able to, but she wasn't.

She slid rapidly out of the bed and grabbed her dress.

"Where are you going? We haven't finished." Foxworthy found his voice, although his knees were still tight to his belly. "Get back here, now."

"We are finished. I am leaving. I should have left before." It was hard to speak. She still didn't feel that mind and body were quite integrated.

"Get back here now," Foxworthy roared as he rose up on his knees. She clearly should have hit him harder.

Violet didn't answer, but pulled her dress over her

shoulders. The back gaped open, and without her corset the bodice hung loose. She grabbed Foxworthy's coat, ready to pull it over her shoulders.

"If you take that I'll have you arrested for theft." Foxworthy controlled his voice, but not the angry red flush that filled his face and chest. "Get back in this bed. I've paid for you and I expect what I bargained for."

Violet dropped the coat. She wasn't sure she could have borne the stench of it anyway. She headed for the door, unable to answer Foxworthy. She needed to be gone.

Foxworthy stood and came toward her, a great naked mass. "If you open that door, everything we agreed to is null. I'll marry your sister and make sure she fulfills my every need. There is nothing I won't make her do."

"You will never have Isabella. I'll see to that." Violet turned on him in fury.

"What will you do? Masters is the only one who has a say over her, and he will do whatever I wish. He'll be relieved that I've changed my mind again." He stalked forward.

Violet fought the urge to turn and run.

"I am sorry," she began, trying to placate him. "I did not mean it to end like this. I don't know what happened, but I just cannot do what you wish."

Foxworthy stopped a foot from her. "I would suggest that you end this nonsense now and get back in my bed.

Are you so dim you don't realize it is not your choice to make?"

No words could have set her off more. "It is always my choice. That is what you and my brother have never understood. Women have choices, and you are not mine."

Foxworthy took half a step forward. Would it be rape? He grabbed her arm and began to pull her toward the bed. He was stronger than she'd expected.

She kicked out, catching him in the shin. He released her.

There was hate in his voice when he finally spoke. "You are making a mistake. I will destroy you and your brother and take Isabella as my spoils."

Violet held her dress tight about her, trying to find a dignity she had long lost. "Do your worst. I've already seen your best and I can't say I am very impressed."

She pushed down the handle of the door and stepped through, a long line of curses following her. She slammed the door behind her.

She wanted to sink down and give in to the hysteria that was rapidly threatening to overtake her. What had she done? She no longer knew what was right and what was wrong. She didn't even know why she had stopped. It felt almost as if her body had acted by itself.

One foot in front of the other, she made it down the stairs and to the door. She'd expected Foxworthy to come after her, but there was no sound from the bedroom.

The door wouldn't open. Her hand moved over the latch and around the door seeking the key in the dim light. She felt the walls, the tables. There was no key to be found.

Resting her head against the cool wood of the door, she felt despair beat at her. She refused to call for help, and nothing short of a firing squad would have driven her back up the stairs to Foxworthy.

She moved from room to room, but each possible entrance was blocked. She ended her journey in the front parlor. She could see the dark street through the window. A solitary lantern cast a beckoning glow farther down the street.

She wanted to pound on the glass, to pound through the glass.

There was a noise on the stairs in the hall. She debated whether to hide. Instead she thrust back her shoulders and drew in a steadying breath. She had survived this far; she refused to fail now.

She strode into the hall. Foxworthy posed halfway down the stair. He must have called his valet for help because his figure was once again well-corseted under his full evening coat. He swung a heavy door key by one finger.

"I wonder what you'd do for this?" He could not have been more composed. Apparently his dignity arrived with his corset.

"I've done all I plan to do." Her voice matched his.

"I thought as much. It's clear none of your husbands trained you well—or perhaps the blame was Masters's. I'll have to be sure sweet Isabella suffers no such fault." He stepped down the stairs toward her.

She stared at him, trying to understand the game.

"Did you expect me to whine like a boy? That is what you're used to, isn't it? I should have realized you could not handle a man."

Ah, male posturing. This she understood.

Was she prepared to play? She eyed the key in his hand. It might be easier to toss a chair through the window.

She stepped toward him. "Are you going out? I would not have expected you to dress."

"I don't know why you think you know what to expect. I am sure that even the most vivid imagination could not foresee my plans." He strode forward, his fingers still locked about the key.

He walked to the door and after a quick twist of the wrist swung it open. "Go find one of your boys. Maybe they'll enjoy your games and your anticipation. I am well rid of you."

Violet walked toward the door, conscious of how close it would bring her to him. The thought of even brushing against him made her shudder.

She stepped forward, paused. There was a barely a foot of space between him and the doorframe. He would not make this easy.

She stepped forward again. He grabbed her, pulled her to him. She felt his lips before she sensed his intent.

"Something to remember me by," he whispered.

The kiss was deep and wet. Vomit rose at the back of her throat.

Suddenly he pushed her forward, almost sending flying down the stairs.

Peter stood on the walk before old Foxworthy's dark house. It was surely another fool's errand. He'd already walked half of London trying to find her. He doubted this suggestion was any better.

Still, young Winchester had sounded sure.

He had called upon Winchester's apartments to find that the man was entertaining, but Violet had certainly never giggled at such a shrill pitch.

Winchester had stood in the doorway refusing him entrance. He'd been tempted to push past and assure himself that the sounds were not Violet, but in his heart he'd known this was another dead end.

He turned away before Winchester spoke. "I'd check with Foxworthy. I have a feeling that's where you'll find what you seek."

"What?" Peter turned back.

"I've a hunch I know why you're at my door, and I can only regret that's not who you'll find in here." Winchester spoke in a hushed tone and glanced over his shoulder.

"I don't know what you mean."

"I imagine you do." Winchester looked him straight in the eye. "She wasn't interested in me or Struthers—she wanted nothing more than a little flirtation. I might have settled for that if she'd seemed happy about it. I don't settle for being any woman's second choice."

Peter's mind raced to keep up with the words. It did sound like he was talking about Violet but, "Why on earth would I find her with Foxworthy? He's old enough to be her father."

Winchester smiled bitterly at that. "Well, with her history she does seem to like them young or ancient. All I know is when I saw her earlier this week she was just leaving a private room. She didn't look happy and it piqued my curiosity. I wanted to see who had put our fine lady in such a state. Your current surprise equals my own when I saw Foxworthy leave the room not five minute after. I'll suggest again you try his abode."

Winchester stepped back.

Peter shoved his foot in the door just as it began to close. "Why tell me this?"

"What can I say? At least you're not Struthers. Besides, I'd rather see her smiling." Winchester spoke with an unexpected softness.

Which was why Peter stood there now, in the middle of the night, staring at a dark house.

He should leave. What would he gain by pounding on yet another door?

Even as he had the thought the door swung open and Foxworthy was silhouetted in the doorway. There was no mistaking that physique. The door open farther and an even more familiar figure appeared.

Peter watched as Foxworthy stopped her and then pulled her into a tight embrace.

The kiss seemed endless. Peter's hands clenched to fists. He didn't know what or who he was going to hit, but it was going to be hard.

The kiss ended and Violet was propelled through the door.

She stood for a moment at the head of the stairs. The solitary light from down the street lit her face. Her hair was a jumbled mass of fire about her shoulders. Her dress hung loosely, held up only by the slim white hand grasped tight to the bodice. Lips swollen by kisses quivered and clenched.

She stepped forward, almost tripping on her dragging skirts. The dress fell from one shoulder, leaving it bare to gleam in the moonlight.

He'd seen her look like this many times—always just after they made love.

Chapter 14

Violet pulled her dress more tightly to her as goose bumps rose on her arms and chest. Her mind seemed incapable of forming a clear thought. No stars were visible in the night sky. Darkness closed all about her.

She took a step toward the solitary light shining bright farther down the street. Was there safety in the light? Or was darkness a better friend? She should not be alone so late, especially not half naked.

The chilled air encompassed her. She drew it in, filling her lungs, wishing it would clear her head. The tall, dark houses rose high on either side of her, quiet monoliths witness to her shame.

The hem of her skirt caught under her foot, almost pitching her forward. She managed to pull her skirts higher with one hand while keeping the other clenched tight at her bodice.

She felt dirty.

So dirty she would never be clean.

She took another step forward, toward the light. All she wanted was to shrink into a corner and cry until there were no more tears.

What had she done? Isabella was in greater trouble than ever before. Foxworthy might have been an undesirable husband before, but now he'd be a vengeful one if he succeeded in his plans. She didn't doubt for one moment that he would take out his injured pride on Isabella.

And what of Masters? Violet had tried for years to pretend that he no longer held power in her life, but the events of the last few days had proved otherwise.

And Peter. She would not forget his face as she drove him away. Another lover. Hah. Since she met him she'd wanted no other man in her bed. She might have flirted, but the thought of another man's touch soured her stomach.

For all her vaunted strength she had failed. She'd given up everything and gained nothing.

Despair ate at her. She should give up.

She took another step forward.

Foxworthy and Masters could not be allowed to win.

She heard the tread of boots a moment before the hand came down on her shoulder. She turned swinging. She didn't care if it was Foxworthy or footpads. She was done playing the victim.

Her fist connected, hard. She turned to swing back

in the other direction, careless of the loose dress and skirts that swirled about her.

Her fist was caught, held.

She kicked out. Pulled a scream deep into her lungs.

"Stop."

Peter. Here. Her foot stopped inches from another kick.

Peter. She stopped moving. Stopped breathing.

He could not see her like this, could not know her degradation.

Was this a rescue? Or a fast descent into hell?

She was so beautiful. It was the most inappropriate thought a man could have, but it filled his mind. She looked frightened, angry, despairing even, but all he could see was her beauty, her strength.

She stood caught in his fingers, one fist drawn back to punch, the other trying frantically to restore some modesty to her attire. Her mouth was swollen and damaged-looking. And her eyes. Her eyes were black in the flickering light. Not black with passion or black with fury, but just black.

He started to pull her toward him, but she resisted. She fought his hold, wanting freedom.

He granted it as he had sworn he always would. Even now, when she so desperately needed him, he let her go.

She stepped back. Her chest heaved with emotion. He raised one arm and carefully held it out to her. She jerked back, but allowed him to stroke her cheek, her lips.

They stood alone in the darkness. He brought his hand to his own lips and kissed the fingers lightly before returning to caress her lips again—the age-old cure of childhood ills.

"Should I kill him?" he asked, dropping his hand.

"What? Who? No." Peter could see Violet's thought process that prompted each response.

"I think I should." He turned back toward Foxworthy's house.

She reached out and touched his arm. "No. Just take me home."

He held firm a moment. There would be much satisfaction in marching up to the door and pounding to a pulp whoever answered. He didn't care particularly who it was. Somebody needed to answer for the look in Violet's eyes.

"Please."

He let his shoulders relax. He always claimed he was not the boy she called him. Responding with fists, not intellect, was the action of a boy.

He shrugged out of his coat and settled it about her shoulders. She looked up at him, trembling. "Take me home."

He took her hand and placed it on his arm, leading her through the empty street with all the poise of a stroll through Hyde Park.

He started to speak once, but she shushed him with a shake of her head. Silence held for the remainder of their journey.

Dawn pierced even the heavy brocade drapes and shone in a slim path across the room. Violet held her eyes fast closed even as the silhouettes of morning moved across her lids.

She still was not ready. The day must be faced. Decisions must be made. But, please, not yet.

She felt Peter behind her. His deep, even breathing tickled the hairs at the nape of her neck. His arm draped about her heavy and safe. Marriage must be like this, waking in security—not worrying about sex, because there was tomorrow and tomorrow and the tomorrow after that.

She allowed herself to nestle back into him, enjoying for a few seconds the safety his warmth provided. His heart beat steady against her back. Even in sleep he was so alive.

It would be so easy to stay in this moment—to pretend this was reality.

But she was done with easy. She slipped sideways on the bed, letting his arm fall heavily to the cover. The wrinkled dress from the night before twisted about her as she moved. It was still unfastened and loose about her shoulders.

She stood, letting it drop to the floor, a heap of golden fabric, all its magic gone. She would never wear it again. She would have it burned. No, that was a gesture of weakness. It gave too much importance to the night. Perhaps one of the maids would take it home and find the enchantment of its glow.

She stretched, feeling the creaks and pains of her adventures. She stepped toward the dresser, eager for the splash of cool water upon her face. She felt so dirty.

Sharp pain radiated up her leg. She glanced down and stopped. Her bare feet were filthy. A large gash ran the length of her left instep.

She had left Foxworthy's house without her shoes. She had walked through the streets of London barefoot and not even been conscious of it. It seemed a preposterous thing.

A loud snore rumbled through the room.

Peter had not realized it either. He would have insisted on carrying her if he'd known.

What was she going to do about him? About any of this?

She took another step to the basin and cupped the cool water to her face. Again. She would never feel clean.

It was not the dirt of the streets that covered her. It was a far more insidious darkening of the soul.

She pulled a light robe off the hook and belted it tight. She did not want to see her own nudity. Last night she had refused to label herself a whore. Today she felt one, a failed one.

She limped over and sank down upon the chaise, staring at the man on the bed. She sat and watched him breathe. She matched her own breath to his. In. Hold. Out. Hold.

She felt his first awakening, counted as the slow, easy breath of night grew more rapid. He reached for her. He didn't even open his eyes before his arm moved out seeking and not finding.

She met his heavy glance as his lids lifted. The time for reckoning had come.

Where was she? Even as the thought filled his mind Peter saw her. She sat in her favorite spot, the well-cushioned chaise. The light of early morning snuck through the drapes, lighting the fires of her hair. Her eyes were heavy and shadowed from lack of sleep.

"You should have stayed abed longer," he said.

"I couldn't. My mind would not be still." Her voice was somber.

He sat up in the bed. He was still fully dressed. He couldn't remember ever sleeping in clothes. Even after the most drunken of evenings his valet would shake him out of his clothing and into fresh linen.

She stared at him. His mind wandered to the discomfort of sleeping in breeches, and Violet looked like her world had ended.

She didn't say anything, she just stared. She never avoided confrontation, so why was she silent now? "Are you going to explain what happened last night?" he asked.

He saw the hesitation in her face, then the decision.

"I told you before. I took another lover. It is not a state secret. I'll ring for tea." She stood and wobbled slightly.

His gaze fell to her feet, to the grubby, bloody toes that peeked out from beneath her hem. His glance shot up to her face. She glared at him, daring him to say something.

He wanted to apologize for his thoughtlessness in not realizing last night. He wanted to take her in his arms and tell her he would fix all her problems. Her eyes dared him, challenging him to make the move.

He swung his legs off the side of the bed. "Be sure you have the maid bring hot water and towels, as well. You know you hate to be dirty."

She stepped back at his words. He'd struck a nerve without realizing he'd fired. He turned from her. She did not want him to see her pain, fine. He could play this the way she wanted.

Ignoring her, he stepped to the door and called for refreshments and water himself. "You should be seated. You don't want to collapse before your first swallow of tea. It really would cause a frightful bother with the staff."

He hoped for at least the glimmer of a smile. He did not receive it.

He sat across from her, waited until the maid arrived burdened with the heavy tray. He waited longer while Violet poured the tea. She took three spoons of sugar, sweetening the drink far beyond her usual.

She wet the towels and began to sponge her feet. Impulse drove him to offer his help, but he held his tongue, held the growing silence.

He could hear the tick of the clock with each move of its gears, hear the splish of the water each time she dampened the towel. If he listened hard enough he thought he could hear each beat of her stubborn heart.

Finally, she spoke. "Will you leave so I can call my maid and dress?"

"I never have before."

"And if I insist?"

"Are you going to?"

She didn't answer. He wished he could tell what she was thinking. Often her thoughts were plain upon her face, but today she was blank, a parchment without a single squiggle of ink to betray its purpose.

Her head dropped forward, hiding her face from him. She looked so weary. Desires warred within him. He should go, give her the peace and solitude she so desired. He should take her in his arms and hold her until time ceased to exist. He should argue with her, shout at her, demand she release the secrets hidden so deeply in her eyes.

"I will not insist," she answered, at last. "I will ask. Peter, will you please go and allow me to dress with privacy? I will not demand you leave my house, just my chamber. Can you please do this for me?"

He stood. "I'll send the maid to you. Do not bother to rise. I'll await you below, at your convenience."

Violet chose an older corset, one that still had slim whalebone stays. It had probably been chosen originally to fit under some court dress, but now she needed its feeling of strength and stability. Her spine lacked the strength to stay upright on its own today. And if ever there was a day for uprightness and strength it had come.

The time for choices was past. Her path was set.

She pointed to a dress of deep brown muslin. It was simple and severe, well in keeping with her mood. The waist of the gown bulged slightly below the overly tight stays, but she smoothed it as best she could, ignoring the clucking of the maid.

She instructed that her hair to be brushed tight and pulled severely back into a knot. She resisted the impulse to pull forward a fringe of curls. She could not afford softness.

Regrettably, her only choice of shoes was the softest

pair of kid evening slippers. She wished for sturdy half boots, but she was not willing to endure their discomfort this day. Enough pain swirled inside her without adding to it.

When she was ready she looked in the mirror. The dress was severe and matronly, despite the deep cinnamon the day's light revealed in the brown. She ignored how it complemented her hair. Some things could not be helped. Her hair was one of them.

She spoke quietly to the maid.

A moment later a small array of crisp white caps were laid before her. She grabbed the nearest one and laid it over her hair. No. That was not she.

She was Violet, Lady Carrington, with all that entailed. She would not change who she was.

He was waiting below. He'd called for another pot of tea and settled in the sunny front room with the day's papers. Each move he made, each page he'd turned had been relayed to her by a servant's whisper.

It could have been the start of any day—her dressing above, him catching up on the day's events below. They'd had many such mornings—they should have had so many more.

Glad of the corset adding steel to her spine, Violet descended. She made no pretense of heading anywhere but to him, to Peter.

She paused in the door. "Do you have the gossip sheets there? Do they speak of last night's events yet?"

He looked up, his eyes sweeping over her stark appearance. His expression did not change. "No, they are still wondering why a certain Lady C found no pleasure with either Mr. W or Mr. S. There is some wondering with whom the fault lay. I suppose I should be grateful that we kept it so private that there is no mention of the cuckolded Lord P."

Peter watched as she came and sat before him, knees only inches from his own, her hands folded neatly in her lap. "I believe you need to be married to be cuckolded in the traditional sense. And we were never married," she said.

"No, we were not. But, then, neither were we traditional."

She sat up straighter in her chair. He wondered if there was an invisible string running to the ceiling that drew her up in such a fashion.

"I will answer your questions, now, if you wish," she said.

Questions. He didn't know where to begin. "You left Foxworthy's house well after two attired in nothing but your gown, and that untied?"

"Yes."

"You had relations with him previous to that exit?"

"Why don't you just ask if I fucked him?" Her voice remained calm despite the vulgarity of her words.

"Did you?"

"I spent the evening at dinner with his friends showing just how desirable I found him. I ran my fingers up his velvet-clad thighs indiscreetly, advertising to all just how little control I had around him. At dessert he dropped a cherry down my bodice and I let him fish it out with his mouth. More than a dozen gentlemen saw him slip a hand up my skirts while we waited for his coach to be brought round. Do you want to know more?"

Each word she said pounded a nail into his chest. He could feel the air in his lungs leak and sputter. Soon he would be unable to breathe. "Yes, tell me all."

"I never knew you were such a voyeur. Perhaps we should have explored it more—it might have held my attention longer."

Peter jumped to his feet in fury and then sat down again. She was spurring him on, trying to get him angry enough to leave and not come back. Why? "Continue with your story."

She paled further beneath his stare, then bent forward and picked up his teacup, bringing it to her lips. She took a long swallow. "He had his hands all over me on the ride back to his home. He liked to describe each move he made, every time he licked me, bit me, caressed me, it required comment. He liked my titties— good full ones like a real woman. Would you like to hear more of his conversation?"

"I am interested in you not him. Why did you do it?"

"Is that really any of your business?"

He stood again, not with anger or with fury, but with determination. He took the step forward that closed the separation between them, let his knees brush hers. "Yes, it is. If you had chosen Struthers or Winchester, I would have held my tongue. I would have accepted that you had the right to choose who you wanted to be with. It would have wrenched the soul right out of me, but I would have let you do it. I can't say I wouldn't have fought—I searched all of London with that purpose in mind—but in the end I would have let you go.

"But Foxworthy"—his mouth filled with bile—"when you choose a toad like that it is my business. When you leave his home alone in the middle of the night, your dress clutched around you and your eyes empty of even tears, then it is my business."

"You are wrong." She lifted her face to stare straight into his. "Nothing has ever been further from your business. I appreciate your bringing me home. I thank you for the comfort of your arms. But it still has nothing to do with you. I have a life and problems that are all my own. I do not need your help."

"But you have it whether you need it, whether you want it." He held her gaze steady. "I have no purpose but to help you."

She pushed up to her feet, the chair groaning with the strength of her grip. "That is not your right."

He placed a hand upon her cheek. Her face was as expressionless as any statue. She gave no indication that she even felt his touch.

"You may be correct that it is not my right, but I have no other choice, Violet. I can't even pretend that I wish it were different. I want to take care of you, to shelter you. Can't you give me even a small opportunity?"

She turned her face away from him, but did not remove his hand. "I belong to Foxworthy now. You must accept that and leave. You must find that girl, that innocent, sweet girl who will give you children and build a family around you. There is nothing in this world that would make me happier than to know that you have found tranquillity."

"I don't believe you."

She lifted both her hands and took his fingers between her own chilled ones. "Peter, no matter what you saw, or think you saw last night, I will return to Foxworthy. I cannot explain my motivations to you, but as soon as you have left I will return upstairs to change. I will put on my most becoming day dress, and in the middle of the afternoon I will call upon him at home. I will be unmindful of scandal, unmindful of my reputation. My only concern will be to persuade him to give me another chance."

"Another chance? What do you mean by that? You look as if your life depends on it. Tell me what hold he has on you. Is it money? Does he hold some vowel that you gambled away? Only tell me and I will take care of it."

She turned from him and walked to the window. Despite the perfection of her posture she looked ready to sink to a puddle on the floor. "What I mean does not matter. It is not my life that depends on it. My life will go on much as it always has. I may be welcome at a few less doors. The comments may be louder and more ribald when I enter a room, but that is of little significance."

She turned and looked back at him from across the length of the room. How could any woman look so strong and so frail at the same time?

She took a single step back toward him. Something in her expression softened, changed. "You will no longer be in my life and for that I am sorry. It is, perhaps, my one regret. I enjoyed our dream in a summer garden, but I must remember it was only a dream."

"Why? Can't you just tell me why?"

"I could, but it would make no difference. You might blacken Foxworthy's eye, but that would only raise his ire. He would take his anger out on me, and so you shall not do that. You will not challenge a man to a duel because I chose him over you, and even if you did I imagine that Foxworthy would laugh it off. He is a man of pride, but not stupidity."

"If it doesn't matter why won't you tell me?"

"Would it salve your pride if you knew that it was not of my own choice that I leave you for a man twice your age and half your value?" She stepped toward him again. "I will tell you whatever you need to make this easier for you. If I cannot make you go in anger then tell me how to make you leave with kindness."

"It is not my pride that needs salving, but my heart." He had nothing to lose. He could feel her leaving him even as she stepped closer. "And your heart."

"Oh, Peter." There was true feeling in her voice. "I never asked you to love me. I told you not to. Please can you not just go and somehow find a way to be happy? I have never been good for you."

"Isn't that for me to say?" He tried to smile, but knew it was more of a grimace. This was really the end and she wouldn't even tell him why. Anger began to rise within him. She would not even give him an explanation of her actions. A thought came to him. "You want me to marry, somebody young and innocent. Forget the sweet, you've ruined me for sweet. How would you feel if I married your sister? She made quite a play for me at Summerton's house party and if I can't have you—"

Her eyes flashed fire, once. He had expected outright rejection, but instead he could see the wheels moving deep inside her head. The feelings she had fought so hard to hide were leaking through.

"That would solve the last of my worries." She spoke

quietly, to herself, her voice almost mechanical. "Why can I not survive that too?"

She took his hands in hers. "It would relieve me greatly if you would marry Isabella. Just promise me you will always care for her. No matter what. She deserves a good life."

He caught the undertone of voice. "And you don't?"

"It is too late for me. I made too many bad choices before I realized they were choices. I found my strength too late. Keep my sister safe until she finds her own strength."

He grabbed her hands and, holding them tight, pulled her to the settee. He pushed her to the seat and knelt before her. "If that is your wish I will promise it to you. You could not have asked a harder thing of me, but for you I will do it. I will even endeavor to love and care for her if that is your wish. But I do have a price. You must promise to explain this whole sordid mess to me. You must explain how in a matter of days I went from feeling I had achieved my one desire to being forced to settle for second best—"

"Do not call my sister second best. She has done nothing to harm you. She deserves all you can give her and more." She spoke with vehemence.

"From the moment we leave this room I will do all I can to cherish her, but first you must tell me the truth. I must admit that from what I have seen of your sister she seems more a gold digger than a victim."

Violet shut her eyes. Her brows clenched together and he sensed she held back tears, tears she would see only as a weakness. "My sister has acted only as she has been forced. You cannot count her actions of the last weeks against her. She is kind and good and only needs a chance to shine.

"I will tell you all now, but you must promise me you will not let it affect your promise. When you leave this room we are finished. You will go to my brother's house and ask for Isabella's hand in marriage." She did not look at him.

He kept his gaze fastened on the clock on the mantel. "I promise."

Chapter 15

Violet watched him, she listened to him, and she felt the love he did not put into words. It was not infatuation or lust as she had consoled herself.

Peter loved her.

It shone out of him. He would put her needs before his own, always. For the first time she let herself accept it, let herself look at him and feel the wonder of it, of him.

For ten seconds she felt giddy with the glory of it.

Then the despair hit. It was impossible. It ruined everything. "I am a fool. The very idea of you and Isabella is ridiculous."

He turned away from the mantel and stared back at her. "Ridiculous? A fool? Do you think I am not good enough for your sister? Not good enough for you, not good enough for her?"

She tried to swallow, but her throat closed halfway. "No, that is not it." It was hard to form the words when her tongue felt that it filled her mouth in its entirety. "I cannot trap either of you into a life without love. I will not force her to marry a man she does not want any more than I would allow my brother to."

"What does Masters have to do with this?" he asked.

"I thought only of myself," she continued as if he had not spoken, "of whether I could survive if you married Isabella. I did not think of her, or of you. I want you both to be free."

"What does Masters have to do with this?" he repeated, his voice rising in volume.

She could only stare back at him. She rubbed her throat as if trying to loosen it. The words she needed seemed to flee from her.

Finally, she walked to a chair by the window and sat, waving him to the seat across from her. "I did promise to tell you. I am not sure I am bound by that, as I certainly have no intention to holding you to your own words."

He moved to the seat and sat. And waited.

"Masters wishes Isabella to marry Foxworthy," she said. "He does not take her feelings into consideration. That is the story, simple as it is."

"What does that have to do with you?"

She stared blankly, his question bouncing around her mind like a rubber ball.

He tried again. "It would seem that all arrangements are between Masters, Isabella, and Foxworthy. Why are you involved?"

"I am involved because Isabella has nobody else to speak for her and she certainly has no desire to marry Foxworthy."

"So she says no. She cannot be married if she does not agree."

Violet picked up the paper he had been reading. She resisted the urge to swat him, hard. "Sometimes you can be so male. Isabella is still a girl. She has no money. She has no choice. I will give her a choice."

"I still don't see why she doesn't just tell Masters no."

"Do you really not understand?"

He paused, considered. She could see his mind working. He might be idealistic. He was not a fool.

"I still don't understand why you were at Foxworthy's," he answered.

"Are you being deliberately obtuse?" She slapped the paper against her knee. His eyes followed the blow. Ah, he knew it was not her knee she wished to hit. "I sought to persuade Foxworthy that he could do better than Isabella. He visited my brother and withdrew his suit in return for my promise. Now he threatens to approach Masters again."

The paper swung, hard.

He watched the paper, imagined its sting. It all made sense, such dreadful sense. He knew Violet, loved her desire to protect those around her. He closed his mind against the image that formed in his mind. He did not want to believe. Still—"Why would marriage to Foxworthy be so bad? Yes, he's older and not the most attractive of fellows, perhaps not the most respectable— but I've never heard anything nasty about his personal habits. There are many such marriages."

"Never heard anything nasty about him? That makes it acceptable?"

He didn't answer.

Violet evidently did not need his answer. "It is not acceptable to marry a girl off without giving her a say in the matter. I will do what I need to for two reasons. First, because Isabella deserves to learn she has choices. If she is forced to marry Foxworthy her whole world will change. I cannot allow that."

"Is that what happened to you?"

"I don't think any man can understand what it is like to be seventeen and full of dreams. The most important decisions in your life involve choosing new dresses and what type of posies to press in your memory book. I remember a cat who had kittens that summer, and I spent hours trying to decide what to name them. Should they be Knights of the Round Table or Shakespearean fairies? I didn't even consider their sexes. I don't believe I would have known how to tell the difference.

"Then my brother came and told me I was to marry Sir Dratton. I have already told you it was not a bad marriage, but it changed everything. I was never able to lose myself in the magic of imagination after that. I was never able to pretend the world was a sun-filled, enchanted kingdom. I learned of reality and I learned quickly. I do not want that for Isabella. I want her to grow at her own pace."

She dropped the newspaper she clutched between her fingers into her lap. There was a smudge of ink in the upper corner.

"You said there were two reasons?" Peter asked.

She looked up at him. "Milber. He is my second reason. I will never risk her having a marriage like that.

"I could tell you stories, but what good would stories do? Most of the things he did would be perfectly acceptable in society. He rarely hit me, and nobody cared if his words were cruel and abusive. He had some practices in the bedroom that were perhaps unusual, but I doubt many of your friends would find them shocking if practiced with a mistress. They would perhaps be shocked that he performed them with his wife, but they would probably consider him lucky to have such a willing wife. Because, of course, a wife cannot be unwilling. It would be unnatural."

Peter slipped off his chair and knelt before her. "I can see that this discussion pains you. Is that why you never talk of him?"

"No, I never talk of Milber because I have made him irrelevant to my life. I cannot say that his actions did not change me—but he is gone and I am here. I do not give him the grace of thought."

"But surely you realize that Foxworthy is no Milber? Rumors do spread and I have never heard—"

She cut him off. "But you don't always hear. I would admit mostly you do, but not always. And, yes, I also realize there is no guarantee that Isabella will not choose a man who has his own secrets, but it will be her choice."

Peter lifted his hands and took them between his own. "So you traded yourself to Foxworthy for your sister. Where is your choice?"

"Don't you see I am making it? I understand fully what I do. Believe me, I could not understand more fully."

"Is it money? Why do you not just pay Masters off? If you need more funds I will give them to you. I doubt Foxworthy can offer more than you and I combined."

Violet tried to pull her hands away. He held tight.

"It is not simply a matter of money," she said. "Although it is at the core."

"Do you need to speak in riddles? We have always been straightforward with each other."

Violet did not answer.

He tried a different tack. "If you won't answer that, answer this." He rubbed his hands back and forth, warming her captive ones. "Explain why you wanted me to marry Isabella."

Violet looked up at met his glance. Her eyes were dark and haunted. "It occurred to me last night that I might be saving Isabella from Foxworthy, but I cannot prevent Masters from doing the same thing again. I had hoped that your offer would be good enough that Masters would agree and Isabella would be safe."

"Then why take away my promise? I would do this for you, do it as willingly as I am able. Then you would not need to go to Foxworthy."

She wanted to believe him. Peter was right, if it was only money, they together could surely offer as much as Foxworthy. But there was still the matter of her brother's possible treason. Would it be possible to buy the man off? She had tried in the gambling hell when they first bargained, but had she tried hard enough? She had offered reasonable amounts—what if she offered the unreasonable? What if she were willing to sell her house and offer all she had? Could any man, even Foxworthy, refuse such an amount?

Her brains were muddled from anxiety and lack of sleep. She knew money was not the solution. Isabella would still be threatened.

She pulled her hands away, this time giving him no choice but to release her. Rubbing her temples, she walked to a corner chair and sat. She picked up a small portrait from the table, her father. It was the only picture of him she had. She ran a finger across the surface of his cheek, uncaring of the oils she left upon the paint.

She thought she had felt safe during his life. The memories were so faint and frayed. She forced her glance up to stare around her perfect room, her perfect house. Could she risk it all, go back to having nothing? Would it serve any purpose?

Peter had said something about Foxworthy. She needed to answer him. If only she were not so tired from the night before, her brain didn't want to think.

She shook her head to clear it. "I fear I need to deal with Foxworthy again, no matter what."

"What makes you think he will see you? He will not be kindly disposed after last night. He will probably instruct his servants to slam the door in your face—if they open it at all."

Violet smiled bitterly. "Do you think so? I don't. I think he will welcome me to his parlor and then shred every hope I have. He is a man who likes to see the pain he causes."

"Then, why—"

"It will be my job to persuade him. I do not delude myself that I will receive an arrangement anywhere near the offer we agreed to before, but I am a woman of—of charm. I think he will listen."

"What are you going to do, strip your ass bare and lay it across his table?" He blinked, stared at her. "My God, that is exactly what you think to do."

She bowed her head and stared at her hands. The beginnings of a plan formed in her mind.

Peter's voice echoed around the room, interrupting her careful thoughts. "I will kill him first."

Anger filled every part of his body; the hairs on his toes twitched with it. Nobody was allowed to make Violet feel like this, nobody. Foxworthy would be the one begging Violet when this was done.

He'd heard Violet's gasp at his words, but he did not take them back. He'd meant every one. He glared at her, letting her see the truth in his eyes.

She turned back toward him. Her voice was calm, reasoning, "And what does that accomplish? You will be in prison. Isabella is still unprotected, and Masters will just find somebody else."

"He will anyway based on what you have said."

Violet turned from him and began to pace back and forth across the room. Normally she was the still one while he sought the constant release of energy. Today anger held him rooted to the spot.

She began to speak as she walked, her pace growing ever faster. "Foxworthy holds something beyond money over Masters—maybe I can persuade him to give it to me. Then Masters would have to wait until Isabella is ready to make her own choice."

"What does Foxworthy hold?" he asked.

"It doesn't matter—I am slightly hazy on the details myself. What matters is that if I can get it, then Isabella will be safe. Yes, if I have it then both Masters and Foxworthy will be without power." Her voice grew stronger and more confident.

Peter grabbed her arm and stopped her momentum. "What you forget is that I truly will kill him before I let you go back to him."

She pulled away at his words. "Peter, I am too tired to argue. Can you not let me do what I must? It will not be so bad. I know last night it was too much, but I am strong. I can do this and survive. I can even emerge from it the winner."

Peter stared down at her, wishing his eyes could speak all the emotions that were in his heart; words were not enough. "I do not think that is possible. Whatever the outcome I doubt you will feel victory, you will be diminished if you do this."

"Peter, I believe that I can win. Do not take that away from me." She seemed to gain strength as she spoke, pulling farther away from him with her final words.

He let her go and turned away. "Violet, I do not doubt you are a strong woman. Always before I have realized that every man you had slept with helped make you the woman you are—even apparently Milber. But this is not in your character—it is why you failed last night. It will destroy you, and I cannot let this happen."

She laughed then, high and shrill. It echoed through the room. "But I am a survivor. I can promise that I will emerge from this."

"But not unscathed." He wanted to shake sense into her. He clenched and unclenched his fist at his sides. "You cannot do this."

"You cannot stop me."

"I can kill him."

She looked straight at him. "But you will not."

"Do not be so sure."

She walked over to the settee and sat, drawing her skirts close in. She patted the space beside her. "Come, sit. Stop looking at me like I've grown an extra head. We need to be calm discussing this. Too many lives hang in the balance to let emotions rule."

He sat, wondering if she was casting a web of manipulation about him. He might love Violet, but he was not a fool.

"Peter," she began, "I should not say this, but I spend most of my life trying my hardest not to think of you. When I think of you I cannot do what I need to do. But I cannot afford to fail."

"How can you decide not to think of somebody?" he asked. His body was still stiff with tension. "When I try not to think of you, all I can do is think of you."

"I've had years of practice. Yes, it was a different thing. I am a master at shutting out what I do not want to remember. I hate to put you in that category, but it is not difficult." She pushed away her failure last night. She should have been able to be intimate with Foxworthy. Her inability had done nothing but create more fences that must be jumped.

But now she had a plan. The goal was not to appease Foxworthy, but to gain whatever documents he held. She would do whatever Foxworthy demanded to gain those papers. And if that didn't work—she wasn't above theft.

"Peter," she began again, needing to persuade him, "That is why I can do this. When it is over I will come home, wash myself, and it will be over. I will not think of it again. It is my choice."

"But I have a choice also. Do not forget that." His foot beat a rapid tattoo upon the floor.

"I do not forget, but I do not believe it is in your nature to kill a man for acting as many others do. It is not Foxworthy who demands this of me, it is I who demand it of myself."

He ground his teeth and did not answer. It tore at her heart to see him like this. "Will you then kill every man I decide to sleep with?"

"This is not your decision—you don't think you have a choice." He barely opened his lips as he spoke.

"You are wrong. It is very definitely a choice." She dropped her gaze. "You told me not long ago that you did not hold my past against me—can you not forgive me this?"

"How can you even ask that? There are some things no man should be asked."

She spoke so quietly she could hardly hear her own words. "I am sorry that my actions do not lead us in the direction you want, but I am decided." She moved to lay a soft kiss upon his lips. A kiss of good-bye.

He caught her face between his hands and pulled back until they stared at each other. He ran a thumb across her lips. He kissed her then, and it was not gentle—consuming, wrenching, passionate, but not gentle.

"Do not do this, Violet. Do not throw all we have into the gutter."

He kissed her again.

She felt her soul in his kiss. She felt it whirl throughout her, flickering with energy and washing away the dirt. She could almost see it, glowing, fresh, and, yes, clean. She had always worried that it was a dirty, tawdry thing, and now it glowed and gleamed. With Peter she could be born anew.

She pulled away from him, waiting for her head to clear. She drew great gulps of air into her lungs. Souls. What a fanciful idea. It was surely brought on by the passion of his kiss. Passion she understood.

When she felt herself again, she examined him—the curling ebony waves of hair, the sun-darkened skin that was just beginning to flake on one of his cheeks, the lips swollen with kisses. And the eyes. Those ordinary brown eyes that filled her with warmth.

If she stopped this game now—found another way to stop Foxworthy and Masters—this would be hers. She wanted to see an idealistic boy, but when she looked at him she did not see a boy—she saw acceptance, a man's acceptance. He looked at her. He truly saw her and still he wanted her.

It was that which made her feel clean again. For the first time someone knew her secrets and wanted her anyway—wanted not just her body, but wanted her. She had to clench her hands to keep them from shaking.

"Don't do this." He said it again. "Violet, I love you. I will find a way to take care of you and Isabella."

Oh, the temptation. He looked at her and she wanted to agree. She wanted his love. She would never say that to him, never even acknowledge that he had spoken the word, but, oh, how she wanted to.

But it was not just Isabella—even if they somehow managed to survive this tangled mess, there was still the rest of the world.

While he might be willing to accept her decisions, society never would. Even after last night opinions about her would be changing. She had appeared with Foxworthy in public and allowed him to fondle her. She had smiled a coquette's smile at another older man and made her intentions clear. Society would not forget or forgive.

And who knew what Foxworthy would demand in return for the papers—he could ask everything she had and she might give it to him. She could be completely ruined.

She could never tell Peter; he would try to stop her.

It was all so unfair.

She wanted what he offered—wanted it all—wanted the dream he spun before her. Marriage. Love. Security.

Damn, this should not be so hard.

The need to move coursed through her. She wanted to pace. Instead she held herself still, forced all that energy into control.

She looked at him again, watched gold-tipped lashes open and close, watched the slight flare of his nostrils with each breath he took, watched his neck move with each swallow. When times grew dark she would need to remember him, remember this. If only she could hold on to this moment, then she could get through anything.

"Peter, it is already too late. We can never go back to where we were before this all began. I will only make you unhappy."

"But—" he started to argue.

"I will not do anything immediately. Please, go now and let me rest and think. And promise me you will do nothing foolish. I need you out of this without any further wounds. When this is done there will be no place for us."

He stared back at her. He blinked once. Twice. He understood what her words did not say. He spoke so softly she had to strain to hear. "So you will sacrifice yourself for my happiness just as you sacrifice yourself for your sister's?"

"Yes."

"Do you then love me as you love her?" The answer rose in her throat, but she could not say it. She longed to, but the word would not come.

Her eyes felt wet and she found herself blinking, trying hard to hold back the moisture. This was silly; she never cried, hadn't cried in years. Tears solved nothing, resolved nothing.

She blinked again. Sniffed.

He reached out and wiped the dampness from her cheek. He brought it to his lips. The look he gave almost ripped the heart from her chest.

Still he did not speak, did not demand an answer to his question. He stood slowly, never taking his gaze from hers.

He walked to the door, his head still turned to watch her.

He paused before easing it open, then he stepped through.

Light from the hallway flowed in behind him, haloing him.

He looked so glorious.

She didn't think she could bear for the door to close, to know that this was over. She grasped her seat to keep from running to him.

He smiled at her. Ruefully. Bitterly. Kindly. She

could not tell through the haze of tears that still welled in her eyes.

"I will go because I too am tired of arguing. But tell me, Violet, why are you the one to make all the sacrifices? Does it ever occur to you that you are so busy making your own choices that you take away mine? And your sister's?"

The door shut without a sound.

Peter stood outside Violet's home. He looked up and down the street, unsure which way to head. His hands clenched into tight fists at his sides. He could head over to Jackson's and find a good fight. A boxing match would clear his head and his need to slam his fist straight into a brick wall. His foot still throbbed from the night before.

She was going to do it. She might pretend indecision, but he knew her. She only wanted him out of the way so she could complete her hideous plan. She truly was willing to throw him away, to throw them away.

He had lost. She would never be his.

He should head to the nearest hell and drink until he couldn't stand. He would probably cease to feel before he finished the first bottle, cease to care before he finished the second. He might manage to forget for days.

He could find a woman—any woman—and drown

himself in lust and passion, show Violet that she was not the only one who could—

God. He sank down on her stairs, taking his head in his hands. The whole world could wonder at his actions and he did not care.

All his thoughts were those of a boy. Violet was right to think he wouldn't handle society's blows if all he could think of was drinking, whoring, and fighting.

His head ached with emotion.

He could not let her do this. Didn't she realize that sometimes it was her turn to be rescued?

Resolution overtook him. She needed a knight and he would not fail her. He pushed back to his feet and headed off down the street.

This time his feet knew where to lead.

Violet didn't move after Peter left. Tears left warm tracks down her cheeks, but she did not move to wipe them. She heard a carriage pass in the lane. A bird called its cheerful morning song. A maid whistled as she worked in the hall.

The world went on and she remained frozen, immobile. It should not be this bad. He was only a boy. One more boy in a growing line of them.

The tears continued to flow unstopped. Could one run out of tears? She probably had enough stored to last for hours if not days.

The sunlight shining through the window was so bright. How could the sun keep shining? The sky should have been dark and gray as it had been all those days at Glynewolde. All except those last ones.

She stood suddenly; the restless energy that had filled her earlier returned. Of their own accord her feet began to pace the room with ever increasing speed.

She had to do something. She had to be busy.

She'd go. She'd do it. She'd be done with it.

Surely Foxworthy would not refuse her. He might demand his goods up front this time, and take everything else she offered as well—but afterward—afterward he'd decide she was worth giving up Isabella. And then she would persuade him to give her what she needed.

She was out the door before she realized she hadn't called for a carriage. She was tempted to walk, as she'd walked last night.

Last night. Peter.

God. She sank down on the stairs, straightened her back. Her neighbors would think her strange enough without her slumping like an ill-mannered maid.

Choices. Why did the word keep running through her brain? And in her brother's voice.

Choices. Choices. Choices.

Violet, you're too young to understand the choices that face us. You don't understand what it will be to have no funds, to have the family name in shreds, to have not even this house around us. I must make the choice for you, therefore. Sir Dratton will treat you well. He'll— Her brother's words ran through her mind.

For a moment she was the scared seventeen-year-old who could only listen and believe. She didn't know better so he made the choices. Had he believed he was acting in her best interests? Was it possible? And what about Milber? Could her brother possibly have thought he was doing the right thing then?

Her mind spun with questions she'd never considered. She'd also never confronted her brother with what her married life had been like. Did he have a single clue what he'd done to her? What he might be doing to Isabella?

Could there be another way?

Was it possible that if she talked to him again he might be reasonable, understanding? She had not forced him to listen to her or to answer to her. What would happen if she did? What if she offered him everything—all the money with which she was prepared to bribe Foxworthy? With money came answers. She didn't know the exact nature of her brother's difficulties. She did not believe Foxworthy's claim that he had committed treason. She might not know her brother well, but he had always loved his country. It was all such a tangle.

The effort of keeping her back straight became too

much. She folded forward, catching her weary head in her hands.

Her brother had not been a monster during her childhood. She didn't have many memories of him, those few years of age had seemed a lifetime, but he'd never seemed evil. She could even remember a smile or two, a doll he'd brought her, being led around the yard on a pony while he held the line. There weren't many memories and none of them flooded her with warmth, but they weren't bad memories either.

Could she have misjudged him all these years? She didn't think so, but could she afford not to consider it?

She was willing to make huge sacrifices for Isabella's comfort. Was she depriving Masters of the chance to do the same?

She pushed herself to her feet and shook out her skirts. She waved gaily at Mrs. Potts, who gaped at her from two doors down.

Now she had two plans. One of them would work.

Chapter 16

Peter stopped, his hand on the knocker. Was he really going to do this? Violet would call him a fool, insist that he acted like the impulsive boy she named him.

She would be wrong. He understood exactly what he did, understood the price he and others would pay for it. To others it would seem the impulsive act of a youth. It was not.

He lifted the knocker. Let it fall.

He heard the sound of response behind the heavy door, the patter of feet moving and a sudden metallic clatter. He should want to run.

He did not. He stood resolved.

The door opened. The porter peered out into the bright sun.

"I've come to see Mr. Masters. Tell him that Lord Peter St. Johns has called." He sounded like his brother the marquess, every bit of manner and aristocracy projected into two simple sentences.

The porter looked him up once, and then again. He should have gone home to change. The wrinkled linen of the night's adventure clearly did not match his tone.

Peter stared at him.

The stare and the tone won. The porter stepped back, granting him entry into the hall before disappearing to seek his master.

He reappeared a moment later to lead Peter deeper into the house. It was a gloomy place, far different from Violet's comfortable abode. There was no smell of lemons and beeswax here among the dark woods and baroque furniture.

Masters sat at his desk writing, pinched between two high bookshelves overwhelmed with volumes. He looked up at Peter's entry. Peter saw something of Violet in the cool direct gaze. Masters's eyes were darker than Violet's, almost black, but there was bit of that mysterious purple tinge about them. And the hair, it too was darker, but with a hint of copper at the ends. Masters was far more like Violet than Peter had ever realized.

"This is unexpected. How can I help you? I imagine that it involves my sister." Masters let his pen drop.

"Yes." Peter let the single word hang.

"I should tell you straight off that I and my sister lead completely separate lives. I do not see how I could possibly be of service."

"Don't tell me stories. I know she lives here with

you." Peter could not keep the impatience from his voice.

"She most certainly does not. Violet has a house of her own, as I am sure you know. Quite a damn bit nicer than this one, too."

"Not Violet, Isabella," Peter replied, turning to look away.

Masters stood. He was several inches shorter than Peter, but still well above average height. "Why would you want to inquire about Isabella? It's Violet you are involved with."

Peter looked back at Masters and glared; so much for all Violet's careful discretion. He waited for Masters to continue.

"You didn't think I knew about that." Masters strolled out from behind the desk. "I've always made it a point to keep an eye on my sister. I don't like unpleasant surprises, and with two sisters life is full of them."

Peter's hackles rose. "Both your sisters are careful of their reputations."

"I would have said you were correct," Masters said. "Violet has shown surprising sense and discretion, but you clearly haven't heard about last night. I imagined that was what you were here about. Although what you thought I could do about it I am not sure."

"Foxworthy."

"Yes, Foxworthy." Masters looked away. His tone was carefully measured. "I'd always felt a bit of guilt at marrying her off to men so much older. I knew it was for the best, though. But between Carrington and Foxworthy she clearly has a preference of her own for older men."

Peter cleared his throat. "I would have thought that you'd understand Foxworthy was also your problem—Violet only pursues him because of you."

Masters choked a little, but then gathered himself together. "Forgive me, but I really would rather not discuss my sister's reasons for choosing her lovers, whether younger or older. You said you'd come about Isabella?"

How could any man display such a lack of emotion while discussing his family? The man could have been discussing spring planting or a new pair of boots. Indeed, Peter had heard both matters discussed with more emotion and enthusiasm.

He tried again. "You really should understand that Violet—"

This time Masters answered with a tightness to his voice that betrayed at least the beginnings of emotion. "I will repeat. I do not intend to discuss Violet and her lovers. The story is already halfway around London that she sat at dinner with Foxworthy's hand, not to mention his mouth, down her bodice and didn't blink once. If anything, she smiled. I hardly think this is fitting conversation. It has nothing to do with me. Now, do you truly wish to discuss Isabella, or must I ask you to leave?"

Peter debated insisting. Masters had driven Violet to the extreme. It was maddening that he'd refuse to discuss it. Peter forced his thoughts to Isabella. Violet needed him to think of Isabella. Masters might deny his part in the whole matter, but it didn't change the outcome. Foxworthy had to be removed from the picture. "I've come to request your younger sister's hand in matrimony."

"Isabella's?" Masters jaw tightened and he turned to meet Peter's gaze.

"Yes."

"But I thought— Well, it doesn't matter what I thought." Masters shook his head as if to clear it and then gestured Peter to a seat. It was clear that Foxworthy had not yet visited Masters again. Masters would not entertain Peter's suit if Foxworthy had already called.

Masters continued, "That is interesting. I was not aware you were of close acquaintance with Isabella. I assume Violet introduced you."

If Masters wanted this played by the rules, Peter could manage that. He bit back all the words he wanted to say and answered, "No, I was first introduced to her by Lady Smythe-Burke. Then we became further acquainted at Summerton's. I am surprised you were not aware of our meetings there. I may even admit that matrimony entered my mind in regards to your sister on several occasions during the party."

"I was otherwise occupied during Summerton's party. I must confess there have been some recent difficulties with Isabella. I might well welcome your interest. I would, however, need to be assured that you could take care of her properly and that there would be no difficulties with Violet. There have been other offers and they were not as they first appeared."

No difficulties with Violet. Peter wanted to swing hard at Masters's emotionless face. It was hard to believe any man could be as frozen as he appeared. "Foxworthy, again. Yes, I understand that you have run into a few slight difficulties there—difficulties that perhaps I can help you with."

It was Masters's turn to blink in confusion. "How? Ah, Foxworthy told Violet. Bloody mess, interfering female." He caught Peter's glance, "Let us get down to the practicalities of the current manner—your marriage to Isabella. Tell me of your estates, trusts, any reason that I should believe you can adequately support my sister in the manner to which she has become accustomed and dreams of expanding upon. I have always been concerned for my sister's comfort in matrimony."

Peter had known from Violet that money was the core of the issue, but still he was shocked at how quickly Masters moved the conversation to the subject. The man darted away from any mention of Violet and right on to finance. Peter would have stood up and stormed out if his goal has simply been matrimony.

He looked around the dark room. Sunlight poured through the window, and still the room felt cavernous. It was, however, in good repair and the finishings were of the highest quality. Masters was not in the poorhouse. He forced himself to speak politely. "I can assure you that I am of more than adequate means."

"Forgive me, but I've learned to be cautious in such matters. I'll need to see accounts, but a personal description will do for the moment." Masters sat opposite Peter.

"I'll have my man visit yours—call the solicitors in. Do the whole thing properly." Peter resisted the urge to roam. He would stay calm and collected, not give Masters any clue how important he found the outcome of the meeting.

"That will be fine for later," Masters continued. "For now I would like to hear from you. I believe a man should know his own worth, the condition of any estates, how much he pays his tailor each month. Do you?" Masters's glance moved over Peter and he felt stripped to his breeches. He could almost see Masters cataloguing each item, before moving on to the next— and not just the clothing, it felt that every part of him was being given a price and the total added up.

Peter fought to keep his voice calm. "I've most often resided with my brother, Lord Wimberley. I did this for convenience, not economy. I do maintain separate apartments, but rarely use them. I also own three rural properties, one a few miles from my brother's home, Glynewolde; one in Devonshire, which has quite a lovely house and turns a tidy profit; and some land on the Scottish border. I would confess I have never been to the last and have little intention of ever visiting. It was an inheritance from a great-aunt I was unaware I had."

"I don't approve of not visiting your estates. How can you be assured they are run well?" Disapproval dripped from Masters despite his flat tone.

Peter matched his tone to Masters's. "I am quite capable of hiring a more than adequate estate agent. All my properties turn at least some profit. I have overseen the books of all and the personal management of the first two. Do you have further questions? Or can I send my man to yours?"

"Oh, I definitely have further questions," Masters replied before beginning on a list of questions that left Peter's blood rising. It seemed there was not a detail of his life that Masters was not prepared to explore. Every crevice, every secret was Masters's to examine. And each question brought Peter closer to the edge—he was not sure how much he would put up with even for Violet. Violet. He bit his tongue and continued to answer. He was not prepared to discuss his past mistresses.

Finally he could be silent no longer. "Did you question Violet's husbands like this? I can't believe another man would have answered any of these questions."

Masters paused and looked up. "I didn't ask Dratton. It didn't occur to me that I could. With Milber I asked and should have checked his answers more scrupulously."

"And Foxworthy?"

"Foxworthy does not concern you. Now, how many chickens do you own?" Masters pulled out his tally.

Peter turned to the window and began to answer again. No, to the best of his knowledge he had never gotten a maid or member of his staff with child. He did not care for politics—left that to his brother—

That caught Masters's attention. "Ah, Wimberley. I was forgetting that opinion seems to have changed greatly about him over the last year—from foolish rakehell to master of intrigue. I am sure there is quite a story there. Why don't you tell it? Is he still a spy?"

That was a step too far. He'd had enough. He might be willing, if forced, to explain himself, but he was not going to give Masters the details of his entire family. "My brother was never a spy. I don't think he need be involved in this."

"But he is. Do you think the proud mamas who have considered you for their daughters do not look at your brother's title and speculate? It may be coldhearted to debate how many deaths stand between you and the title, but I assure you it has often been discussed."

Peter curled his fingers into the edge of the chair. "The answer is two. My brother is in perfect health and has become father to a son. If a title is necessary, I am afraid that I am sorely lacking beyond the honorary one.

"Foxworthy did not have a title," Peter continued.

"No, Foxworthy did not have a title. He had other attractions."

"What attractions? I know there was more to his offer than money." There, it was out in the open.

Masters paused and gave Peter a long, penetrating look. "Do you truly desire my sister? This is not merely a passing fancy?"

Peter avoided thinking of which sister he desired. He answered the only way he could. "I am proposing to marry her."

"That means something, but not everything. I am sure you know of many marriages that are based on anything but emotion."

"Such as the one you proposed with Foxworthy?"

Masters pursed his lips. "Exactly. If we are being frank, I do think he would have made Isabella an adequate husband. He might not be the man she dreamed of, but he would have cared for her needs and kept her safe. She needs a calming influence in her life. But, yes, there were other matters involved."

"Matters that you expect me to take over." Peter leaned back in the chair, his own lips tight.

Masters came and sat across from him. "That is actually the difficulty. While I am sure you are looking forward to rewarding me for the delight I will bestow upon you, there are other matters you cannot help with. I have, however, heard things about your brother, Wimberley, that imply that he might be of service."

"Political things." It was the only possibility.

"Yes, political things." Masters leaned back, duplicating Peter's posture. "Do you think that Wimberley, once we became family, would feel an onus to help his newly acquired brother out?"

Peter wasn't sure that Wimberley felt an onus to do anything. He might occasionally dabble in political matters, but Peter had always felt he did it strictly for his own amusement. "Wimberley is at Glynewolde celebrating the birth of his son. It will be several weeks before he returns."

A faint smile formed on Masters's mouth, the first that Peter had seen. "Ah, you are good at not answering. Still, it will have to do. I can't imagine that Wimberley will want a disgrace in the family. He will keep things from going too far. It's not as if I have much choice."

Peter had to lean forward to catch the last part.

Masters looked directly at him. "Well, I imagine that you are eager to be on with the rest of it. Give me the name of your agent and I'll have the documents drawn up. It may be necessary to await your brother's return to Town. Foxworthy must be dealt with before any of this can be made final."

Peter nodded and stood. "Then perhaps you should

send for Isabella. We must discover her feelings on this sudden turn of events."

"Surely there is no need to speak to her today," Masters began. "I imagine that you will want all the papers signed first."

"I would like her answer to the matter before we proceed. I do not want an unwilling wife. I must know that this is her wish."

Masters pushed to his feet and moved to the door. "In most instances I would demand you wait, but your background does grant you certain leeway. I am sure that once promises are spoken you would never dream of breaking them. Am I wrong?"

"No." That was the crux of the matter. Once he had spoken to Isabella he would hold true to his word—no matter what.

Masters paused at the door. "Do you have reason to think she'll refuse you? If that is why you are impatient, I can assure you she will not." Masters opened the door and stepped into the hall. The transaction was complete.

Transaction. He was thinking of it as a transaction. Peter felt like he'd taken a quick blow to his stomach. This was not what his marriage was supposed to be. It went against everything he'd ever believed, imagined.

Masters paused on the other side of the door. "I'll have Isabella summoned. Would you like to do it here or in the garden?"

"Send her here." Peter turned away and walked to the window to wait. He felt chilled despite the bright sun pouring into the room.

He could do this. He would do this—for Violet.

It might seem reckless, but this was the one way he could protect her. He would save her, no matter the cost.

There was a rustle at the door. He turned. Isabella had replaced Masters. She stood still, staring at him with serious eyes, but with a slight lifting at the corner of her mouth. She walked into the room, letting the door shut behind her. Had her brother told her the purpose of his visit? She looked about the room as if to choose a seat. Was it his imagination or was she trying to choose one that would give him room to drop to his knees before her?

A large wing chair in the far corner was her choice. She sat down graciously, adopting the stiff posture that Violet favored. She did not giggle or titter. She watched as he walked toward her, measuring each stride he took.

He stopped a few feet before her. Her hair shone far brighter than her sister's. It was much lighter in color and lacked the curls that gave such life to Violet's. She had the barest sprinkling of freckles upon her nose, surprising given that her skin looked as if it had never seen the sun.

Violet loved to loose her bonnet. A warm golden glow colored her all summer long. Isabella's complexion looked as if it could be January, the sun shrouded for months.

Her figure was slighter than her sister's. He doubted that she ever sat for hours over dinner sampling and savoring each delight in life. In fact, Isabella didn't look as if she savored much. She looked so solemn and thoughtful as she sat there awaiting his question. A library seemed the proper place for her. He wondered if she was as studious as she appeared.

He hadn't thought so at Summerton's. He'd thought her one more girl among many—perhaps more amusing than the rest, but not significantly different in any way. Except that she was Violet's sister.

Violet. Isabella.

Could he really love one and marry the other?

His plan didn't seem so brilliant as he looked down at Isabella's quiet face. He couldn't imagine kissing her, much less anything else.

"Are you ever going to speak or will you just keep staring at me? You were not so forward when last we spoke," Isabella said, breaking the silence. "I can assure you I am unchanged since last we met."

"Actually, you have changed," he answered.

"Nonsense. Now, did you have something you wanted to say?" The smile was threatening to overcome her stiff lips.

He should have remembered the girl who placed his hand on her breast, the girl who kicked him in the shins trying to escape from behind a curtain to her own ruination. He was all too aware that each word he spoke fastened the shackles tighter about him.

"Are you asking me to hurry?"

"I'd rather be done before my brother returns. He will not leave us alone for long. I do want this to be done properly." She gestured to the space in front of him.

Damnation, he'd been right. She wanted him to kneel.

After the cold interview with her brother it was too much. He almost turned away—almost. He had to remember why he was doing this—he would set Violet free.

He looked at Isabella again. She remained stiff despite the curve of her lips, not at all the look of a girl about to receive a proposal. Maybe they could discuss this sensibly, plan how it would work. No, he had promised to love and care for Isabella. From the moment of his proposal he must convince her that this was what he wanted. He must make this be what he wanted.

He bent down to one knee. "Will you, Miss Isabella Masters, do the honor of agreeing to become my wife?"

"Yes." The smile that finally escaped to fill her face was radiant. Her whole demeanor changed in a moment, relaxed but brimming with happiness. Peter could see in her what must inspire Violet's devotion.

"You have filled me with joy," Isabella continued. "I was scared you didn't really like me. Lady Smythe-Burke said you claimed affection, but it seemed so unlikely. I've been so scared that—Oh, none of that matters now—please, kiss me and make it real." She leaned forward, lips parted, eyes wide open.

The house was just as imposing as ever, tall, thin, dark—it seemed to overpower the more delicate abodes surrounding it. She had lived there for a few months before her marriage to Dratton. The house had seemed incredibly grand, then. It had been her only trip to London and she'd been busy planning how perfect life would be once she was a married lady, one who would take London by storm.

She stepped onto the path to the house. The plantings were neat, but unassuming—carefully manicured greens, so different from the bright colors and scents surrounding her own home.

The door was a neatly painted red, the knocker polished to a high gleam. She lifted it once and let it fall.

The door opened.

"I'd like to see my brother please, Jones." It was the same porter who had served all those years ago. Masters never liked change. She stepped forward, giving the startled man no choice but to grant her entry.

She waited while Jones went off to find her brother, then followed. She would not give Masters the chance to refuse her, if she was going to risk the dragon in his lair, then by God she was going to have the chance to fight.

She halted at the library door. Jones had passed the room by, but she knew what the closed door meant. Masters was inside. Jones probably had instructions not to admit her and was simply putting on a good show. She must have been right about her brother all along.

She filled her chest with air and turned the handle, swinging the door open with vigor. She was strong. She could face her brother, face anything.

Telling her brother what her life had been like should not be too difficult. Then she would beg him to tell her the truth behind Isabella's engagement to Foxworthy. There was something not right in what Foxworthy had told her. Maybe for once she and Masters could work together to find a solution.

Yes, she could face anything. She pushed the door wide.

She could not face this.

If Medusa had stood before her she could not have turned to stone with more surety.

Peter was kissing Isabella, perhaps not with the enthusiasm to which Violet was accustomed, but kissing Isabella all the same. As Violet watched, her sister wrapped both arms around his neck and drew him closer, slender fingers threading through his dark curls.

She wanted to breathe, wanted to release the air that filled her lungs, but stones did not breathe. All she could do was watch Peter, strangely posed on one knee, while her sister, the sister she had given her all to protect, pressed herself toward him like a limpet to a rock. As she watched, he raised his arms and placed them around Isabella.

Finally, life returned to her feet as she stepped back—right into a firm male chest.

"What are you doing here?" Masters asked, his tone flat and unemotional.

She couldn't find the words to answer.

"Do you want to wish your sister well on her upcoming nuptials?"

Violet couldn't form another thought. She needed to be gone. She glanced back at the couple. Peter was turning toward her. Horror shone on his face. It only made things worse.

Peter heard Masters's voice. He twisted his head around, his heart plummeting into his boots as he saw Violet standing there stiff and proud. He'd known she was there even before he saw her. He pried Isabella's fingers from his hair and moved her aside just in time to see the skirts of Violet's dress disappear behind the bend as she fled.

He started up after her, only to find himself sandwiched between Isabella and Masters. Neither one looked ready to let him leave. Looking as expression-less as ever, Masters stood in the door barring his way.

It would have proved a simple matter to push him aside, but Peter held back. This maturity was not an easy business.

"Why are you running off? Did I do something wrong?" Isabella's tone rang with hurt innocence—genuine, if he was not mistaken. He turned to look at her.

Questioning hazel eyes filled her face. A new fiancé was not supposed to break away in the middle of a kiss. He should still be learning her lips, not dashing from her arms. She placed a soft hand on his sleeve.

He wanted to run off to Violet to tell her—to tell her what? He couldn't very well tell her she hadn't seen what she'd seen or that she'd misunderstood it.

She hadn't.

He was betrothed to her sister.

He had been kissing Isabella with passion, or at least trying to.

He could tell her that he had not enjoyed the kiss, that his body did not respond as it had with hers, that he would much rather be in her bed, in her arms. Some-how, he doubted any of that would help.

She had told him it was foolish for him to marry Isabella, that she did not wish to trap either him or her sister in a loveless marriage. He began to wonder if she had been right.

The prospect of years of thought-out kisses was hard to imagine. Would he ever manage to lose himself in passion with Isabella as he had with Violet? It seemed impossible.

No, he would endure, and even if he faked passion he would be sure that Isabella never knew.

She pulled lightly at his sleeve, and he realized how long he'd stood without speaking. "I am sorry, my dear. I was surprised by the interruption and reacted badly. These matters are difficult for a man."

"Oh, of course." Isabella smiled patiently, but she looked unsure.

Peter turned to Masters. "Was that your other sister I saw in the hall? She left quickly."

"Yes, she did," Masters answered. "She came to speak to me and then she wished to congratulate the two of you. Unfortunately, she remembered a forgotten engagement and needed to leave. I am sure she'll return later with well wishes."

Peter was not so sure. He could only nod.

"We should celebrate. Might we have champagne, Masters?" Isabella had recovered from her momentary lapse and shone with high spirits.

Masters looked down at his sister, his expression unreadable. "If you wish, dear sister."

"Doesn't that sound wonderful?" She smiled up at Peter.

His stomach sank. How could he celebrate when

he felt closer to tears than he'd been since leaving the schoolroom behind? He put on his best smile. "I am afraid that you've reminded me I also have an appointment. I wasn't expecting everything to move with such speed this morning." He watched her lips begin to quiver. "Of course, nothing would please me more than to spend the afternoon delighting in my good fortune. A man has arrangements to make if he's to take a wife."

"But where are you going? You should take me with you. It is not proper for us to be parted now. You must stay." Isabella's voice shook.

"I am afraid I really must go—alone." He moved toward the door.

Isabella caught at his shirtsleeve. "Where are you going? Is it a secret?"

"I am sorry, my dear, but I must be off. I'll explain later."

He nodded to Masters, kissed Isabella's hand, and made it through the door. He almost stumbled on the steps. The whole world seemed to sway before him; it had become a most unsteady place.

He wondered how many measures of whiskey it would take to steady things up.

Chapter 17

The back garden looked as beautiful Violet had ever seen it. The roses were at the peak of bloom, full, lush, heady. Simply breathing was enough to transport her away, away to someplace magical. A place where wishes came true, families loved each other, and hearts never cracked.

At least it was a nice thought. It wasn't quite working that way, but Violet kept trying. She leaned her head back against the trellis, uncaring of the thorns that pulled at her hair and stared up through multicolored blossoms. The gardeners had done amazing things. Several different bushes grew together along the trellis, each gifting a different color, a different scent.

If anyplace on this earth could have brought her peace and safety, this would have been it. She inhaled again, hoping for the magic of her fantasies. She was home. She was safe.

It made her even more melancholy. She'd been

happier married to an eighty-two-year-old man she'd wed for his fortune than she was now. Than she ever expected to be again.

Emotion trickled back into her. Closing her eyes, she fought against the image of Peter wrapped in Isabella's embrace. The image only grew brighter.

Bah. She opened her eyes and sat forward, letting the tangled thorns pull her hair from its pins. Self-pity would not be allowed.

She was back to choices.

She pushed all thought of the last hour from her mind.

She could decide to sit here and mourn something that could never have been or she could take action.

Only what action?

Peter was marrying Isabella. There was nothing she could do about that.

Running from the house had been the coward's way out. She should have stayed and congratulated them. If only it had not been so unexpected, so painful.

She leaned back again, tilting her face up to the sun, wishing the warm light would wash away her troubles. The scent of the flowers was overpowering, maybe the scent would force her to faint and she could lie asleep while the world went on around her.

Her lips curled at the thought.

She drew in one more breath. No fainting, not even a little light-headedness. Pushing up, she looked again at the perfection of her garden, and prepared to return to the house.

"I thought I'd find you here." Peter's voice called from the back corner of the garden—the gardener's entrance from the mews.

"I am not receiving," she answered, trying to school her features into nonchalance.

"That's why I didn't come to the door. I'd hate to embarrass your servants by refusing to leave. They still haven't quite figured out what to make of me." He walked toward her. He smiled, but his eyes did not.

"You should not have come. Thank you for the reminder. I'll make sure that the staff knows exactly how to treat you should you ever try my door again."

"So hospitable."

She turned to face him fully. "You proposed to Isabella. You could not listen to my advice?"

"I listened, but decided that for once you needed to be taken care of. I wanted to help you." He stopped only a few inches from her, blocking the sunlight. On any other day this would have led to kisses and grass stains.

"It does not help me at all." She turned from him.

"You don't have to trade yourself to Foxworthy now," he said, reaching for her.

"Perhaps—perhaps not. I have not had the chance to consider the whole situation. What matters now is that you have affianced yourself to Isabella."

"And you have difficulties with that?" There was a belligerent note to his voice.

She turned to stare at him. "Difficulties? I know you are not an idiot. Do you truly not understand what a mess you have created?"

"I understand completely the price I will pay and the one your sister may pay. It is my choice. You always speak of choices—well, this is mine. If the only way I can grant you freedom is to marry your sister then that is what I will do."

"So you purchase my freedom with yours and my sister's? I never wanted that. And I am not even sure it will work. Who knows what Foxworthy will do now? Through my own actions I may have made him even more determined. He could still be dangerous."

"Then don't you think it's time you tell me the whole story in detail?" Peter reached out and snapped a full-blown rose from the stem. He looked like he wanted to crush it in his palm.

"God, it seems a little late for that now. Perhaps you should have waited to find out everything before taking action." Violet edged slowly back to her bench. "I've already told you that Foxworthy holds more than money over my brother. Foxworthy claims Masters has invested unwisely—some might even say traitorously. I am not sure the extent of the treachery—although I do believe my brother unknowing. He is a cold fish, but not a traitor. Foxworthy mentioned a noose, but I doubt it would come to that. Masters is too highly placed and there are many who do not want their finances examined closely."

"Why is Foxworthy involved?" Peter plucked a petal and dropped in her lap. It stood like a bead of blood on the pale fabric of her skirts.

She caught the petal between her fingers, shredding it. A stain spread faint crimson across their tips. "I don't know how, but he has proof of the transactions—whether he laid a trap or was merely lucky I am unsure."

"I thought you did not care for your brother—and after our encounter this afternoon I daresay I understand. Why would you try to protect him?" Peter dropped another petal, his large hands pulling it from the stem with utmost delicacy.

She remembered an early fascination with his hands—so large and capable. They looked like they should be holding a cavalry saber but they could perform the most intricate of tasks with ease and gentleness.

She loved his hands.

She left this petal to lie. "I am surprised to find I do actually care, but that was not the reason. I do it for Isabella. Masters would have sold her to protect himself, and even if he did not, his good name is her good name—to ruin one is to destroy the other. And now"—she smiled bitterly—"now I may have made everything worse in trying to protect Isabella. If Foxworthy decides to attack it is my duty to protect you all. It would not do for the Marquess of Wimberley's younger brother to be wedded to treason. Can you imagine the gossip? The cartoons? You'd probably fill a window at the barber."

Peter answered forcefully, "So again you chose for us all—the willing martyr. Does it matter that I would willingly give up my reputation and position—should it come to that—for you? And your brother is capable of paying for his own mistakes. I think he may even have his own plans." He dropped two petals.

"And what of Isabella? In asking for her hand you have taken responsibility for her. You do not decide simply for yourself, you decide for her. What has she done to deserve to be linked to treason? Where is her choice?"

"I think your sister is more capable then you credit her," he said.

"How can you say that? She is but a girl."

"She may be young." He ripped the remaining flowers from the bloom with one hard pull. "She may be innocent. But she is not naïve. If you would only stop and listen to yourself I think you would see this is not the disaster you paint it. I think you would be surprised by Isabella's strength of will and her ability to plan her own life."

Violet spread her skirts and waited for the petals to fall. "I don't want her to have to be strong."

He looked down upon her steadily. "As you were once forced to be strong." He let the petals flow down like rain. "But that is part of maturing. Do you not want her to grow?"

"Yes, but at her own pace." She stared down at her lap full of the crimson petals. In other circumstances romance could have blossomed in the pile—now all she saw was their stain.

"Do any of us grow at our own pace?" He pushed aside her answer. "Was I ready when my father died? I was still in my teens. Was my mother ready? Were any of our young men who went off to fight the French ready? I don't believe you've thought this out calmly. Is this about your sister or what was done to you?"

Violet tried to ignore the latter half of the question. "So you think I should have left her to Foxworthy? Is that what you think?" She shook her skirts, and the petals settled on the white gravel about their feet.

"No, but you didn't have to handle it alone. Do you think I wouldn't have helped? Haven't I shown by now that I would do anything for you?" He stared down at the remains of the rose.

"Yes, I know you would have helped. I understand now what you would do for me." It tore at her heart how deeply she now understood. "But what could you have done?"

"I could have beaten the bloody man to a pulp, killed him if necessary. Oh, I see in your eyes that is not the answer you want, but I promise that if he survived he would have thought twice about threatening mine again. And as for the rest, what of my brother? I think Foxworthy would think twice before interfering with the family of a marquess—and that would have held just as true had I married you."

She paused at his words. She could feel their truth—but wanted to ignore it. With all that she had suffered it could not have been so simple. "I am not your brother's problem. And it might be that Foxworthy would use this as a chance to gain power over him too."

"Do you think so little of him, of yourself? Wimberley is more than able to care for himself, and my brother cares for you, as does his wife. And they want my happiness. You are that happiness. Why can you not let us help?"

"I've never depended on anyone for help. I have always been enough." She had to look away from him.

Peter suddenly sat on the bench beside her. She had not seen the move coming and so had no defense against it. She tried to move aside, but he sat on her skirts, trapping her, thigh to thigh.

He reached over and lifted her red-stained fingers to his lips. "Do you know I've finally realized the problem? You work so hard to be strong. In fact, you are stronger than any woman I've known. But deep inside you are still a dreamer. You spoke of how hard it was when you were married to Dratton, about how the part of you that believed in enchantment disappeared or died. It didn't. It is still there at the core of you."

He kissed the tips of her fingers with the softness of a butterfly's wing.

She should pull her hand away. She could not bear the tenderness of his touch. They had already said their good-byes. None of this could matter now. She traced her finger along his lips. "You are wrong."

"No, I don't think I am." He kissed her fingers again. "You've focused your dreams on others for the most part, on your sister, on me. That is why you can't bear for us not to have perfect lives. You want us to live your dreams."

She bowed her head and did not look at him.

"But look at you," he continued. "What did you say you wanted when you were a girl—a sun-filled enchanted kingdom? Look at this magical home you have created. I've never felt as contented as I have here. The cushions are soft, the linens fresh, the air always smells like lemons, or flowers, or biscuits, or something far different than the streets outside. Your servants smile, yet keep every speck of dust at bay. Your cook always has the perfect dish to set upon the table and she whistles while she does it. You have taken a dream and made it a reality."

Could he be right? She'd come to realize how clearly he saw her, could this also be true? "I just like things to be comfortable."

"You've taken comfort and made it an art." He smiled down at her. "The only problem is you still dream of being the woman who takes London by storm. Perhaps that is why you chose to live the slightly scandalous life you did after Carrington's death. You wanted the attention one way if not the other."

"You could be right. I have never thought of it."

"I will ask you then, Violet," he said. "Do you still wish to move into that inner circle of high society? Is that what you dream?"

She drew in a deep breath and felt the question fill her. "No, it is not what I want any longer. I am happy with the friends I have, the world I have built."

She stood suddenly, yanking her skirts from beneath him, treading over the fallen petals. Her skirts spun about her as she turned and began to pace. "For a moment I became so caught up in your words that I forgot Isabella. Maybe you were right. Maybe between you and Wimberley you can take care of Foxworthy. I would never have asked, but you are correct that it might be possible. But there is still the folly of your engagement. Whatever else happens, you are now bound to my sister."

Peter lost his smile. She could see his mind spinning with thoughts, but it did not matter. They were still trapped.

She walked away from him, over to a small, carefully kept pool of golden fish, a gift from her first lover.

Oranges and reds swirled about in the dark water, graceful and glistening. Did they know of their captivity or did they think the small, deep pool the world?

Was it better to know? Would she have been better if Peter had never come into her life and she had never smiled back at him?

"I can call it off. If it is known there will be a scandal and I will never be welcome in the inner circles of society, but we can be together, build our own circle." He spoke cautiously.

"Could you really do that? Having given your word, could you take it back? I have never known you to break a promise." The fish swarmed at her feet, eager for food. She stepped back, not wanting to tempt them with treats that were not to be.

She felt him come up behind her. The heavy safety of his presence surrounded her without so much as touch.

"I might," he whispered into her hair. "For you I think I would sell my soul."

She closed her eyes and dreamed. He was right. The dreamer did still live, but she had learned to make do with reality. She opened her eyes again and turned to face him.

"I cannot ask that of you. I know what your honor means to you, and there is still Isabella. There is a chance that no one will find out, but what if she has already told her friends, if Masters has consulted his lawyers? You speak of what the scandal will do to you, but what of her? People will always wonder and whisper at what she did that caused you to commit such an act. No one will want her."

"The fact that I love her sister beyond all reason will not be seen as reason enough?" Even as he spoke the words she could see the knowledge of what must be simmering in his eyes.

"I am not the only dreamer." She held out her hands to him. "Come and give me one last kiss. We will stay in this dream for but a moment more. Come and give me a lifetime of comfort and strength in a single instant."

He inched forward, but still made no move to touch her. "Tell me, Violet, promise me and mean it. Promise me that you will not go back to Foxworthy. Leave me to deal with it. Let me do this one last thing."

She could not make her mouth form the words.

"Will that make you promise?" he persisted.

"Will you promise to never let my sister know of us? To always keep Isabella first in your thoughts?"

"My thoughts, but not my heart. I cannot change my feelings, Violet. I do not know that I would if I could, but I cannot."

"God, what a mess." She leaned forward and rested her cheek against his chest. The sun had warmed his shirt, and the scent of spice and musk wafted from it. Not even all the flowers in the garden together smelled so good, filled her soul in such a manner. "I wish that I could want you to change your heart, but I am greedy. If my heart must ache, I want yours to also."

He bent his neck and placed a light kiss upon her temple. "What are you saying, Violet?"

"I am saying that I love you, you fool. Now that it is too late and nothing can come of it, I am saying that I love you." She tilted her face up to his.

Peter watched Violet's eyes sink closed as she waited for his kiss. She loved him. His heart cried joyously. He knew he should feel despair. The situation was hopeless, but he could only bask in the wonder of the moment.

Violet had never looked more beautiful to him. The sun had brought out the peaches in her complexion. She looked ripe and ready for a bite. Instead he laid his lips upon hers with utmost gentleness. If this was to be their last kiss as lovers, he would make it linger. He didn't press at all as he enjoyed the sensation of her satin skin so soft against his own. She pursed her lips, bringing them tighter against his. He was so caught in sensation that he could feel each muscle tighten and pucker. With only a puff of sound he completed the kiss and drew back.

He stared down into her eyes, deep purple and filled with passion. He kissed her again. Lightly. Sweetly.

"Is this how friends kiss?" he asked.

"I don't normally kiss my friends," she answered.

"We'll have to do something about that." He pulled her back into his arms. This time it was not gentle. He brought his lips down fiercely. He would have devoured her if he could.

She met him, opened for him. Her hunger was apparent in her every move, every touch, every stroke. Her hands slid around him, slipping under his jacket to caress him through the soft linen of his shirt. A trail of liquid fire followed her touch.

The desire to take her here, to push up her skirts, and let passion win fought through him. She would not resist. He could sense that for this one last time she was his to do with what he would.

One last time.

He pushed away. "We can't do this."

She stared back at him, her eyes filled with suppressed desire. He watched as reason slowly returned to her.

"Isabella." She said the single word, and it lay like a blade between them.

He turned away, stepping toward the wall of climbing roses. He needed to put space between them. He was surrounded by beauty, but filled with blackness.

The sound of a door slamming echoed through the garden, startling him from his melancholy. He glanced back toward the mews. "I must not have closed it properly. The breeze has picked up."

He stepped toward the trellis and sought the most perfect bloom he could find among the flowers dancing in the wind. Not too red. Not too pink.

None seemed to fit.

He heard her moving behind him, but refused to look. He focused solely on the flowers. Maybe a yellow one? Yellow symbolized friendship. And that is what they were to be: friends.

Yellow did not suit her.

White was too bland.

He moved back to pink. Romantic love. Could they manage the love that would always be there while avoiding the downfalls of the passion that could no longer be?

He could feel her breath on the back of his neck. The air was warm. The breeze steady. And still he could feel her, know how close she stood.

He reached up and plucked a deep coral rose from high on the bush, the petals edged in a color so deep it was almost fuchsia. Friendship, love, and passion. They could not be separated.

He stepped to the side, away from her, and turned to hold out the blossom. "We can't do this," he whispered, wanting to yell.

"You just said that," she answered, stepping toward him again. The flower remained in his outstretched hand as she stared at it, then at him.

"No—I mean, yes, I did, but I meant something else.

I mean you were right in the beginning. I cannot marry Isabella. How can we deny what is between us?"

This time she stepped away. "We will not ruin my sister's life."

He returned to the bench and sat, stretching his legs before him. "It is I, not we. It is I who would cry off. You don't really have a say in the matter."

She opened her mouth, and he could hear the anger of her reply before she even spoke a word.

"I only"—he cut her off as the first sound left her lips—"want you to realize that basic truth. For once it is not your decision. However, having said that, I realize that we must decide a future plan together. It is not my purpose to make us all miserable."

She stepped farther away. He could feel the invisible wall forming between them.

She pursed her lips. "Come into the house. Let us sit in the parlor—with the door wide open—and discuss this like reasonable adults." She turned, her skirts spinning out around her, and walked up the pebbled path toward the house. Red rose petals scattered in the breeze as she walked by.

Judging by the pace and the sway of her hips, he wasn't sure how reasonable she intended to be—unless reasonable was defined as "doing things the way she wanted."

He looked down at the bloom he had selected, cupping his hand around it. Was it really too much to want it all? He didn't see that giving up even a single piece would make any of them happy.

Not even Isabella.

He leaned back against the trellis. He would give her a few moments, let his suggestion wrap around her—entangle her in its possibilities.

Finally, when he could wait no longer, he stood and turned to place the flower on the bench. No. He twirled the stem between his fingers as he checked the garden gate to make sure it had latched properly. Violet would not want any unwelcome visitors.

Violet walked into the house, resisting the urge to stomp. He had gotten them into this mess—well, that was not strictly fair, but she needed it to be. She needed to be angry if she was to get through this.

How dare he say they couldn't do it? What choice did they have?

Choice.

She lived her life seeking choices and now she never wanted to hear the word again. She didn't want to have to decide to do the right thing, the hard thing. Why couldn't somebody else force the blasted issue?

Swinging wide the double doors that led into the parlor, she sailed into the room. She might have almost given in to passion in the garden, but that had been a momentary weakness. It would have been a betrayal of her sister.

From the moment Peter had asked for Isabella's hand, he had ceased to be hers. His motivation did not matter.

She paced about the room awaiting his arrival.

Why was he making her wait?

She paced more.

She was almost ready to seek him out when she heard his heavy footsteps following her. The room offered many possible locations for their discussion. She chose a spot on the window seat with care. She spread her skirts wide. It would not stop him from sitting next to her, he had proved that in the garden, but it did send him a message. The window seat had been designed for solitary pursuits. The nearest chair stood a good eight feet away.

She almost smiled when she saw his expression as he took in the situation.

He looked at the chair, looked at her. He placed the rose he still held on a side table. Then he picked up the chair and turned it, setting it down only a few feet from her hems. She should have known he was a man to rebuild the situation to meet his own needs.

He sat, setting his feet squarely in front of him. The air nearly quivered with the intensity of his expression. "We can't do this," he repeated.

"Then what would you have us do? What can we do that will not ruin Isabella's future?" She stared at the hands neatly folded in her lap. A viewer in the street outside would think she had no worries beyond choosing a pattern for embroidery.

"It is not even a few hours since I first put my proposition to your brother. He cannot have had time to make an announcement. In fact, I doubt he will do anything until he speaks to my man of business and is assured that all is as I have told him. We do not know whom Isabella has told. As of this moment only us few know of my proposal."

She looked up at him. "That is true."

"I would suggest I hurry back and prevent him from making any announcement. I can either tell him the whole thing is over or at least delay his announcement until I have a chance to speak with Isabella and see whom she had discussed the matter with. Then I will tell her the truth."

"The truth?" asked Violet. "I am trying to spare her feelings."

"For the most sensible of women you are being remarkably shortsighted. Do you truly think it is better for her to marry me? Do you think she will never notice the way we look at each other, the heat that springs up between us?"

"Then I will leave, go abroad." Her heart screamed for her to accept his plan, but she refused to believe it. It would make the whole matter too simple. The solution could not be so easy. "I was considering it as I sat in the garden before you arrived. I would rather leave than watch you and Isabella."

He leaned forward. "Then listen to me and think. Do you really wish your sister a husband who does not love her, cannot love her? I only propose that we give her the choice. I will explain the situation and give her the choice. Is that not what you believe, that people deserve choices? I have caused this tangle, let me straighten it."

Choices. It was that haunting word again, but this time fragile hope rose in her breast. This was not the situation she would have wished, but perhaps Peter was right. It could not be fair to Isabella to condemn her to loveless marriage without giving her the chance to seek more.

Or was that only her personal desires speaking? Was she truly seeking the best for her sister or only giving in to what she wanted? Violet leaned her head against the window, relaxing the rigid posture of her back. Each bone of her spine shifted, and she sighed with the relief it brought.

Blocking out Peter and the bright room, she closed her eyes and tried to focus on nothing but Isabella. Love brought no promise. Isabella could marry a man of her choosing and still end up miserable.

If Isabella married Peter, Violet knew he would do his best for her sister. He would never deliberately hurt Isabella or betray her—but what about inadvertently?

She imagined Peter and Isabella years from now surrounded by their children, happy and— She could not picture them happy. She could see contentment and pleasantness, but she could not imagine Peter smiling down at Isabella as he did at her. She tried harder, but the image would not come.

How hard would it be for Isabella to be told the truth? If it had been she, Violet would have wanted to know. It was hard to imagine being tied to a husband who loved another. And he did love her. It had taken time to accept that reality, but now that Violet had accepted it she could not turn back. "You love me."

"Yes," he answered.

"It is not lust or passing fancy. You love me." She said it calmly as if reciting the evening's menu to Cook.

"Forever."

She sat up and bent forward toward him. "Then you had best go. If Masters has made an announcement, all this is moot. If not, I will concede that Isabella deserves a chance to decide."

"I will be off then." He stood.

"Wait, there is one more factor. I will trust you can take care of Foxworthy, but should you fail, I will do whatever is necessary to make peace with Foxworthy. Whatever."

He stared down at her, his eyes fierce. "I understand; therefore, I will not fail. But you must understand I will do whatever I deem necessary to accomplish that. Whatever."

A challenge. Violet felt her breath quicken. If anything had been missing in their earlier relationship it had been this—challenge. She wondered if Peter realized that in always seeking her pleasure he had almost lost her.

That was one secret she would never share. He could figure it out on his own. A woman needed to hold on to some advantages.

She nodded her agreement.

Peter replaced his chair and walked to the open door.

He stopped, turned. "You do realize my words are not permission for you to visit Foxworthy now?"

She looked away from him. Stared at the fireplace, the window, a book on the table—anywhere but at him.

"Violet." He said her name firmly, with more command than she had ever heard in his voice. Something deep inside her shivered.

"Do you need me to actually promise?" She still did not look at him.

"Actually yes, I do. I will believe you if you promise."

She closed her eyes for the briefest of moments. "I promise I will not go to Foxworthy—not until I know more."

"And then?"

"I don't know."

He walked back to her and took her hands. "We are a team, Violet. Do not do anything alone. I will be there with you."

She shuddered slightly at his words. She had never needed protection, but now as it wrapped around her she wanted nothing more. "I will not do anything without letting you know. Is that enough?"

He ran a finger over her palm. "Letting me know before you act—that would be enough."

Tilting her face up at him, she smiled. "Go." She said a single word and realized she imagined a future, dreamed a future. The dreamer lived after all.

Chapter 18

"**W**here is she? I know she must be here." Masters burst into the room upsetting both a small table near the door and Violet's calm. She placed the book she'd been distracting herself with on the shelf and turned to him, her back straight.

She watched as his chin jutted out and he glared at her. It was a gesture she knew from her own mirror. They were more alike than she would ever have credited. "I don't know what you are talking about," she replied.

"Isabella. I know she was coming here." Masters yanked a piece of notepaper from his jacket pocket and waved it at her. His normal composure was as disturbed as his neckwear. Violet had never seen him in such disarray. He continued, "She said she was coming here as soon as she finished with Foxworthy. There was no answer at his door so she must be here."

"I truly don't know what you are talking about," she said quietly, resisting the urge to snap back at her brother.

He stalked over to her and glared down at her. He waved his papers in her face. "I know you are behind this. Every time I believe I have things running smoothly you interfere."

Violet took three deep breaths—it had been an incredibly emotional day—and moved to her previous place on the window seat. "Why don't you tell me what this is about? I do have plans for this evening."

"It's a note from your sister." Masters waved the note in Violet's face again.

"I am sure it is not the first note you have received from Isabella. What is so special about this one?" Had Peter already spoken to Isabella? Surely there hadn't been time. It could not be twenty minutes since he left.

"As if you don't know."

Violet smiled up at her brother, pretending that her chest was not vibrating with emotion. "Actually, I don't. Why don't you take a seat and then you may explain to me calmly what this is all about. We have other things to talk of as well." She gestured at the seat set a good eight feet away.

Masters stalked over to the chair and sat, still glowering at her from halfway across the room.

"You must know about this. She visits you and Foxworthy and runs off. It must have been you. There is no other reason she would do such a thing." Masters waved his piece of paper in the air again.

"Why don't you tell me what that is, brother, and

then I can tell you if I know what you are talking about." She reached out her hand toward Masters.

Masters stared at her outstretched fingers, but in the end he rose. "It's a letter from your sister."

"So you've said," Violet answered, her hand still held out.

"It says that she isn't going to marry St. Johns and that you know why. She says she's not coming back. How could she not be coming back?" Masters handed the note to Violet. His voice wavered a little, and Violet wondered if his anger might be fueled by concern.

He returned to his chair.

Violet perused the note quickly, her heart speeding with each word she read until at last it felt ready to spring from her chest. Isabella was calling off the wedding, refusing to marry Peter. It seemed impossible. Isabella, for reasons of her own, found Peter unsuitable. Unsuitable! How could anybody not realize how perfect Peter was?

It was at that point that Violet's heart slowed.

Isabella was calling it off! Peter was free.

Violet went back to the note. There was not much more. Isabella finished by saying that she was leaving London forever and that Masters should speak to Violet if he had any questions. It ended with a command not to follow her. Violet closed her eyes and could hear Isabella saying the words as forcefully as she had proclaimed that Violet could not stop her from leaving.

What was going on?

If Peter had spoken to Isabella this would all make sense, but he hadn't. The timing was off.

Something was wrong, very wrong.

New worries formed in her chest. Isabella might sound strong, she might think she was strong, why, she might even be strong, but that didn't mean she should be traipsing about alone. She was in no way prepared to face the world on her own.

What was going on?

"How could you let her leave?" She turned the problem back on Masters.

"Let her leave? Since when have I let that girl do anything? This marriage to Foxworthy is the only thing she's even pretended to do that I want, and you know how that ended up. I hear in the clubs that the man is ready to have me strung up—even if he hasn't yet told the world why. You talked to him. Do you really think he has the power and the evidence to do that?"

So Masters's concern was not solely for Isabella. "I don't really know. He only ever told me the basest details about your dealings. I don't know how strong his evidence is, or how guilty you are. As for power—he doesn't have much of it, but he knows how to use what he has."

"You're so reassuring, sister. And I asked Foxworthy not to discuss his evidence with you. It is something that it would not help you to know."

"Shouldn't I make that decision?"

"I know you always think you know what's right, Violet, but it this case, no—there would be no purpose. It is my burden to bear.

"Only you don't bear it, do you? You let me bear it first, and then Isabella."

Masters ran a hand through his hair, mussing the smooth waves. "I know that's what you think, and frankly I doubt I could change your mind. I don't think you will ever believe I acted in your best interests."

"No, I don't suppose I will."

"Then there really isn't much to say now. I cannot change the past and I don't know that I would if I could. I did what I thought was best and what was necessary. I am sorry that it didn't meet your lofty standards."

A heavy wave of hair slipped forward over her eyes. She blew at it. "It is not my lofty standards that must concern us now, but whether Foxworthy has evidence of treason."

"Yes." It was only a solitary word, but it seemed that all the starch leaked out of him.

"You committed treason?" She could only state it as a question, not as a fact. It seemed unbelievable that the brother who had raised her could have done such a thing.

"He has evidence of treason and he will use it if he can, now that his desires have been thwarted. It is long past the time when money could contain him."

Violet pushed back the curls that were slipping forward on her face. She drew in a deep breath, ready to order her brother to go. She should leave him to fend for himself just as he had always left her. He'd brought it all on himself, and despite everything, it did seem unlikely that Foxworthy could really bring him up on treason. Wimberley would see to that. It was much more likely that it would make the gossip rounds and ruin Masters's social standing and position. That did not seem an unfair price for him to pay.

And Isabella—Isabella was gone.

Social standing and ruin seemed so trivial when she thought of her sister alone somewhere on the streets, taking a carriage by herself to God-knew-where.

Foxworthy would still need to be dealt with, but other concerns were much more pressing.

She took that deep breath and prepared to order Masters away.

"I've been to your brother's house and nobody is there. I even tried his club. They haven't seen him this day. I don't know where else to look." Peter walked into the room without knocking. He had a ready smile on his lips, but his eyes were troubled.

He stopped suddenly as his eyes lit on Masters. He turned to Violet with confusion in his eyes.

"Did you have questions about planning the wedding?" Masters's question caught Violet by surprise.

How quickly he'd gone from worry to trying to gloss over the entire situation.

"No, I was coming to—"

Violet cut Peter off. "She's cried off. That is one worry we no longer have."

"Cried off?" A flare of hope gleamed in Peter's eyes.

"Don't worry. We'll find the girl and bring her back and all the nonsense can be cleared up. Everything can go back to the way it was." Masters's voice rang with desperation.

"I would never dream of pushing a girl who didn't want me." Peter was close to grinning like a schoolboy, although his eyes still sought answers from Violet.

"What Masters is not saying," Violet interrupted, "is that Isabella has left a note saying she doesn't want to marry you, and has run off. It does not say where she is going. We must find her." She stretched out Isabella's note to Peter. "Did you talk to her? Is that why she has done this thing?"

Peter reached out and took the missive. His knuckles were grazed. She brushed her fingers over them.

"I am afraid I punched the wall when Masters was not at home. He grinned sheepishly, then scanned the note. His face tensed with comprehension. "No, I have not seen her. As for why—I don't know. Surely you don't blame yourself for what is probably a whim. Perhaps she simply realized we would not suit."

"Then why would she leave? I don't believe she would leave just because she decided not to marry you."

"You blame yourself. I hear it in your voice." Peter caught her hand and held it tight.

"No. Yes. I started to, but then I realized that I cannot control her choices. That doesn't mean I can't try to stop her, however. She is too young to know what she is doing. We must go after her."

"Do you know where she has gone? Does she have any contacts she might have prevailed upon?" Peter turned to Masters as he asked this last question.

"None that I know of. She has a friend, Annie Westers, but I've already inquired there, and I am convinced the girl knows nothing. It is why I came here. Her note clearly says you'll know why she left, Violet."

Violet turned to her brother. "I wish I did. I can't even imagine a reason she'd leave." As she spoke she turned and glanced at Peter for reassurance.

He smiled at her and came toward the window seat. She moved her skirts aside so that he could sit. He looked between her and Masters and then deliberately put an arm around her.

It was a moment of truth. Violet leaned into him.

She could see the muscles in Masters's neck tense as he prepared to blame this whole mess on her. She turned her face toward Peter. Her nose rubbed against the fine linen of his shirt. It smelled like him. Safety and comfort were in that smell. Normally things smelled like things, leather, musk, horses, smoke, but he smelled like safety and comfort.

It was an odd thought. Her mind must be delaying the moment that she would raise her head and confront her brother.

Sensing her movement, Peter placed a finger under her chin and raised her face up to meet his. He planted a soft kiss on her nose. "Nothing he can say can hurt us. We are together in this."

"I am not so confident." She spoke to him softly, ignoring Masters, who hung back stoically, completely. "It feels like my life is hung from a series of threads, and I don't hold the end to any of them."

"We will just have to wait and see. Life is about adventure as well as choices." He laid the softest of kisses against her forehead. "What matters is that we are together. We will find your sister and somehow work out this mess with Foxworthy."

Violet knew she shouldn't believe him. He made it all sound so easy, but surrounded by the soft smell of his shirt all things seemed possible. Together they could do this. For the first time today it seemed really possible that they could do this. Together. The knots that had formed in her belly began to loosen.

She raised her face and stared at her brother, awaiting his comment. He met her glance and said nothing.

He seemed to sink further into his seat. He turned and looked at Peter. "I don't suppose your brother, Wimberley, will still help me with our problems?"

Violet could feel Peter pull a deep breath into his chest before answering. "I'll make no promises, but I wouldn't want to see Violet or Isabella pulled into your mess. I will see what can be done. The St. Johnses protect their own. Foxworthy will be disarmed."

Masters seemed to deflate like a balloon at his words, the tension leaving his body. "I never meant it to turn out this way. You may not want to believe me, but I always wanted decent lives for my sisters—thought I was doing the best thing."

Violet's eyes met Peter's. She wanted to say something to Masters, to ask how he could ever have believed that marrying Milber and Dratton was best. Instead she continued to stare at Peter. If she had not lived the life she had, she might not have ended up where she was, and that would have been a shame.

She said nothing, and the three of them sat in silence for a moment. Then Violet turned to Masters. "What matters now is finding Isabella. Are you sure she didn't say anything when she gave you the note?"

"She didn't actually give it to me. She raced out of the house a few minutes after the two of you," Masters said. "She refused her maid, saying she needed a brisk walk in the park to clear her head. Getting engaged was apparently heady stuff. I tried to insist, but she was gone before I had a chance."

"She must have come back to write the note," Violet challenged.

"No, a boy brought it by about half an hour ago. He scampered off before I could question him. Evidently my reply was not required," Masters answered.

"Is the stationery her own?" Violet inquired.

"No, she uses some pink nonsense with a floral cutout edge. Quite atrocious."

Violet bowed her head to consider. Where would Isabella have gone? Did she know anybody in the country who might take her in? It seemed unlikely from what she knew of her sister's life.

"Foxworthy—you said something about her visiting Foxworthy before coming here." Her stomach tightened again. Did it always come back to Foxworthy?

Masters waved her comment off. "Yes, but that doesn't matter—there was no answer at his home. Not even a servant."

"That's strange," Peter said.

Violet glanced at him. "Yes, it is very strange." She turned back to her brother. "And how did you know that Isabella was going to visit Foxworthy?"

"It must say in the note."

"It doesn't."

Masters raked his finger through his hair. "I don't

know then—perhaps the boy said something. I just know that's what she was doing."

Violet's eyes met Peter's. They clearly had the same thought.

Peter spoke first. "Go back to your house and wait for Isabella." He addressed Masters. "I find it hard to believe Isabella won't return to fetch a bonnet or some such."

"But—"

Violet turned on her brother. "Just go. She might be there now. Peter and I will take care of the rest."

Masters looked up at her in confusion. "The rest?"

"Foxworthy." Violet and Peter spoke in unison.

The house was dark. It was the middle of the afternoon and Foxworthy's house stood still and empty. Peter glanced from house to house along the street, trying to decide what made this one different. It was too early for lights to show even if lit, and the sun reflected off the windows the same as any other home on the street.

Still, something was different.

"Won't he think it odd that we are here together?" Violet laid a hand on his sleeve. "Should I just go up to the door alone?"

"And having you call, alone, in the middle of the day would be less odd?" He turned and looked at her squarely, spoke firmly so there could be no doubt. "No, we go together."

Did she look relieved? She'd tilted up her chin defiantly, but deep in her eyes he saw something else. He placed a hand over hers.

Side by side they walked up the path to the stairs. Violet stepped aside as he knocked. There was no answer—not even the bustling sounds of servants.

He knocked again, harder. The door shivered. He glanced at Violet and then instead of knocking he pushed. The door swung open.

Still, there was no sound from inside.

Violet clutched his sleeve more tightly. She nodded toward the interior.

He stepped forward. The fall of his step echoed through the empty hall. The rustle of Violet's skirts followed behind.

"His study is this way. It seemed the most lived-in room of the house." Violet pulled him toward the back of the hall.

The door was halfway open. He pushed it the rest of the way.

Isabella stood there, not moving, a statue.

She didn't seem to even see them as they stepped through the door. Her gaze was fastened on the floor to their left.

Peter glanced over. Foxworthy.

The body lay sprawled across the rug, the head turned at an impossible angle. Even without the thin line of blood that marked the brow, it would have been impossible to miss what had occurred.

"He's dead." Isabella spoke without even a glance in their direction.

Violet stopped short next to him. She appeared almost as still as her sister, but he could feel the rapid beating of her heart.

Peter moved toward Isabella. She was right. Foxworthy was dead and needed no aid. Isabella, however, looked like she might topple at any moment.

Violet pulled a chair from behind the desk, and he maneuvered Isabella into it.

"Did you—" Violet started to speak.

Isabella cut her off. "I saw you in the garden."

"I don't understand," Violet tried again.

"You should have told me." Isabella's voice held no emotion.

"Told you what?"

Isabella didn't speak, but started to pick at her skirts. Her hands were smeared with blood. Each touch left a smudge on her skirt. She appeared not to notice.

Peter wrapped an arm around Violet, drawing her close. Worry seeped from her like a palpable thing. She reached out for her sister's hand, unmindful of the blood. "You still haven't said what I am supposed to have told you."

Isabella jerked away violently. There was a slight tear along her sleeve, the lace hung loose.

Violet stared at it in fascination. Peter could feel the questions she longed to ask but she held silent, waiting.

"I am not stupid, you know." Isabella's feet began to tap a nervous tattoo on the floor. "Although . . . maybe I am. It never even occurred to me."

"What never occurred to you?" Violet's voice was soft, comforting.

"That you and Lord Peter were attached, and that you would risk all that for me. I never really thought you cared."

"Of course I care. How could you even think such a thing?" Violet watched as her sister began to worry the fabric of her skirt again. She longed to ask Isabella what had happened, but Isabella was clearly lost in some world of her own.

"You rarely visited and almost never wrote." Isabella became still for a moment as she stared at her sister.

Words escaped Violet. It was true that she had always been a poor correspondent, and she had not visited frequently because she disliked feeling herself under her brother's thumb, even for a short time. She should have tried harder. "I have always loved you. You are my sister. I would have done anything for you."

"I know that now." Isabella looked at her strangely. "I always thought I was on my own. I thought when you didn't want to help me find a husband it was because you were too busy. Only Lady Smythe-Burke ever wanted to talk to me, and I always feared that she simply wanted somebody to talk to. I think anybody would have done. It didn't matter that it was me."

Violet stroked Isabella's hair. There was a long rip at the neckline of Isabella's gown. She hadn't noticed it before.

Peter drew a breath in. He'd seen it too.

"I wasn't busy." What had happened here, and why was Isabella talking about everything but the body that lay in the corner of the room? Still, the important thing was to keep Isabella talking. Violet continued, "I just didn't understand the situation with Masters, and then, once I did—"

"And then, once you did, you did everything you could to help. I wish you had just talked to me about it. I never thought you would offer yourself instead. I could have said no to them. I simply thought it would be easier to find a different husband, one that I wanted. I had no idea what you would do."

Violet's hand fell still in her sister's hair. "You would have said no to Masters?"

"Yes. I know you seem to think I am a ninny, but I am very capable of standing up for myself. I don't know why everybody seems to think I can't take care of myself. I've done very well for years."

Violet remembered Peter's words. He had said that she misjudged her sister. "I only wanted to take care of you."

"And a great mess you made of it." Isabella's foot began its rhythm again.

"How did you—"

"I followed Lord Peter when he left this afternoon. He sounded so mysterious about his errand. If he was to be my husband, I deserved to know his secrets."

Staring at her sister, Violet was slowly filled with comprehension. "You followed him."

"Right through the back gate of your garden. I heard everything."

"Oh." What else was there to say? Violet tried to remember exactly what had been said when.

"I came right here, to Foxworthy's house. I needed to know if it was all true, that you had really done that for me. And I needed to know about Masters. Could he really have done something like that?" Isabella began to shake, deep tremors that ate at Violet's soul.

"I didn't do anything." Violet spoke softly.

"But you tried. I never dreamed anybody would do something like that for me." She pushed away Violet's hand and stood. She turned to face the body. "You did leave Foxworthy very angry. I didn't know half the words he used. He did intend to ruin us."

"Did?"

Isabella reached into her ripped bodice and dropped several sheets of paper on the table. A bloody thumbprint marked the corner of one. "Did. I had to stop him. When he said those things about you, I just—"

Violet was reached for the papers just as a loud voice

sounded from the hall. "Foxworthy. Where are you, you old fool?"

They all froze at the sound. Peter put a finger to his lips and moved softly to the door. "Open the window to the terrace. Go out that way," he whispered.

Violet grabbed the papers, rammed them into her reticule, and reached for her sister's hand to pull her away. Isabella resisted, walking back to Foxworthy's desk and scooping up a large handful of papers and a couple of thin notebooks from a drawer. Violet gestured for her frantically. Stuffing as many papers as she could down her bodice and into her sleeves, Isabella finally followed, as Violet slid the lock and with a heave pushed it open. It was an easy matter to slip out. Isabella followed.

It took a moment to realize that Peter had not followed. He still stood at the door to the hall, his ear pressed to the crack. Violet started to climb back in.

"I must go." Isabella's voice sounded strong in her ear. "I can't be caught here."

"No, wait. We must get Peter."

"I must go now. I can't be caught here," Isabella repeated. Her voice was firm and heavy with conviction. Whatever spell had held her was broken.

"But if we leave they'll think—" Violet reached for Isabella's arm again.

"They won't think anything, because they won't know we were ever here." Isabella stepped out of Violet's reach. The trembling girl was gone completely, replaced by a cold-eyed woman. "And what would they think if they knew that I killed him? Well, whatever they thought, they'd be right, because I did. Foxworthy is dead because of me."

"Don't say that. I know that whatever happened was not your fault. It was an accident." Violet reached again for her sister. "Just let me get Peter. I promise we'll take care of everything."

"But I don't want you to take care of anything. No matter what you say you cannot change the facts. I was found alone in a house with a dead man. It would serve nobody if I told the full story of what really happened. Please trust me. It is time for me to live my own life. Everyone will be better off if I leave."

"Just stay for a moment. Give me a chance to—"

There was a loud slam. Somebody had just shut Foxworthy's front door, none too gently. There was more noise from inside the house. Why wasn't Peter leaving? They needed to be gone.

Violet turned toward her sister, ready to beg her to stay. Isabella turned her back and walked toward the road.

"Don't go. I can help if you'll just tell me what happened," Violet called after her sister.

"It's better this way. You don't want to know." Isabella stepped in the street, waving frantically at a hack. "I am sorry. I would have acted differently if I'd known you truly cared."

There was the clatter of another carriage pulling up in front of the house. She had to get Peter to leave. If she didn't he would be caught. Violet glanced once more toward her sister. She knew instinctively that the moment she went back through the window Isabella would be gone.

She climbed over the sill.

Chapter 19

"Why didn't you just come? I don't understand why you took so long." Violet leaned back on the settee. They were home and safe. She'd managed to pry Peter from the door just in time. By the time they'd made it make out the window the door had been opening. She hadn't waited to see who entered.

"I recognized the voice. I know I've heard it before. I just wanted to know who was there—see if there might be another explanation."

"You mean besides my sister killing a man." There, she'd said it.

"You don't actually think that she—" Peter sat beside her, pulling her legs onto his lap.

"She said she did. I can't imagine her doing so, but I've never known her to lie. It must have been an accident. Oh, I don't know. Why did she leave if she didn't?" Her voice was trembling and she had no power to control it. She turned her face into Peter's chest, seeking safety. "If you could have heard how cold she sounded when she said that she'd killed him. Why would she say something like that if it wasn't true?"

"I am sure there are a million reasons. Maybe she even thought she did. Or maybe she lost her senses when she found the body, and isn't even sure what happened herself."

"We just need to find her and ask. She can't have gone far." Peter sounded confident, but she knew that he pretended this firmness for her benefit.

"I've messed up this whole affair from the beginning."

Peter sighed, but did not disagree. "I think we all have. And that includes Isabella—if she was willing to say no to Masters she should never have involved you."

"Still, if I hadn't—"

"Didn't you say Isabella wanted to live her own life?" Peter ran a finger over the top of her foot.

"Yes, but my sister may have killed a man because I—"

"Stop right there. You don't know what happened. I don't know what happened. I do know that the man who came seeking Foxworthy sounded angry enough to kill. We don't know that he hadn't been there earlier."

Violet considered for a moment. "If he'd killed him why would he be looking for him?"

Peter continued, determined. "Maybe he wanted to cover his tracks. Or maybe he wasn't sure if he was dead. There must be a dozen reasons."

"I don't know." Violet knew her voice was filled with doubt.

"That is the point. We don't know. And until we do let us not make any assumptions. Our priority needs to be finding your sister, not wallowing in guilt."

Violet relaxed her back into the cushions. He was right. There was no point in beating herself over what had happened. That was the past. They could only move forward.

Peter removed her slipper and began to massage her foot. It felt so good. Maybe that was the problem. It seemed so unfair that she had Peter and poor Isabella—

"Ahem," the stiff, ladylike sound echoed through the room.

Violet jerked away from Peter, swinging her feet to the ground, as Lady Smythe-Burke strolled into the room and turned to stare at Peter. "So you were after the older one after all. I told you I'd approve of that match. Very suiting. I may take credit for it anyway. I always did take you for a man of sense, and a man of sense would know that my dear Violet is far more the woman you need to keep you on your toes. A man must be kept on his toes at all times." She addressed this last part to Violet.

Violet wasn't sure what to say. Lady Smythe-Burke had never visited her home before. They did have a past relationship, but it was based on convenience and favors, not actual friendship, and the last thing she needed now was an hour of polite chatter. "How may I help you, Lady Smythe-Burke?" That was always a polite way to begin a conversation.

Lady Smythe-Burke turned toward her. "It's not how you may help me, but how I can help you."

"Help us?" Peter asked as he stood and tried to assist Lady Smythe-Burke to a chair.

The lady avoided him and continued to stand. "Then you have not heard?"

"Are you talking of my sister's disappearance?" This time it was Violet who spoke.

"Oh, that, not at all what I meant, but we will get to that in a moment. I was speaking of the attack on Foxworthy. He was murdered this afternoon." She peered back and forth between Violet and Peter. "I wanted to be sure your servants will say you were home all afternoon? Good. It would be so awkward if they didn't, given your history."

"Foxworthy murdered?" Violet felt compelled to repeat the phrase as the knots formed again deep in her belly.

"Yes, he was found in his library, a knife stuck in his chest and his throat slit. All quite mysterious—nobody would know a thing about it if the parlor maid hadn't gone screaming down the street when she found him. Yes, quite mysterious." She turned a penetrating eye on Peter.

"He was found by a maid? His throat slit? A knife in his chest?" Peter asked. Violet could see the question in his eyes—there hadn't been a knife when they'd been there. Isabella certainly hadn't stabbed the man. Something must have happened after they left. But what?

"And why do you think this concerns us?" Violet calmed the quiver that threatened her voice.

"Well, you were seen acting out of character with the man only last evening, and you, Lord Peter, have never been known to have the calmest of tempers." Lady Smythe-Burke stared pointedly at Peter's bruised knuckles. "Even forgetting the magistrate, I daresay there will be rumor and gossip."

"Will we be suspected?" Peter asked, his voice tight.

"You, I am sure not. Violet, well, from what I hear, it was quite a performance you gave last night. Still, I fancy you can manage any question that comes your way. Can't you, my dear?" She turned back to Violet.

"I imagine I can."

"And besides, I can't imagine that either of you would have reason to rob the man," Lady Smythe-Burke continued, "although it was more his papers than his valuables that the thief was after. I gather only a scattering of petty coins were missing. His desk had been rifled through, however. It's rumored he had a collection of vowels from half the young pups in the land in his top drawer and maybe even secrets of a more damaging nature."

"I am still not quite sure why you came here." Violet fought the urge to say more. Why had Isabella grabbed those papers? And had she taken any coin? Violet didn't think so.

"Ah, did I mention that the maid reported that a young woman with red hair had been in to visit Fox-worthy—of course she was reported to be quite a few years younger than you, my dear Violet. Quite mysterious. I might almost have thought of your sister if—"

"If what?" Violet interrupted. The knot in her stomach had turned into a hopeless snarl that twisted further with every word spoken.

"Why, if she hadn't been with me. Quite the girl, your sister. I do have hopes for her someday."

"When did you see her? She was with you this afternoon?"

"Didn't I just say that? She came by and spent the whole afternoon," Lady Smythe-Burke said, staring pointedly at Violet. "You modern women never listen. When I was a girl if you didn't listen you got your ears boxed good and hard. My sister once looked like she'd grown cauliflowers out of the side of her head when she kept thinking about boys instead of listening to my father. I never did like cauliflower. Is it a vegetable or is it a flower? And if it's a flower, then why are we eating it? Maybe we should make wedding bouquets out of them. That pale creamy white with just a hint of pastel ribbon."

"Forgive me, Lady Smythe-Burke, but could you tell us when you saw Isabella about?"

"Oh dear, was I wandering?" Lady Smythe-Burke smiled slowly, but her eyes were deadly serious. "It's a wonder I can keep track of anything. I might even confuse the time of a visit if I am not careful and think it was even earlier than it was. Dear Isabella showed up at my home quite distraught. Apparently she'd followed Lord Peter out of her house. She wanted to see what was so urgent he couldn't stay and kiss his fiancée a few more times—she hoped to get a peek at her betrothal ring. Very sensible on her part, I must say. Girls today don't always have the gumption to do what must be done. In any case I can imagine you know right where you led her, Lord Peter. Couldn't you have used the front door instead of the mews? Isabella's hems were quite the sight after she'd been traipsing through muck for a good while and she must have scratched herself on a rosebush—her skin was quite marked. She'd even bloodied her skirt."

"Did my sister mention where she might be headed?" Violet asked. It was clear that Lady Smythe-Burke knew far more than she would say.

"Oh, she's gone off to take a position." Lady Smythe-Burke stared straight into Violet's eyes as she spoke. "Isn't that the most wonderful idea? I wrote her a brilliant reference. I am sure she'll be hired in no time. Unfortunately, of course, all the positions I know of are far from London."

"A position?" Violet didn't know what else to say.

Lady Smythe-Burke glared at her. "Isabella is a properly brought-up lady who has run into difficulties and possible scandal through little fault of her own." The lady paused and gave each of them a stern look. "She wishes to have her own life, and I decided she should have it. She'll make a wonderful companion or governess or whatever she chooses to do. Whatever."

Violet glanced at Peter at that final whatever. Her stomach was churning, but words seemed to escape her. All she could do was grasp his hand.

"Do you know where she was heading?" Peter asked. "We would like to know where she is going, be sure that she is safe."

"Oh, that would have taken away her adventure. I gave her a list and some currency, and told where to catch the stage. She is a sensible girl and she will be fine."

"Surely you could give us some idea where she went?" Violet swallowed as she forced the words out. This whole situation was impossible. It was not long ago that life had seemed so normal.

"Let's see. I gave her the direction of a friend with five children in Newcastle, of an older woman who needs some help in Caernarvon, of a finishing school in Launceston, and of a good friend who always needs help with something in Maidstone. I am sure she'll be at one of those locations."

"I am surprised you didn't send her to Norwich and complete her tour of the kingdom," Peter stated.

"I did consider it, but the Winglehams live in Norwich and I really didn't think she'd suit. Hmmm, I'd forgotten Clara Westington. You're friends with her, aren't you? I always did like that girl. She's in Norwich. I should have sent Isabella there but I didn't think of it. Oh well, it's such a pity that I can't remember exactly which direction she took. I'll never be able to tell anyone where she went."

"Yes, that is a pity." If Violet didn't know where her sister was she'd never be able to tell anyone. Violet stared at the clasped hands in her lap. Peter's were so much bigger and darker than her own.

"It's almost as much a pity as that you didn't just talk this out with Isabella in the beginning. It was such a shame to see her sense of betrayal that you hadn't trusted her with your plans and feelings. She could have helped avoid this whole mess if you'd only spoken to her—or consulted me—I don't know why people never realize what a help I could be." Lady Smythe-Burke turned and swept from the room. She stopped only once to say, "I do hope the two of you remember that if you should run into difficulties—I can be quite helpful, particularly with matters of society and opinion, and even on occasion with those of a more political nature. You should ask Wimberley. I've helped him a time or two. A word from me can go a long way toward smoothing a scandalous past.

"Oh, and Isabella said you should check your reticule."

As the last tap of her shoes faded from the house, Violet reached over and retrieved the small bag. She shook it open and pulled out the papers she'd removed from Foxworthy's house.

Peter took them from her and glanced over them. A strange expression passed across his face. "Not quite what I expected. I imagine these are what Foxworthy held over Masters. Your brother is safe from prosecution—but I expect he has always been so." Peter scanned through the papers, paging back and forth. "There are receipts for investment in some foreign company and letters indicating a knowing involvement in French treachery."

Violet reached out a trembling hand. "How can you say he is safe if—if he knowingly helped the French?"

Peter turned the pages toward her. "Look at the dates and the signature."

"It's my father's. Why would Masters have—?" She ran a finger across the name. "But, of course, he didn't. He lied. He made Foxworthy lie. I told him I might speak to Foxworthy, and he spoke to Foxworthy first. What I don't understand is why?"

"I am sure your brother had his reasons—and Foxworthy too, perhaps," Peter answered. "We shall probably never know the full truth unless Masters cares to tell us."

"That is unlikely. The one thing we do know is that it was not my brother's name he was trying to protect."

"No, it appears it was your father's, and perhaps the whole family's. What would have happened if this had come out? Your father is dead, but I do not know if that would have made the Crown more forgiving. It is possible all his properties would have been seized."

Violet was quiet for a moment, trying to remember those days after her parents' deaths. There had been so little money left anyway. What would have happened if that little had been taken away? "Could it matter after all this time?"

"I don't know. I can ask Wimberley. We can trust in his discretion. I expect, however, that the answer is yes. Treason casts a long shadow."

Peter dropped the papers between them and reached again for Violet's hand. He clasped it between his own and held it tight. He made no move to bring it to his lips or caress it in any way. He merely held it tight.

"I am sorry. I can't even imagine what this means to you," he said.

"I am not sure I even know. It all seems so long ago and far away. I had little intercourse with my parents. They never displayed interest in their daughters." She gripped Peter's fingers tighter. "Do you really think Masters was trying to protect us?"

"Why don't you ask him?"

She drew in a deep breath. "I'll do that. I've been meaning to have a long talk anyway. It is time we settled the past. And I've a feeling that with having to track Isabella we will have plenty of time to talk."

Peter lifted her fingers up to his lips and kissed them lightly. "I can just imagine your very proper brother traipsing across the country." A smile lit his eyes. "You do realize what all this means, don't you? There is no longer any obstacle between us," he said.

"I know."

"Isabella is gone, but despite her prattle Lady Smythe-Burke will have taken care that she is not in any danger." He squeezed her hand once more and then let it fall back into her lap.

"I am sure you are right, but I cannot help worrying. We still don't know if—" Violet wished he were still holding her fingers tight. The small movement of a hand had left her so much more alone.

Peter brushed a finger over her lips, silencing her. "We don't know what happened. Maybe she came by afterward and the papers were lying there, or maybe he gave them to her earlier for some reason she didn't have time to explain."

Violet longed to feel the truth of his words, but her mind could not hide from what it knew. She had seen Isabella gather up even more papers. The explanation was not as simple as the picture Peter painted.

"Don't look so despairing." Peter's fingers moved to brush her cheek. "Even if it is true, she only did what she had to do, I am sure—as we all do what we have to."

Violet dropped her eyes from his. Yes, they had all done what they had to. It only remained to see what happened next. She wasn't sure that she was ready to move on, or that she was brave enough to take that next step, to accept Peter and all that would mean.

As if sensing her thoughts, Peter picked up the garden rose he had picked earlier—it seemed a lifetime earlier. A maid must have found it and placed it in a vase. He held it out to her. "I know it has been an impossible day, an impossible few days, and that both our emotions are still unsteady, but that has not changed my feelings. Are you ready to accept my friendship, my passion, and my love?"

Violet's hand shook as she took the rose and brought it to her nose. He could be so foolish, so romantic. She waited for the doubt to fill her; instead she smelled a summer dream, one she had long feared forgotten. "I will accept them," she said, then added honestly, "I am just not sure what I'll do with them, but give me time." She kissed him on the cheek. Everything had happened so fast.

He turned his face until their lips almost touched. "I am not going anywhere. There is no force on earth that will take me away from you."

Chapter 20

"**T**hat didn't go so badly." Peter turned to Violet with half a grin.

"You mean only two matrons pulled their daughters out of your path for fear you'd ask them to dance and our corrupting influence would be spread?" Violet steered him away from another group of young girls. She couldn't decide which was worse, those who lowered frightened eyes at their approach or those who boldly lifted flirtatious eyes toward him.

He was worth flirting with this evening. He'd chosen a coat of deep brown velvet embroidered with golden leaves. On one shoulder a rose bloomed—all reds and golds and pinks—their rose.

She drew in a deep breath and turned toward him. "You truly don't mind?"

"Mind what?"

She gestured at the crowd. "I am used to always

having to choose who will speak to me and who will only give me the briefest nod. There are some who will not even do that."

"We were invited. Is that not enough?" he asked.

"We were invited as part of your brother's party. Nobody denies the Marquess of Wimberley. It is not the same." She drew slightly away and stared across the full dance floor. Skirts spun and gentlemen laughed. It was a picture of gaiety. Why did she feel excluded? It had never bothered her before.

She turned and stared at Peter, at her lover. It had been almost a month since Isabella disappeared. Masters still traveled after the broken path she had left.

Violet was still unsure how she felt about the whole situation—there was guilt and worry, but she couldn't see where she could have acted differently. Was the whole situation inevitable?

Inevitable.

She looked at Peter. Were they inevitable? She couldn't imagine any other ending to the story— although she still wasn't exactly sure what that ending was.

Was it too soon to have taken him back? Violet had welcomed him into her bed again this past week, had agreed to accompany him in public, but still stalled at the final step. Could he really be happy in her world?

She was beginning to think that he could.

He'd stood with her when she'd talked to Masters

and come to comprehend all the secrets of the past. She might not understand some, if not all, of her brother's actions or be fully ready to forgive him, but she could see that he'd done as he thought best for everyone, just as she always had. And it did make up for a lot, knowing Masters was traveling from one end of the kingdom to the other in a bumpy carriage. That was bound to knock some of the starch from his spine.

She glanced back at Peter. He was still smiling. He'd put up with her family and her slightly tarnished reputation and still grinned and laughed—and gave her time—and let her have her way. Or at least he let her have her way some of the time—he was beginning to make her fight for her win.

And shockingly, she was finding she rather liked that.

A chuckling voice roused her from her thoughts. "This one doesn't look too sweet. So did you finally take my advice?" A rather rotund gentleman she did not know had come up behind them.

"Lady Carrington, it gives me pleasure to introduce you to Mr. Henry Edwards. Mr. Edwards, let me introduce you to my dear friend Lady Carrington."

Peter didn't hesitate over the introduction. He spoke with complete confidence. He didn't seem to care what others might think.

She glanced over at his face. He looked comfortable.

In fact, from the moment they had walked into the ball he had seemed perfectly at ease. It was she who had doubts, not him.

She watched him chat with his friend. They were discussing Lord Summerton's mother, a lack of champagne, and how these all conspired to mean poor Summerton must find a bride. She didn't understand at all. But Peter looked happy. Even as she watched he threw back his head and let out a true belly laugh. Several surrounding couples turned to stare, and he just shrugged his shoulders.

He said his good-byes to his friend and led her toward the refreshments. "I should warn you even my brother probably cannot get us into Almack's. Lady Smythe-Burke might be able, but she'd probably require us to actually name a child after her first, and that might produce some difficulties."

He filled a glass with lemonade and handed it to her. She sipped. Sugar was the only discernable taste. She wasn't even sure a lemon had been waved over it. "It's awful."

He grinned. "Yes, it is, and still it's better than Almack's. Did you ever try their swill during your long-ago season?"

"Once, I believe. Right before Dratton offered."

"Do you have any desire to go back and dance on those wobbly floors?"

"No, I can't say that I do," she answered.

"Then we won't. This matter of not having children does make everything easier."

She stopped in her tracks. "How can you joke about this, about everything? Don't you know these things are important?"

He grabbed her hands and led her toward the stairs leading to the high mezzanine that surrounded the ballroom. "Do you mean these people? They are only as important as we make them. I would admit I would hate to be completely cast out. This is the world I know, but I honestly don't care if Lady Bellwise thinks that I've overstepped the bounds of propriety in making you the woman that I love.

"I am sorry if talk of children upsets you. I only wanted to show you that I can joke about it. I would love for you to have my child, but I don't need you to. You are what I need."

They reached the top of the stair and Violet moved along the balcony. They were so alone up here above the swirling crowd. "You've said that so many times. You need me. I almost don't believe it anymore."

He grabbed her shoulders and turned her to face him. "Do you believe that I love you?"

"Yes."

"Do you love me?"

"You know I do."

"Can you imagine a life without me?"

She turned her face away. "Yes, and it is not a life I wish to lead."

He placed a hand on each of her hips and turned her back toward the crowd below. He pressed her forward until her hips were in firm contact with one of the heavy marble pillars holding up the railing. He placed a hand on each side of her. "Then accept that I need you. I cannot imagine a life without you, Violet. You are the center of my being."

"But what do you want from me?" she asked, her voice dropping an octave as she felt the front of his hips settle against her buttocks.

"Why don't we see if you can guess?" His body weight trapped her as one of his hands slowly began to ruck up the side of her skirt. The iridescent spider silk slid up her leg, setting each nerve ending on fire.

"We can't do this here. I don't want to be seen," she gasped.

"Haven't you realized that it's not always about what you want, my love?" His fingers slipped down to stroke the outer edge of her thigh. He leaned forward so that she could feel his hot breath against her neck. He didn't kiss her or make any other move above the waist. His hands, though—the places his hands were traveling. "This is about what I need from you."

"What do you mean?" She sighed as he separated the globes of her buttocks, trying hard to make no sound that would carry to the dancers below.

"What are you willing to give me?" he asked, sliding one finger forward into the moisture between her legs.

"What do you want?" She would give him anything if he kept this up. She'd never realized how powerful it could be to let someone else take control.

"Wrong question—I want to know what you offer freely." His fingers continued to work their magic.

She could feel the strength of his erection pressed against her. He was still fully dressed and she had her skirts about her waist. He was lucky she had not worn her drawers tonight. His finger slid back and forth again. Or maybe she was lucky. "Are you trying to seduce me into answering a question I don't understand?"

"Actually, I am trying to get an answer before I seduce you. And I think you do understand. I am simply having a hard time holding myself back."

She thrust back against him. He groaned softly—yes, a very hard time. She pushed again, enjoying her power over him. This was a game for two. "What do I want from you, Lord Peter?" She rotated her hips. "I think I want all of you—including perhaps even your name. Do you think you could handle that?" She drew back, leaving him gasping.

She moved forward again. "Do you think you could handle me forever?"

He stepped back and for a moment she feared she had lost him, then she saw him, bent over, below the edge of railing, making a quiet approach. His breath hit the small of her back as his hands spread her legs farther apart.

He bent further and kissed the inside of one knee, then the other. She felt his warm kisses move upward, his tongue leaving a trail of warmth and delight.

When he reached his goal he only blew softly, setting her curls and her nerves astir. She gripped the cold railing tight and prayed that nobody below could see how tight she bit her lower lip.

He blew again. "I think we'll have to see who has trouble handling whom, Violet, Lady Carrington soon to be St. Johns. This time we're doing it the way I want."

She wanted to protest, but as his warm tongue hit spots his breath had prepared, she rather thought they would do things his way—at least for now.

At Avon Books, we know your passion for romance—once you finish one of our novels, you find yourself wanting more.

May we tempt you with . . .

- **Excerpts** from our upcoming releases.

- Entertaining **extras**, including authors' personal photo albums and book lists.

- Behind-the-scenes **scoop** on your favorite characters and series.

- **Sweepstakes** for the chance to win free books, romantic getaways, and other fun prizes.

- Writing **tips** from our authors and editors.

- **Blog** with our authors and find out why they love to write romance.

- **Exclusive content** that's not contained within the pages of our novels.

Join us at
www.avonbooks.com

AVON

An Imprint of HarperCollins*Publishers*
www.avonromance.com